THE DREAM WALL

Graham Dunstan Martin

UNWIN PAPERBACKS
London   Sydney

First published in Great Britain by Unwin Hyman, 1987
First published in paperback by Unwin Paperbacks, an imprint
of Unwin Hyman Limited, in 1987.

UNWIN HYMAN LIMITED
Denmark House, 37–39 Queen Elizabeth Street,
London SE1 2QB
and
40 Museum Street, London WC1A 1LU

Allen & Unwin Australia Pty Ltd
8 Napier Street, North Sydney, NSW 2060 Australia

Unwin Paperbacks with Port Nicholson Press
60 Cambridge Terrace,
Wellington, New Zealand

British Library Cataloguing in Publication Data

Martin, Graham Dunstan
 The dream wall.
I. Title
823'.914[F]   PR6063.A714/
ISBN 0-04-823337-4
ISBN 0-04-823363-3 Pbk

Set in 10 on 12 point Palatino by Grove Graphics, Tring, Herts
and printed in Great Britain by
Biddles Ltd, Guildford, Surrey

*To the fifteen million
peasants who died
in the great Russian famine,
1929—1932*

Contents

Once upon a time I, Chuang Tzu, dreamt I was a butterfly, fluttering hither and thither, conscious only of following my fancies as a butterfly, unconscious of my identity as a man. Suddenly I awoke, and there I lay, myself again. Now I do not know whether I was then a man dreaming I was a butterfly, or whether I am now a butterfly, dreaming I am a man.

———————— CHUANG TZU ————————

Author's Note

It is not the least of ironies that the quotations from Trotsky are all drawn from his *Defence of Terrorism* (Allen & Unwin, 1921), and hence are not attacks on, but apologies for, the behaviour of the Bolshevik Government of the time.

As for the fictional characters who inhabit this book, no resemblance is intended to any living person, though it may well be intended to some as yet unborn.

Finally, my warmest thanks to Mike Falchikov for his expertise in that little known subject, twenty-second-century Russo-English slang.

G.D.M.

PART ONE

Reality and Dream

Event One

Not everything has been properly adjusted here.

— KONSTANTIN CHERNENKO —

Freeday, 2 Marx 2116

At about 7 pm on Freeday, 2 Marx 2116, John Mathieson's identity was snatched away from him, and the onward march of history was transformed.

Or rather his identity card was snatched, but that was the same thing.

The problem was that the plumbing in Mao Apartment Block had had 'the Muscovite jumps' since early February. First it had developed a racking cough, and the water that vomited in spasms out of its taps was no longer yellow, but greenish brown. Then the frost had clenched and unclenched its fist upon the pipes, and the greenish water had coursed down the walls of the top seven storeys. A week later an official team of people's hydrotechnic metricians had visited the apartment block. The water flowed for eight days without protest, then a death rattle ran down the pipes, and everything, even the water soaking into the plaster-work, came to a stop. The metricians returned twice without result, and then returned no more. John headed a delegation to the Leninpool City Hall to 'put the problem before the authorities', but nothing was done. Perhaps the metricians had gone on holiday to the Crimea, perhaps they had been arrested or promoted to the Sewerage Service, who could say? At all events, Mao Block was waterless, and there was nothing for it but to visit the Public Revolutionary Bath-House.

For, that evening, John had a date with his girlfriend, and in

3

preparation for this he could be satisfied neither with brown water nor with none. Sighing, therefore, and patting the pocket of his overalls (pale grey, baggy, regulation issue, uniform of a petty clerk or 'chinaboy' Grade 17) to make sure he had his Proletarian Pleasure Pack with him, he caught the trolley-bus to the corner of Irreversible Progress Street, walked three blocks and turned in through the heavy gothic portals of the building, which had once been devoted to the 'worship' (whatever that was) of 'God' (whoever that had been). Over the arch you could just make out the words

YOU SHALL BE WASHED WHITE IN THE BLOOD
OF THE VICTORIOUS PROLETARIAT

They had once been picked out in triumphant scarlet, but the rain, in its resentful capitalist—reactionary fashion, had by now almost erased them.

Once inside, John wrinkled up his nose at the smell of stale sweat and athlete's foot, undressed among a crowd of other males, and passed his bundle of clothes over the counter to a yawning attendant, who handed him in return a plastic disc on a piece of string. Here there was a slight hitch, for he had forgotten to bring any soap with him, and the attendant reminded him of this public duty with the word 'Parasite!' before offering him a small cake, grey, the size of a postage stamp.

Then he attached himself to a queue of naked and shivering men. Bourgeois decadent deviants or 'queers' were particularly fond of such places, and it was best to gaze ahead of you, just three inches over the scalp of the man in front, and not permit your eye to drop to eye level, chest level or — Marx forbid! — lower down. At the same time you must take the utmost care not to lose your place in the queue, for the proletarian elbow had not forgotten its sharpness these last hundred years.

When at last he arrived at the shower cubicle and had wedged himself in, holding the door closed with one shoulder, he found that his soap refused to lather and that when you turned the switch to HOT, the water stopped. The building was unheated save by the reek of human bodies, and it was a particularly chilly Marx day. John tried his best to wash thoroughly before towelling himself to some degree of warmth. He joined the out-queue.

Here there was a more worrying hold-up. Having exchanged his disc for a bundle of clothes, and having hastily dressed — for the outer door was open, and an icy wind was blowing down the corridor all the way from Soviet Union Street — he found himself in a fourth queue — an unexpected one this time. He glanced down at his watch — Perpetual Revolution Time-Keeper, made in Russia. Yes, he still had plenty of time. He peered down the shadows of the corridor towards the lighted doorway.

Four of them!

Sky-blue uniforms. Peaked caps with a band of scarlet round them. Sam Brownes and machine-guns.

People's Friends!

'Your documents, cond,' they were saying to the man at the head of the queue.

As John edged closer he could see that this young man bore some resemblance to himself. He was dressed in the same clerk's overalls, like him he looked undernourished and was slightly balding. The man seemed distinctly worried as he felt first in one pocket then in another, without success.

'Mislaid your identity, have you?' said the officer. He winked at his colleagues.

'No, no,' stammered the young man, 'here it is.' He produced from an inner pocket a wallet containing the requisite seven cards — Personal Identity, Family Status, Housing Permit, Certificate of the Ministry of Productive Labour, Marxist Activity Record, Certificate of Subscription to *Truth*, Social Quotient . . . His hand was shaking so much that the wad of cards spilled on to the wet concrete floor.

John, feeling a similar alarm, felt for his own documents.

Sweet Marx! Blessed Lady of Krasnoyarsk! Where were they?

As he clapped his palm to different levels of his anatomy, testing feverishly for that familiar comforting thickness which would tell his hands (almost without his brain knowing it) that here was his true self — recorded on paper, stamped with official recognition — he thought to himself,

5

'Not tonight, Sue.'

For clearly his plans were off. A visit to the cells for a start. How many days would it take while they made 'the standard inquiries'?

Wearing his regulation issue overall, he was no longer naked, but positively transparent, like a bottle full of World Peace Vodka — the burning liquid in his guts was fear — and he felt as if the People's Friends could look right through him and measure its level with their eyes.

At the Workers' Party, they were having a party workers' party. At the doors, jackbooted troopers cradled their machine-guns in their arms like babies while they checked the guests' invitations. Inside, a hundred-piece brass band was roaring out *Land of Hope and Glory* (long since liberated from its imperialist associations), the buffet tables groaned with stuffed pheasant, truffle pâté, lemon chicken à la Mao Tse-Tung, and the righteous of the Party struggled to tread the correct line through the fumes of alcohol that had been steadily rising since five that afternoon.

There were fifty-two social grades, and to this party only the top three had been invited with their wives. None of the guests, therefore, was less than two proletarian metres round the waist. The exception to both these rules was a number of Grade 11 female secretaries who lent both party and Party its grace and charm, and who were here for their sturdy socialist accomplishments both in and out of bed.

Two such heroines of labour were Rusalka Smith and Ludmilla Hecklestone. 'A pair of nice titsers', as they put it in Party circles. The girls, that is, and not what some proletarian, ignorant of the beautiful Russian language, might suppose.

Said Rusalka to Ludmilla, 'How's OBL? Surely *you* must have heard the latest?' She said this in a discreet whisper.

OBL was short for Our Beloved Leader, or Vladimir Potter-Krasnovsky, for two years Chairman of the British Workers' Party, President of the Truly Democratic Republic of Great Britain and All Ireland, who now, at the age of 85 . . .

'Boris says he's settled down,' confided Ludmilla. 'Stable condition. For the moment.'

'How many days do the doctors give him?'

'Oh, at least another week.' Ludmilla touched the good luck charm that dangled from her bracelet. It was in the form of a tiny silver book, inscribed KAPITAL.

'I'm asking Innokenty to send me to Switzerland — just in case. Why don't you do the same?'

'Oh, Boris needs me here,' said Ludmilla.

Meanwhile, the two men in question were greeting each other with a warm 'Zdrastye, Tov,' and inquiring after each other's families. 'Mine are in the West Indies,' said Innokenty Fisher-Bukharin. Adding by way of explanation, 'Delightful weather at this time of year.'

Physically, the two men were in contrast. Fisher-Bukharin, Generalissimo of the British Red Army, was heavy-cheeked, deep-jowled, wore his huge paunch with pride and style. Boris Clegg-Molotov, Minister of Social Harmony, on the other hand, indulged himself less than some and had a naturally ascetic frame. His face was deeply furrowed as if it were made of cloth that had been out in all kinds of weathers. What both men had in common was a clear head unaffected by infinite quantities of alcohol.

'And your own loved ones?'

'Marxbreak has taken them to Switzerland this time. The skiing's at its best this time of year.'

A flicker of mutual understanding passed between the two. Both knew that at this critical juncture in the State's history, it was advisable for one's nearest and dearest to be out of the country. A man did not rise to the great offices of state without knowing how to take precautions. Both Switzerland and the West Indies were among the few insignificant countries that were still capitalist. Nothing would go wrong, of course. But if it did, such a country would be less likely to extradite small children for a political offence committed by their parents.

'So all is ready?'

'That depends, dear Innokenty, how much longer you require.'

'Another twenty-four hours should do it. Are you sure he'll last that long?'

'I shall see he does,' said Clegg-Molotov solemnly.

For the last few exchanges he had, out of the corner of his eye, been watching the stately advance of the Russian Ambassador across the floor. Now, as Comrade Vorkuta stood at his elbow, he burst into fluent Russian, turned and embraced him in warm Muscovite style, the smacking kiss on both cheeks, the rib-breaking bear-hug, perhaps even a small discreet tear in one eye.

'My dear Arkady!'

'Borís dorogóy!'

Some way across the room, Mrs Winch-Kalashnikov stood and watched this warm greeting with some disapproval. 'Shocking, I call it,' she breathed to her husband. 'And OBL not yet cold in his grave.'

'Hush, Sandra. The Nation grieves, but we cannot snub the Ambassador of the great Socialist Motherland.' He helped himself to another slice of pheasant.

Fat Sandra wished, not for the first time, that her husband would not always use his official Party manner. It was like never taking your socks off, even in bed. She turned back to her friend, Mrs O'Boyle, and began to unburden herself. She was so worried . . . Her daughter Natasha . . . The silly girl thought she'd fallen in love. How petty bourgeois could you get!

'And do you know who it is?' Dramatic pause. 'A worker! A common working man from the Islington sock-factory! Heaven knows how they met! We've given her everything, Sasha and I. Dresses, culture, holidays abroad. Always taken care to introduce her to the right people. And now she thinks she can turn round and snap her fingers in our faces!'

Mrs O'Boyle flickered her artificial eyelashes in sympathy.

'A young man of absolutely no position. Not an idea in his head. I'm at my wits' end.'

Mrs O'Boyle listened understandingly till her friend had pumped the whole story up into a satisfying state of inflammation, and then suggested *sotto voce*, 'Maybe you should drop a word in C-M's ear.'

'Clegg-Molotov?' exclaimed Mrs Winch in alarm. 'Isn't that a little drastic? Holy Karl!'

The young man fourteen places ahead of John Mathieson was on his knees now, scrabbling around after the precious documents that he had spilled all over the muddy bath-house floor. The People's Friends stood over him in their clean blue uniforms, smiling faintly, waiting for him to finish.

'There you are, Tov,' he babbled at last, shoving them into the hands of the officer. The latter turned them over, sorting them.

At John's shoulder, the man next in the queue commented under his breath, 'Our boys in blue are worried tonight, aren't they? Must be why they're worrying us.'

John hardly heard him. A great pang of relief surged through him as his left hand encountered a bulky wad in his inside pocket. Surely . . . But he hadn't put them there, he always kept them on the other side. But was it? Holy Karl, he breathed, he'd found his real self again!

Really, however, it was very curious. How had he come to put them in *that* pocket? Perhaps it was the unfamiliar experience of visiting the bath-house. He must never mix up his pockets again. Such errors could be bad for one's heart.

He did not therefore hear the name that had just been pronounced at the head of the queue. The young man who slightly resembled him heard it, however, and looked astonished.

'No, that's not me, Tov,' he was protesting. 'That's not me. My name's Ivan Lumsden.'

'Not what it says here,' said the officer, grinning, comparing the identity card with his list, and turning it in his hands so that his colleagues could have a good view of it.

'Ivan David Lumsden,' insisted the young man, ' "chinaboy" Grade 15, about to be posted to London to the Bureau of Social Harmony. I . . .'

'Call me "Tov Captain" when you speak to me.' Behind the unfortunate Comrade Lumsden, one of the People's Friends moved abruptly, and the young man went down, kicked off his feet on the slippery concrete. The four 'blue-boys' roared with laughter, and the men in the queue felt constrained to join in too. You did not keep a straight face when a People's Friend laughed.

No PF could resist a joke. And this was a joke in the best possible taste, Citizen Lumsden, as he called himself, slithering about on the greasy concrete, unable to keep his footing. Every time he made to get up, another of the People's Friends kicked him off balance.

The officer wiped his eyes. 'So you're not . . .' he said, tapping the card in his hands. The name was inaudible behind the laughter of his colleagues. 'You must be a thief, then, for you've got his cards in your pocket.'

'Now I tell you what I think, you slumchick,' he went on, addressing the grovelling man. 'You think you're having a joke with us, but I think we're having a joke with you. Your number's come up,' he said, tapping his list. 'You've won the state lottery. John Mathieson,' he repeated, staring at the card. 'Take him away, men.'

Fourteen places back in the queue, the real John Mathieson froze. His jaw dropped, his face went white. Lenin preserve us, it's me they're after! How the hell had this man got hold of his cards? Of course, there must have been a mistake at the door when we handed our clothes in. Two brand-new, identical, badly fitting pairs of overalls. It explained why the documents hadn't been in his usual pocket.

He glanced down at the cards and for the first time checked the name upon them. Holy Karl! Every one of them was made out to the name of Ivan David Lumsden.

At this point John, despite his alarm, was about to do his civic duty — more to the point, his human duty to Ivan Lumsden. He was about to step forward and explain his mistake. 'Tov Officer,' he would say, 'I've just looked in my pocket and I find . . .' No, that wouldn't do it. How could he put it so they wouldn't beat him up when they got him to the station?

And what was this about 'winning the lottery'? That was really alarming. It looked very much as if he, John Mathieson, had had his name put on some List or other — not the List of Inadequate Political Commitment, surely, for his Social Quotient was in good shape — but could it be *the* List, the Tally, the Directory of Directories, the roll-call you couldn't avoid however hard you tried?

Or so people said. To tell the truth, the Great State Lottery (in which there were no winners, only losers) was only folklore, had never been officially confirmed. But people solemnly whispered that, no matter how many 'unreliables' were picked up every year, the quota of arrestees was always made up to a round 0.5 per cent, and that the names to make up this total were (so to speak) drawn out of a PF's cap. It was a kind of seal-cull, only these were two-legged seals. It was further rumoured that, when the terrible stresses of high office fell more harshly on the grandees of the Party, *the quota was raised*.

So had they put him on this mythical 'List'? Was that really what the gun-jack's joke had meant? Or was it because he had complained about a plumbing problem? But that was unheard of. There wasn't anything political about that. Unless they'd changed the rules.

Which they might have done.

Still, he must, he must step forward. His conscience demanded it. He had a duty to the — no, he had a duty to Ivan Lumsden. He tried to speak up from his position in the queue, but the link between his conscience and his voice had been broken by some animal reflex of fear. He pushed at the man on his right, trying to press past him.

'Here, mate, wait your gramsci turn,' swore the man, scowling, blocking his way.

For John to grasp the situation, to check his identity cards, to comprehend what had gone wrong and why, took a few seconds. Then fear delayed him a few more. But in the meantime events had moved on too far and too fast. The false John Mathieson had clutched the officer round the knees in the time-honoured gesture of supplication. 'But I'm not him,' he cried. 'Check me out at my bureau tomorrow. Please, Tov Captain . . .'

As John would be able to guess later that evening, young Ivan Lumsden knew that, however innocent he might be, if he were arrested that would be the end of his splendid new job in London. The arrest (though unjustified) would be automatically added to his record, and he would be reposted to some god-forsaken spot like Harrogate. It was desperately important that the matter be settled here and now, before his name was entered on some official 'List'.

11

'Get him off me,' said the officer softly.

Behind Lumsden, a blue-boy swung the butt of his gun. The blow looked casual but, through long practice, was perfectly timed as by a cricketer hitting a six. There was loud crack, like a wooden plank splitting. The young man went sprawling. Silence. He lay quite motionless.

Thoroughly frightened, John Mathieson checked again. It occurred to him that he would be for it even worse now. But somehow, having seen Lumsden felled, he just couldn't get his legs to move.

'Hmm,' said the officer thoughtfully. Lumsden continued to lie still upon the filthy concrete. One of the People's Friends stepped up and turned him over with his boot. Quite gently, for once.

The blue-boy who had felled him examined the butt of his gun to see if it had sustained any damage. Everyone else gazed pensively at the young man's body, as if meditating on some text of the prophet Engels.

The officer, who had bent down for a closer examination, straightened up, adjusting his uniform. 'Call a Health and Sanity Vehicle,' he said to the bath-house attendant. 'Not that it matters now.' Pause. 'That yobber must have had an eggshell for a skull. Not our fault.'

Then, to everyone's surprise, he motioned to the silent queue. Perhaps he felt that honour had been satisfied. Perhaps the quota had, in a sense, been filled. He waved them past him and out of the narrow doorway with the muzzle of his revolver. 'On your way, conds. Get a move on. No hanging about. Straight home.'

The real John Mathieson slunk by him, unable to concentrate on anything but just getting away, out of this place, into the wet black streets of Leninpool, getting away to think what next to do, if ever there was anything now that he *could* do.

'Excess of zeal,' the captain was saying to the gun-jack who had dealt the blow. 'Quite commendable really.'

'Expect they've just raised the quota,' said the man at John's elbow. 'Must be because the Leader's on his last lap. Enough to give you a dose of the trotskies.'

Up in the People's Palace (once called Buckingham) they were operating on Potter-Krasnovsky for the second time that week. Professor Jaurès MacPartland was afraid that gangrene might be setting in in the President's left leg. Until C-M could settle the succession, however, the People still needed their leader.

'Oxygen,' said MacPartland. 'Saw. Oh Holy Marx, not another power cut.'

Leaving Equality Street, where the top people's Party — or rather the top People's Party — had been holding its rave-up, Ludmilla Hecklestone thought privately that the English Rolls-Royce was still the best in the world, settled luxuriously back into the pneumatic ease of its back seat and, taking her lover's hand, moved it directly over to her Bermuda triangle. Communists aren't queer, that's one thing you can say for them (she gasped to herself). Hair and thrill-juice. Muscles and mussels. 'Mh!' she uttered, wiggling and shifting, lifting her mouth to be kissed.

'Oh luby,' she cooed in C-M's ear, 'you're so good for my career.'

She had been hand-picked last autumn from a shortlist of ten, after exhaustive personal interview (it had been a hard choice, Boris remembered). He had not regretted it, however, and six months on she was still his Personal Secretary no. 1. In the office they joked that Personal Secretary no. 2 wrote, while Ludmilla lay, on the sheets.

Satire betrayed a prematerialist worldview, thought C-M. One must be serious about this aspect of early twenty-second-century socialism. It was essential that those who directed the State, who raised the political consciousness of the masses, who drove it to ever higher pinnacles of achievement (in close co-operation with the great socialist motherland of the USSR) should not be distracted from some urgent task by the sexual instinct. Now if you are not to be distracted by sex, comrade, you will simply have to have as much of it as you want. 'From each according to her ability, to each according to his need,' as Marx had said in his prophetic way.

We are, after all, three centuries on.

'Three *what* on?'

'Oh Gramsci! Are you still there, Ludmilla? Since Marx, I mean.'

They were in Ludmilla's bedroom, in the richly appointed flat that Party funds had assigned to her just off Holborn. Lights muted but warm, blankets tossed back into the shadows, a splendour of golden brocade sheets, matching curtains and bed-hangings, a huge gilt mirror staring down at them both from the ceiling. The scenes it could have re-enacted! But this mirror only reflected and took no film, unlike the other similar mirrors that Boris's People's Friends had installed over the beds of all his colleagues' mistresses.

And yet, and yet . . . with all the advances since Marx's time, with all the dissident elements they had jailed (three hundred thousand in British re-education camps at this very moment), with all the People's Friends they had (8 per cent of the population), Utopia had still not dawned. All those deaths too back in 2009, ten million when the IRA had won at last in Ireland and had carried its revolution to England. An entire class eliminated. And yet the world was still not perfect!

'A revolution has to be made in every generation,' said C-M sadly.

'What? We made ours back in 2009!'

'But would you think it, seeing those people there tonight!'

'People? There weren't any People!'

'Exactly, my love. To hear them talk, you wouldn't think a Revolution had ever happened. Sometimes it's almost more than I can bear to hear them going on about how lazy their servants are, and how the miners don't mine and the plumbers drill holes in the pipes. Meanwhile, they stuff themselves with pheasant, and . . .'

To himself he thought: Potter-Krasnovsky. He actually likes corruption in his ministers. He's always had gangrene, particularly on the left.

'Luby, the phone's ringing.'

'Keep him going,' said Boris through his teeth. 'Take his other leg off. No, maybe better not.'

'Yes, yes, our society is corrupt. Too much bribery and blat

14

and string-pulling. Old Mao was right, permanent revolution's the only way.'

'I do love you when you talk politics to me,' sighed Ludmilla, her eyes shining. 'It proves how much you trust me.'

'Now, Ludmilla, don't be silly. As Minister of Social Harmony . . .' He checked himself on the verge of telling her that the jackboot was on the other foot, that listening was just as implicating as talking.

The telephone rang again.

'Yes, tov doctor, I put him entirely in your hands. Do as you think best.' And if it doesn't turn out right, he thought, so much the worse for you.

Ping.

'I'll tell you what I think, sweetheart,' he went on, 'the body politic requires a good cleansing purge. An amputation or two, like poor old Potter-Krasnovsky. I . . .'

Brr Brr, Brr Brr.

'Okay, I'll come right over. — Sorry, Ludmilla darling, but at this critical juncture in the nation's history . . .'

'Tell me you'll protect me whatever happens.'

'Whatever happens,' replied C-M, not knowing what might happen.

A kiss. A last whiff of sexual alcohol from the bedroom. Life was exciting, especially if you rode its Striding Edge. The dance, thought Boris, the dance between pinnacle and chasm. On your left the Chairmanship, on your right — but a man like himself was the equal of the Great Khan, of Josef Vissarionovich himself.

What the Truly Democratic Republic required was youth at the helm. They had been governed for too long by cautious old geriatrics who liked a quiet life in their declining years. What was needed was a young man like himself, aged 52 and at the peak of his powers, to tear corruption out shrieking by its hair-roots, to cleanse the body politic, to bring to birth at last that blessed day — the dawn, bright crimson-red, of Marx's dream.

Stalin had been a bastard, but still, you had to admire his single-mindedness.

15

He phoned General of the Truly Democratic Republic Fisher-Bukharin. He phoned Len (short for Lenin) Thoresby, Minister of the Interior. He phoned Scott-Chuznevsky, Brendan Lynch and Liam Donovan. Then he rang for his Rolls and pulled his trousers on in four seconds flat.

Ludmilla sighed and spread herself, wriggling, gazing upwards at the pale and shapely elegance of her own image in the mirror. In the muted glow of lamplight, the eyes of her reflection seemed to be shadowed and shut. It was as if she were glimpsing another Ludmilla, in another world, buoyed up and floating on a tide of sleep. And that other Ludmilla was dreaming of this one.

'What shall I do?' John Mathieson's thoughts were shouting in his head. All drenched black sky above, all patches and puddles of electric yellow beneath, Leninpool lurched by under the rainlight. He was sitting on the top deck of a trolley-bus, headed out towards the wilds of Cheshire, seeking the solitude of a two-hour journey to collect his thoughts, to struggle towards a decision. In the black and yellow night outside, the monotonous streets swept past, block after block, pavement after glistening pavement. Prostitutes sometimes, blue-boys more often, stood transfixed as in a photograph under the honey-coloured cones of the street-lamps. The drizzle materialised out of the darkness and could be seen dropping through the bilious air. And the PFs' pale blue rain-capes were turned lime-green, slime-green under the falling light.

What shall I do? To all intents and purposes a corpse, laid upon the concrete slab of the Public Revolutionary Bath-House. Or rather, my own ghost, crouching here on the top deck of the bus, gripping in my hand a part written for some other actor. I should have had the courage to make myself known. Then I would have been hauled along to the Bureau of Popular Friendship, would have had my face slapped . . . 'Your face isn't red enough, cond,' the gun-jacks would say (it was supposed to be an old Chinese proverb). 'Beating determines consciousness' (and that was a modern Russian one). On the other hand, there are cases of people who've had their legs broken by a slap in the face from a blue-boy.

But it's not as bad as that. I'm overdramatising it. I could perfectly well not have noticed I had the wrong identity till later, till just now on the bus for example. Or till tomorrow morning. Just go along to the Bureau. 'Last night in the bath-house somebody stole my documents.' Yes, the sensible, rational, commonsense thing.

Simple.

Mind you, the very thought of willingly approaching, let alone entering a Bureau of Popular Friendship, caused a wave of panic to swell up in his mind. But that was a purely psychological problem. He would have to fight it.

Why was it that the rational course of action seemed so unattractive? People had lost their identity cards before now. Ah yes, he knew. It was because of the Great State Lottery and the myth of the List, and the words of the man beside him in the queue: 'Expect they've just raised the quota.' Exactly. That was the reason why he was so mysteriously, so unaccountably reluctant to appeal to the friendship of the Friends.

I'm a coward, he decided. If only I'd spoken up before Lumsden was killed, then . . . But really, looking back over it, he was pretty sure he hadn't had the time. Holy Joseph, he felt awful about it, though.

On the other hand, feeling guilty wouldn't bring Lumsden back to life. Just have to go and play the innocent tomorrow morning. The trouble was that when a PF was staring into your eyes, it was hard to feel innocent even when you were. To the blue-boys, as the saying was, nobody was innocent until proved guilty.

Maybe I'm not a coward, he thought, but I'm certainly scared out of my wits.

Once John had seen a man registering a 'No' vote in an election. Though hard to credit that such things could still happen after a hundred years of socialism, it was true — he had seen it with his own eyes. There were a number of things the People's Friends might have done. They could have had him sentenced to Balvraid, the notorious camp in the Grampians.

17

They might have let it go for the moment, and arrested him later at the favourite time of three in the morning. In the event, they had simply marched the man out of the polling booth and shot him there in full view of the people (of all ages from 7 upwards) queuing to register their votes.

A fanciful picture crossed his mind. You could always quit Leninpool and turn up in London. There must be ways of getting past the checks at the station barriers. Once in London . . . You needed a work permit for anything legitimate, but there were said to be all sorts of shady organisations there — people who could forge documents and so on. The East Enderworld. He put it out of his mind with a shudder. No place for a coward, that.

The trolley-bus had emptied now, and John was left alone on the top deck as it jolted and swayed its way out into the Cheshire countryside. Reflections of steel bars and ripped leather seats tipped and swung, floating on the darkness of the night. They rocked along on both sides of the bus at a crazy angle, as if the real bus and its reflected images were quite incompatible. John turned his face and gazed at it in the mirror of the night. Pale, young, slightly balding. The face of a coward. The world was reduced to himself and darkness, on which was projected a triple vision of the trolley-bus interior, shiny, artificial, somehow false. The motor ground away, vibrating beneath him, and the only thing that told you there was a road beneath its wheels was the shaking and jolting. It was as if nothing else was there at all.

Except the image of Sue in John's mind. Ah, there now, there was something real. He had been going to see her tonight. But how could he do that now? Not till he'd decided what he might do, whether he'd be safe from investigation. Because he mustn't compromise her. Whatever he did, he mustn't put her in danger.

All was silent for a while inside the bus. It had reached its terminus, and the driver downstairs, locked away in his cab for fear of vandals and muggers, was puffing away at a Shamrock fag. No one climbed onto the top deck, and the silence was absolute. Pressing his face to the window, he could see four or five detached houses, each one set back behind a pair of tall iron gates and a twenty-foot hedge. The houses were large and, peering at them through the falling rain, John could make out their style — mock Tudor, with frowning eaves, their half-timbering picked out in black and white. They were like fierce blind faces, their cheeks and foreheads tattooed with zigzag bars. The huge hedges around them would conceal, he knew, an electrified fence. For this was plainly a suburb favoured by the local Nomenklatura. Further off to his left, a row of street-lamps showed where the terraces of more ordinary mortals were to be found.

Yes, the outside world had become faintly visible again, though ominously so, like a stage set left deserted and half-lit. More out of boredom than curiosity, John stuck his hand in his pocket and pulled out the identity cards that had belonged to Ivan Lumsden. At least it was something to do.

Ivan David Lumsden, born Engelsburgh 21 April 2091, age 24. Family status: unmarried. Father: Vladimir David Lumsden, Clerk Grade 13, died 2112 at the age of 40 after a simple operation. Mother: Janet, died of causes unknown a year to the day later.

John paused, suddenly affected. A family tragedy, simple and deadly as the PF's gun-butt. And now their son had followed them.

One sister, unmarried, a china-girl in Glasgorky.

Here was the Certificate of the Department of Productive Labour. Clerk Grade 15. Appointed to a post starting on 5 Marx 2116, Department of Social Harmony, Community Spirit Avenue, London. Holy Karl!

No wonder poor Ivan Lumsden had been so anguished in his appeals to the People's Friends. A step up in the world. No wonder he had been so frightened. For if he lost this, when would another such chance come his way? Moreover, it must have been promotion on merit.

John shook his head at the enormity of the thought. Merit? But it must be so, for Lumsden had not done the obvious thing when charged with — with being himself. He had not said, 'Ring Tov X, he'll vouch for me.'

He felt sorrier than ever for poor Lumsden. But there was no point in that. To tell the truth, the saddest thing of all was that there was no point in being sad.

He turned over the other documents. Credits in the Truly Democratic Bank: dear me, yes, he had saved. 100,000 Phunt, a trivial sum, but it amounted to a lot of effort. Social Quotient excellent for a clerk whose grade had been, until this promotion, 17th. Meant he was either a bastard, or knew how to keep his head below the parapet. Impeccable record of contributions to the Party coffers — sensible man!

What did he look like? Like everyone and nobody, I expect. Your quintessential conformist.

John had had only a momentary glimpse of him from fourteen places back in the queue. A laddy of his own age. Insignificant, underfed. He felt, however, a kind of superstitious awe as he opened the identity pack and gazed at the blurred, ill-reproduced photo of the dead man.

Yes, a conformist. A coward. Eyes intense, watchful. Thinning hair. Holy Karl!

John turned to gaze at himself again in the mirror of the night, holding up the ill-taken photo of Lumsden beside his own reflection. Sweet Marx, there was more than a slight resemblance, as if the dead man were some cousin of his own. And that might even be so, since his own family came from the Scottish Borders.

The sound of voices rose from below, and there was the sound of boots climbing the stairs. John put the cards hastily in his pocket again, making sure to close the zip-fastener firmly over them. Two young men, both cheerfully drunk, appeared at the top of the stairs and threw themselves heavily onto the seats, laughing and swearing. After a couple of false starts the engine of the trolley-bus hummed and vibrated, and the vehicle began to rattle and jolt its way back on the road towards Leninpool. The reflections in its windows tipped and veered as it swung out onto the main road, and it was there, suddenly, as he glanced once more at his reflection in the glass, that John had his great idea.

Vissarionovich! No, no, be sensible, John, keep your feet on the ground and your eyes firmly on the Party flag.

And yet, on the other hand, why not? The notion was crazy. It was a piece of lunacy. But it could be done. Frowning, staring fixedly into the depths of the bus but seeing nothing, John went over the whole thing in his mind, working out the consequences, puzzling out the snags. For the life of him he couldn't see any real conclusive reason . . . Why, you risked worse things every day crossing the street — particularly when there was a People's Friend standing at the other side of it.

Two hundred miles away, in the palace that had once been Buckingham, a man lay dying. Around him stood his Court, expressions of triumphant sorrow on their faces. Though he was the Leader, he had spent the last month of his life in the hands of the surgeons. A prolonged session of torture, such as he might himself have decreed for some Enemy of the People. It had not been politic to let him die in peace.

Event Two

*The worker does not merely
bargain with the Soviet State;
no, he is subordinated to the
Soviet State, under its orders in
every direction — for it is his
state.*

——————— LEV TROTSKY ———————

John had met her on a bus last midsummer. Seeing her sitting
there, half undressed — no, that wasn't true, she was merely
dressed for summer, a girl, biscuit-brown, revealed to the knees.
Above the white skirt she was wearing nothing but an athlete's
vest, sweating slightly into the middle of her cleavage. When she
smiled at him, she revealed white teeth that were a little
crooked. Svelte as a statue. But alive, her big brown eyes
luminous, taking in the man who was looking at her. Skin like
white coffee, shining black hair. He wondered, not for the first
time, how it was that young women could look as glossy-
skinned as porcelain. But porcelain had been invented long *after*
young women were invented, was modelled on the smoothness
of their skin. She was Wedgwood, Meissen and Ming. Unlike
porcelain, however, this five-foot figurine had muscles in her
thighs and a consciousness in her head. She breathed, felt and
reacted. She saw him as he saw her.

They had smiled at each other. He had moved into the seat
beside her.

In a sense it wasn't the first time he had met her. Seeing her
there on the bus he had had for a moment that sense of *déjà vu*
— what was it? — it was on the tip of his memory! Then it
dawned on him. He had seen her in a dream two nights ago. He

remembered the uneven white teeth, the frank brown gaze.

Later he told her about it, laughing, for it made an amusing story.

He was startled when she took him seriously, nodding her head rapidly and saying, 'Yes?'

'Yes what?'

'Yes, tell me more. What was I doing in your dream? Where was it, and was it summer there too?'

'I don't know,' he had said, unable to penetrate the mist of sleep that stood like a wall between him and his image of her. He was silent for a while, frowning, then shook his head. 'I can't bring back anything else at all. Only — it's very odd — a perfectly ordinary little word. *Set*.'

'Gosh.'

'Why, is that important?'

'Och, it isn't *set*, you see, it's *Sète*. It's a town in France. Was I very brown in your dream?'

'Yes, browner than you are now.'

'Look,' she said, moving to the shelf and taking down her old school atlas, tattered and dog-eared. She pointed to a small dot on the Mediterranean coast, sited between a huge lagoon and the sea, halfway between Béziers and Montpellier. 'And you didn't even know it existed!' She added wistfully, 'For some reason I've always wanted to learn French and go there. I don't know why.'

'You take these things very seriously, don't you?' he said with some unease. 'What would Marxist—Leninism say about it?'

'Those gowks!' she laughed at him. 'I expect it's my Scottish blood. I come of a long line of seventh sons of seventh sons, all with the second sight, so don't you cross me, John laddy, or I'll read your fate in my teacup!'

'But what's your theory?'

'Theory? You don't need a theory to make out truth from untruth.' And that was all she would say about it.

And now it was the month of Marx, and her skin was as white as ice-cream — like the girl in that picture he'd once seen, tipping water out of an urn she held upon her shoulder. Like Highland snow, he thought, as she opened the door.

'John! You are late, I thought you were never coming.'

23

He put his finger to his lips and slunk in like a burglar. 'Your flat-mates aren't here tonight.'

'No, I sent them off to the pub with their boyfriends. But we can go there too, if you like.'

'Not tonight. I'll tell you why in a moment. But perhaps you won't want to know me after what I've got to say. I hope it isn't dangerous for you, my coming here.'

Sue McKinlay shared her flat with two other girls. It was fifteen feet square, but then, there had been a housing shortage for the last hundred years, caused (according to a complicated argument put about by the Ministry) by the constant fall in the birth-rate.

'What does that mean, John? What have you been doing? You don't look quite yourself this evening.'

'I'm not myself at all, and shan't be any more. The first thing you must get used to is calling me "Ivan" from now on. If you want to go on knowing me, that is. And *never* slip up.'

'Holy Karl, J — Ivan. You haven't decided to become one of those Pseudo-Russkies, have you; with their Potter-Krasnovskys and their Clegg-Molotovs? Amusing really. When the policies change, there's nothing quicker on two legs than a Pseudo-Russ switching his name from Molotov to Khruschev and then back again!'

'Don't blether, woman, this is serious.' The tensions of the evening collected their strength and suddenly stabbed him through the stomach, so that he doubled up with pain.

'I'll get you a cup of tea,' she said. '*Ivan*,' she added, frowning with the effort. 'At least it's easier to say than Yevgeny.'

Ivan told her his tale from beginning to incredible end while she oohed and aahed and said 'Christ Jeezus' in her old-fashioned way throughout.

'But, J — Ivan, you'll have to take the cards back tomorrow. Sweet Marx, I hope it's all right,' she added, worried.

'No, Sue, I'm not taking it back tomorrow.'

'Leninday, then.'

'No, love, on Leninday, 5 Marx I shall be in London starting my new job as a Chinaboy Grade 15.'

'Ivan, could you please repeat that? I thought I heard you say you'd be in London starting your new job.'

'Yes, that's exactly what I said.'

'Jings!' she squealed, and dropped her full cup of tea all over the floor, as if the handle had suddenly become red-hot. The full weight of his meaning had struck her. 'But you cannae do that, John. They — they'll find out! Jeezus, what a mess! Wait till I get a cloth.'

She got down on her knees scrubbing the bare floor-boards while he explained to her quietly just why he thought he could. First, he, John Mathieson, was officially dead, and if you were officially dead you were *dead*, right? Secondly, he looked as like Ivan Lumsden as two peas in a tin. Thirdly, the man had no living relatives, save a sister in Glasgorky, which was — what? — four hundred miles from the capital. Fourthly, how could he go along to the Bureau and claim he was who he really was? Fifty-fifty he was on the List, and if he went in by that door his next sight of the open sky would be from halfway up a freezing mountainside, at Balvrain Re-education Camp. How many people ever came back from there? Fifthly and sixthly . . .

'Am I convincing you?' he asked, as she settled herself down with a second cup of tea.

'Man, you're daft, and so must I be, cos you *are* convincing me, right enough.' She shook her head sadly.

'Do you think I did the right thing coming here?' he asked. 'What shall we do now?'

'I don't know, what do you want to do?' she said vexingly.

At this point there was a knock on the door, businesslike, peremptory. Sue became absolutely motionless, the hand with the teacup in it freezing one foot from her lips. With her other hand she made a gesture like a conductor commanding an orchestra to silence. *I'm fast asleep*, she mouthed silently at Ivan. He turned to stare at the door. After a moment, its handle rattled and twisted as the person outside tried it. 'Cond McKinlay? Cond Porter?' came a confident male voice from outside.

It must be Redman.

Petya Redman (his real name was Peter Greene) was the chairman of the Apartment Block Committee, and made it his business, as a good chairman should, to revolve every night among the flat-dwellers, inquiring into the state of their Marxist consciousness, discussing knotty problems in *Kapital* with them, and talking over new ways in which the Block could show its loyalty to our glorious socialist motherland. At the same time he kept an eye on them, as a good Party man should. That eye was not so very fatherly where his younger and prettier tenants were concerned.

'I shall have to change flats,' muttered Sue under her breath, swearing. 'But how? Redman has the housing department's ear.'

'You know fine well I *want* you to change flats,' replied Ivan. 'Listen, darling, I want you to marry me — or at the very least come to London with me.'

So there, he had said it.

He added, 'But only if you think it's safe. I know what I'm proposing has a certain risk attached. I can't bear the thought of living without you, but I don't want to put you in the slightest danger.'

So there, the shocking truth was out! There was something he found more important than dialectical materialism!

She did not seem to notice this lapse from good Socsov principle, however. She got off her chair and into his arms, and for a while spoken communication gave way to another kind.

'You know I like that,' she said giggling. 'But listen, you awful man, you know we have something to discuss. First.'

'First,' he agreed.

'Well, you know . . . Listen, how can we talk when you're . . . I think I'd better go back to my own chair.'

With imitation primness she separated herself from him and resumed her position on the hard little chair, shoeless, knees and ankles held together, feet curving downwards, almost as if her nether limbs were about to turn fishy and finny like a mermaid's. There was a silence while both of them contemplated the problem.

'You know very well that getting married does nothing to help. You can't live together if you haven't got a job and a work permit. Why, you know poor Mrs Lloyd along the corridor? She's been trying for fifteen years to join her husband in Marxeter. And *she's* got three children!'

'The point is,' said Ivan, nodding, 'do you *know* anyone?'

'Luckily I do. Department of Productive Labour. He'd fix it for me, I'm sure.

'Or at least he'd take a lapper.'

Was it the crudity of this word, or the bourgeois nature of its moral implications that made Ivan wince? 'How much will it cost?' he asked, and reached into his overalls, for among the treasures he had found in the unfortunate Ivan Lumsden's belongings was a thick wad of thousand-phunt notes, all safely used, all prettily stamped with waving flags and advancing workers' militias. This inspiring effect was spoiled by the presence in the foreground of Potter-Krasnovsky's brooding, melancholy jowls. No wonder Ivan Lumsden had been on his way to London! When John had come across this treasure-trove, he had amended his view of the man's character. No, he had not risen by merit, after all. He had plainly been useful to somebody. He felt slightly less pity, slightly less guilt at the thought.

'A bourgeois invention, but it oils the wheels of history.'

'No, no,' she said then, putting up her hand to check him. 'You'll need that for my wedding present.

'Och yes,' she explained, 'I have a wee nest-egg put by. A girl has to look to the future. So long as we don't have to live in the East Enderworld, that's all I ask.'

'I'm afraid that man in the Labour Department may put your future in his pocket. But — oh Sue! I hadn't noticed! You've just said Yes, haven't you?'

'Of course I have, you daft thing. You males aren't very observant, are you? I suppose it's because you spend your time watching our legs instead of our lips. Soft things, the lot of you.'

A kiss at this point was not merely apropos or delightful, it was positively necessary. One thing leads to another, and all this heady emotion was sealed by a breathless pulling-off of clothes, and by the only sport where you lose if both sides don't win.

He had to prove that he wasn't soft, too.

Afterwards, as they sweated harmoniously together, Ivan asked her, 'Do you think I'm being immoral?'

'*What*?' Sue was prepared to look insulted if he had no explanation.

'Oh, I don't mean *this*. I mean cheating the State.' That wasn't

quite what he meant, either. Rather he was thinking of Lumsden, the dead man, whose papers and money he had taken, whose
signature he would have to learn to forge, whose ghost leaned
over them both at this moment. Resentfully? No, smiling, surely,
and happy that some*body* might be profited, and not some*thing*.
Lumsden, destroyed by the Great Whatever-It-Pretends-To-be,
hovered in the musty air of the flat. Signing his name, forging
John Mathieson's useless signature, he made over his worldly
goods to Ivan Lumsden the Second. Fight them for me, mate.

'Are you daft, John? Ivan, I mean. Of course not, they don't
give a damn who anyone is. It's the sort of state,' she added
bleakly — and Ivan watched her disentangling herself, pulling
on her panties and skirt — 'It's the sort of state you have to
swindle to stay honest. Poetry and justice, jings, they don't often
come together.'

Sueivanly sticky, Ivan drew his clothes on in his turn. Yes, as
you grasp the woman you love with both hands, let's grab this
chance. Smile back at fate while it smiles on you, or Marx knows
what will happen. Marx knows exactly what will happen.

One small shadow. Unspoken between them lay the possibility that this man, this so useful anonymous man from the
Department of Productive Labour, would not be satisfied with
a purely monetary bribe. Ivan shrugged his shoulders. Life was
as you found it, and if that was to be so, he simply hoped she
would never tell him. Of course. She was a level-headed girl, she
knew the social etiquette, she never would.

Event Three

*Even torture has facilitated the
invention of the cleverest
mechanical contrivances, giving
productive employment to a host
of honest workers.*

———— KARL MARX ————

Freeday, 22 June 2116

As his bullet-proof Rolls purred into Pollittburo Street, swung
round Piccadilly Circus past the famous statue of Class Warfare,
and plunged down Stalinsbury Avenue on its impatient way to
Beatrice and Sidney Webb Prison, Clegg-Molotov admired the
huge hoarding that closed off the end of one block.

COMRADES,
it shrieked in ten-foot letters of scarlet,

IF YOU ARE WEARY, THINK OF POTTER-
KRASNOVSKY, AND HE WILL GIVE YOU COURAGE.

IF YOU ARE DOUBTFUL, THINK OF POTTER-KRAS-
NOVSKY, AND HE WILL GIVE YOU TRUTH.

'POTTER—KRASNOVSKY SAID' — THAT MEANS THE
PEOPLE THINK SO.

'THE PEOPLE SAID' — THAT MEANS POTTER-KRAS-
NOVSKY THINKS SO.

Not very snappy, but it gave the right idea. Workmen were
swarming all over it, removing the name Potter-Krasnovsky and
replacing it by Clegg-Molotov.

Unaware of any biblical overtones, Boris nonetheless mused:
What a sense of humour History must have! When you thought
of the site of London's central prison — the Web, as it was

29

fondly known — for so long the British Museum had stood there filling up with the assembled knowledge of the centuries — till the revolutionaries of 2009 had broken in, hunting down white-haired professors between the bookstacks, then burning the place to the ground — sweeping it away along with the rest of the repressive bourgeois past. It was a symbol, thought C-M — one mode of knowledge replacing another. Interrogation techniques — now there was the real knowledge, the knowledge of man's minds and hearts.

You had to admire the revolutionaries of 2009. They had had a keen awareness of the symbolic import of their acts. Razing the Houses of Parliament had been another such. It would have been useful to conserve these buildings, to turn them over to the Workers' Assembly, but the power of that place as an emblem was too great. Before long the People's representatives might have started arguing with the decisions of the Government, and then where would democratic centralism have been? C-M recalled the solemn warning of the Old Bolshevik, Lev Kamenev, back in . . . 1919? 1920?

'For if they say today, let us have democracy in the Party, tomorrow they will say, let us have democracy in the trade unions; the day after tomorrow, non-Party workers may well say: give us democracy too . . . and then the myriads of peasants . . . '

Once let democracy get one little foot in the door! Boris shuddered to think of it.

So the proud classical colonnade of the British Museum was no more. Instead a wall fifty feet high, bearing metal spikes upon its coping-stones, ran the whole length of Guy Burgess Street and Anthony Blunt Place, capped at intervals by even higher watch-towers. And if you revolved to Philby Place on the other side of the block you could see the prison itself staring down at you — a vast oblong of stone twelve storeys high, half a kilometre in length, 90 per cent of its windows shuttered and blinded at any time of day. Above it all there fluttered the flag of the Truly Democratic Republic, crimson with a hammer and sickle in one corner and a shamrock in the other.

The guards at the gate saluted, the Rolls swung into the courtyard. The PF Captain on duty stepped forward to open

C-M's door, saying as he did so, 'Warmest congratulations, Tov Chairman, on your appointment.'

'Thank you, Tov Captain,' said Boris modestly. 'Thank you in the People's name. I hope it will enable me to serve the Revolution.'

With some emotion he raised his eyes to the vast blank menace of the web. Ten thousand cells, the ghosts of 10 million prisoners, men, women and children. His domain, now to be turned over to his successor. Here, thirty years ago, he had performed his first interrogation. Here (he recalled with a sentimental catch in his throat) he had struck his first prisoner. Here he had returned (after a lapse of time as Minister of Health and Sanity) to take over control of the whole vast organisation of Social Harmony, with its 900 prisons, its forty-two re-education camps, its ammunition stores, its eavesdropping equipment, its private morgues, its 2 million employees.

But, of course, he consoled himself, this was not exactly goodbye for ever. He would be keeping a close eye on the acts of his successor. None closer.

From the dark shadow of the archway, that same successor now stepped forward, offering in his turn congratulations on C-M's promotion to the post of Head of State.

'So early in your career, Tov Chairman. A mere — what is it? — 49?'

'Fifty-two,' replied Boris. Vassily Forson knew his age as well as he did his own. 'Some of the Presidium argued, of course, for an older man. Experience, continuity. There's much to be said for it,' he pronounced humbly.

'But you pointed out to them the advantages of youth.'

'Of efficiency. Innokenty had the kindness to mention our production record at Social Harmony. It swayed the day. One thing I am delighted about, that it has cleared the way for so dedicated an official as yourself.'

Vassily expressed his gratitude for this kind remark, while thinking to himself, How pointed!

They proceeded down the echoing state corridor, lined with doors, each bearing its gnomic lable: INFORMBURO, STREET SURVEILLANCE, E.A.R., DEPARTMENT Z, PHYSMETH,

31

PSYCHOSP, JUSTLIAIS, ARTICLE 58, INTEXILE, RE-ED, CAMPDEP, SPECIAL DELIVERIES, CLOSED FILES. At one of these many doors, Boris paused for a moment, then gently opened it to reveal within a roomful of cadets about 18 or 19 years old, all listening with grave attention to the Comrade-Colonel-Tutor.

'One should never underestimate,' he was saying, 'the initial difficulties a tov may have in performing interrogation duty. When you are first called upon to apply physical methods, you may find yourself assailed by pity. I can assure you from my own experience that this is a most disturbing sensation. Don't smile when I say that some young officers have been known actually to cry. Don't worry, this is quite normal. The majority of people are subject to such emotions, which have perfectly good physio-chemical explanations. The thing is not to be over-concerned, not to agonise too much about your feelings. You can rest assured that, with practice and experience, such emotions will dissipate themselves.'

C-M closed the door softly, nodding his head.

'We shall miss you, Tov Chairman,' Vassily was saying enthusiastically. 'The professional's professional, if I may say so. I was just telling Patrick Shillito this morning how you still love to roll your sleeves up and get down to the job just like any ordinary officer.'

'Kind of you, Vassily,' Boris murmured, soaking in this praise while at the same time giving himself the pleasure of disapproving adulation in the abstract. Feeling flattered but despising the flatterer. The best of both worlds.

But now to business. Both men turned in at a door marked ADMIN(OFFMIN), outside which a couple of guards with tommy-guns came respectfully to attention. This morning C-M was to complete the complex business of checking his successor through the secret files. While he did so, he ruminated on the question of trust.

Such problems could not be compared with those of capitalist times, when relationships were exclusively of class—social and male—patriarchal power. Nevertheless, he had always found it advisable for his own safety to encourage the loyalty of subordinates and the esteem of colleagues by tokens of his gratitude. Marx (to use a tautology) was right. It was the *economic* relationship that was fundamental to human life.

Vassily had often expressed envy of C-M's datcha, that large estate in the north of Wales which contained a huge Victorian castle. Built on so lavish a scale that no Norman baron could have created it unless he had all the riches of the Indies as well as those of his own conquered Welsh serfs, it had once been owned by Lord Penrhyn, a particularly oppressive mine-owner. It had the advantage of its own private harbour — ideal if you were, like Vassily, a sailing enthusiast. Over coffee (People's Indian Ethnic Collectives of Brazil) C-M dangled this carrot in front of his successor, then hinted with an ominously cheerful smile of darker things.

Vassily's hands were not the cleanest. Ministers of Social Harmony had ended up before this in their own cellars.

'Take a look at this,' said Boris.

'This' was a dossier or, to use the correct expression, a person by the name of Doherty, James Colum. Vassily Forson, speaking no word, uttering neither a 'Hm' nor a 'Hah', thumbed it rapidly through, with the practised eye of a man who can compute another's fate in twenty seconds. Certain entries leapt at once to the eye.

'Utility Rating A. Disposability Rating A. Age 21. Milieu: East Enderworld. Drug Addict (Source of Supply, PF). Criminal Assault (x 7). Certified Psychopath, Grade 2. Trained Marksman (Source, Crimworld, PF). Suggestivity Rating A. Political Status: Class-Hostile Element.'

'You see what a dangerous man he is,' said C-M. 'The guard is to be doubled on the First Secretary's office. He must be arrested *before* . . .' He let this sentence hang on the air.

Vassily almost winked. He remembered a number of things: his Byzantine dealings with the black market, his wife, his delightful 12-year-old daughter, and last but not least *Tropicana*, his forty-foot motorboat, a floating vodka palace, the apple of his eye. He remembered that C-M knew more about him than he did himself, and that everything he knew must be by definition true.

Boris looked Vassily in the eye and disliked what he saw there — which was satisfactory. Speech broke out again, and they chatted for a pleasant ten minutes, but somehow more meaningfully than usual, of datchas, vodka palaces and 12-year-old daughters.

After such intensity it was natural that they should part upon that token of mutual esteem, of comradeship tried and tested over the years in the selfless struggle for social justice — the brotherly communist kiss.

Event Four

*The 'free State', whatever is
that?*
──────── KARL MARX ────────

Sartreday, 23 June 2116

'Do you suppose beer used to be green in the *old* days, under
capitalism?'

Geoff and Ivan stared suspiciously at the seventy-centilitre
glasses the barmaid was pouring. It was no good complaining.
Even the prettiest barmaids were paid employees of the PF. At
least the pub was comfortable, being that historic London inn
called 'The Hammer and Sickle' (not far from 'The Soviet
Worker', 'King Charles III's Head' and 'The Red Lion').

'And two thirties of cider,' added Geoff, glancing across the
room to the table where Sue and Polly were already ensconced,
under the notice reading

PEOPLE'S NUTRITIOUS ALE PRODUCTS
WARRANT OF EQUALITY
STATE CERTIFICATED FLAVOUR

The blonde and brunette heads were close together, the lips
moving volubly. Female secrets.

'A friend of mine,' Polly was saying, 'was sent to Thurso!'

'Thurso's a fine wee town,' said Sue defensively. Scotland was
better than London any day, and what could be known of such
things by mere southerners like Polly, who came from Tashcanter-
bury in the county of Tashkent?

'Maybe,' said Polly doubtfully, 'but even a rabid Scot like

yourself, Sue, must admit that it's a bit much when her husband was left in London. "The needs of the People take precedence over the needs of the people," ' she mimicked in her most official voice. 'And all because she wouldn't sleep with that horrible man in the Labour Department. Mind you, when I got to come here with Geoff, it was because I knew Someone. And do you know — you'll hardly credit this! — he arranged it all for nothing!'

'Sweet Karl!' breathed Sue, amazed.

'I won't ask what *you* had to do for *your* Someone,' Polly insinuated, blue eyes sparkling with curiosity.

'Sh,' said Sue, 'here come the men.'

A new friendship was always exciting. The interest of finding out whether these people, apparently so interested in you, were really state informers. For two whole months the two young couples had revolved about each other warily, taking all kinds of precautions over what they said and thought. Now all reserve was thawing under the pressure of Sue's wit and Geoff's humorous gentleness. Calm of character, vast of shoulders, he might well have been a rugby forward before the game was banned as class-élitist.

'Cheers,' he said now, and, leaning forward, murmured in reverent tones, 'Don't look now, the barmaid might be embarrassed, but don't you think what it really is is an *ear*?'

They all glanced over to the emblem above the bar, badge of this pub as well as of the Truly Democratic Republic. You know, Geoff was quite right, it wasn't a hammer and sickle at all, it was the stylized image of an enormous ear, clapped to the wall above the bar as it was to every official building in the city.

'Straining its drums just now, isn't it?' said Ivan.

'What's the hammer, then?' asked Sue pertly. 'A hearing aid?'

'That's right, it's a hidden microphone.'

Geoff laughed and began to tell the latest story. 'Do you know why it's just been decreed that all bread shops must have at least three kilometres between them?'

'No, why?'

'So that the queues don't get mixed up.'

And had Sue given the functionary more than money? Ivan

had never asked her, and she had never told him. For suppose he had asked her and she told him — perhaps truly — that the official had not demanded any favours . . . then what about the next time or the next time after that? One of these days you might, by dint of asking all these impertinent questions about officials, catch sight of the ghost of an untruth in the corner of your wife's eye, and that would spell the end of marital trust. No, it was one of those things you simply didn't talk about.

What was important was that she had been assigned an excellent job in a London restaurant, and so could be with him.

Two evenings later was Discussion Group, where they met Geoff and Polly again, as novitiate members of the Party being instructed in its inner dogma. It wasn't hard if you had a good memory. Indeed, Polly was so good at pronouncing long words with calm panache that Geoff had started calling her 'Polly Syllable'.

This particular Leninday was *literally* a red-letter day, for Sue and Ivan, Geoff and Polly were at last inducted as new-fledged members of the Party, with the right to be called 'tov' instead of 'cond'. They rode home on the bus clutching their brand new scarlet cards in their hands, printed out in Russian and English, feeling a considerable emotion. You deserved to feel it, but precisely what kind of emotion was it? Officially and aloud you called it 'pride'.

The Underground was not very safe these days. Since Sue had joined Ivan two months ago, there had been three crashes, the last involving a fire and some loss of life. They preferred, therefore, to take the bus, up Sloane Street, crossing Knightsbridge (renamed Sinn Fein Street after that memorable blow against the exploitation of the poor, the IRA's Christmas Bomb of 1983), north through Paddington, and home at last to Kilburn, where it was only a short step to the door of their apartment block. There they said goodnight to Geoff and Polly, and walked hand in hand four hundred yards along the road, past the strolling pairs of People's Friends, each cradling his beloved tommy-gun, past the ageing apartment blocks of De Valera Road, still pitted and pocked with bullet-holes after more than a hundred years.

The flat that had been assigned to them (Imagine, in the old pre-Revolution days, you had had to look for your own accommodation!) was very old-fashioned too. Just as well, thought Sue; I wouldn't like to live in one of those glass bowls across the street! For on the other side of De Valera Road, it was the most up-to-date of comforts: walls all glass from one side of the room to the other, and special curtains that were transparent, so that every cond's life was on show from sun-up till sundown.

'NEW DWELLINGS FOR THE NEW MAN AND WOMAN' said the notice at the door. 'In the People's Truly Democratic Republic we have NO SECRETS FROM EACH OTHER. Here is the new life of SINCERITY, TOGETHERNESS, COMMUNITY SPIRIT. APPLY TODAY FOR TOMORROW'S WORLD.'

Not that anyone ever did apply. Besides, such buildings were assigned, like any others.

'They say *their* electricity always works,' said Sue. 'I prefer power cuts.'

So there were two things to be grateful for, first, that they had a two-room flat, second, that it wasn't in TWENTY-THIRD CENTURY BLOCK. The luxurious size of their new flat was due, of course, to Ivan's rise in grade. Only a couple of steps, but that and a wife ensured . . . As well as entry into the Party.

She threw herself down on the aged sofa with a gasp of relief. 'Oof, I'm so tired! Be a darling, Ivan, and brew us up a cup of tea. Enthusiasm!' she complained. 'It takes a lot of energy. "Clegg-Molotov" — clamorous shouts. "The Truly Democratic Republic" — plaudits, extended clapping. "Long Live the International Workers' Federation" — storms of applause. And all this political theory!' She wrinkled her nose. 'How can you remember it? What does it *mean*? Sometimes I wonder if there hasn't been a kind of switch in worlds, and we live in *this* one, but our theories belong in the other.'

'Didn't you find it interesting tonight, though?' asked Ivan, bringing the tea. 'The history of the British Revolution!'

'Och,' she said dismissively, 'you know what the doctor says when he's doing his job properly? "I'd like another opinion." '

'Mm, but I think we can form our own. We have to go

through it anyway, because we need to recite it back on Engels-day.'

'Give me my tea, then I might be able to think.'

'Here you are. Do you want to start, or shall I?'

'Well now,' said Sue. 'Back in 2006 — if I go wrong, just tell me, Ivan — there was so much automation there were 10 million out of work, and women weren't counted as unemployed at all. And if you didn't have work, you had to beg for charity or else you starved. At the same time there were lots of plutocrats with grouse moors and yachts and datchas . . .'

'Hush, Sue, you mustn't call them datchas, they were "stately homes", remember?'

'Industry was owned by the Americans, but salvation was at hand. In Northern Ireland there was already a revolution going on, led by the Irish Republican Army and the National Libera-tion Front. The British Army had gone in to massacre the Work-ing Class, and were being assisted by a gang of class-traitors called . . . called . . . help me, Ivan.'

'Called "protesters", I think,' said Ivan, frowning.

'So then Will Murphy, known as the People's Will, who was leader of the National Fuelmen's Union, called his members out on strike. Hey, Ivan, what's a strike?'

'I don't know,' said Ivan.

'Anyway, he called them out on strike, and he had to pretend he'd called it against closing mines and oil wells and factories, because striking against the government was forbidden. Right?'

'Left,' said Ivan, which was the accepted response these days.

'And the government granted all Murphy's demands, but he still wouldn't send his members back, and they'd been out for nine months. Late 2007, and there was an election looming.

'Then, just before polling day, the New Left Labour Party suffered a terrible loss. Their leader, Arnold Briggs, was assas-sinated by the Tory terror machine and in anger the people all voted New Left.'

'I don't understand,' said Ivan, shaking his head. 'How could the Secret Police have allowed it?'

'Shut up, Ivan, you can give your version later. This is the praveelny one. Murphy became Prime Minister and the govern-

39

ment took all the factories away from the Americans and gave them to the People. They sent the Yanks packing with their atomic bombs. And they withdrew the Army from Northern Ireland and disbanded it because its experience there had taught it a vicious hatred of the Working Class.

'Then the Secret Police began to use terror against the British Working Class, and . . .'

'No, you've missed something out. What about Ireland?'

'Oh yes. The Protesters defeated the IRA and began to massacre the Irish Working Class. Then the Irish Government could stand by no longer. Their troops crossed the border into Ulster, but the Protesters defeated them, and marched on Dublin.

'Then there was a mass-proletarian rising on this side of the Irish Sea, led by the freedom-fighter Brianston-Pedley. The Great Class War had begun — the Last Act of History — the final confrontation. Things hung in the balance, though, till the government called in the freedom-loving USSR.'

'But they wouldn't have been able to, unless,' Ivan prompted her.

'Och yes, I nearly forgot. All the countries in Western Europe had given up their atomic weapons under pressure from the International Workers' Peace Movement, so the Russian army found it quite easy to come to the help of the toiling masses. The existing state machine was dismantled, and the exploitative classes were liquidated. And that was how the Revolution of 2009 began, and how Murphy's Law became the law of the land.'

'I wonder how many people died?'

'They didn't say, did they? Listen, do you suppose there *was* a Secret Police?'

'Och, Sue, be reasonable, how could you govern without a Secret Police?'

'I don't know,' said Sue in her turn.

'Do you suppose if we read it all upside down . . . "Militarist — colonialist terror against the Irish workers . . ." What if it was the other way round?'

By an automatic reflex, Sue went pale.

Subdued, frightened by such audacity, they had a second cup

of tea. She peeped out at the big glass house that reared, twelve storeys high, across the street. Twenty yards away she could see a wife and husband sitting drinking tea. A couple of just their own age. They too were silent, but as if in their case they never spoke at all, but spent every evening sitting there, facing the transparent curtains, not daring to utter a word lest the night outside the window should be watching and know what they thought of it.

She had the strange sensation that, over in Twenty-Third Century Block, it really was the future already, and that she was looking out of the past into that time of which the prophets spoke, when there would be no more darkness, when all would be clear and simple, pitilessly illuminated by the glaring daylight.

Then, where would the darkness go? That was obvious: it would run and hide, inside the skulls of men.

Dream One

What relief! And so hot too! Only two days ago, the skies had been wringing their gloom out over London, like dirty water out of a sponge. But here in the Midi, the sand struck dry white sunlight at your eyes and burned the soles of your feet, the blue water glittered as if every wavelet held cupped within it a bobbing miniature of the sun. Sue grinned her crooked grin and quoted incomprehensible Frog at him:

'Le Temps scintille, et le Songe est savoir.'

'What? Darling,' John said humorously, 'are you trying to educate me or something?'

The dream, or his attention, shifted.

The glare of the blue sky had receded now. It floated above the roofs at the summit of a cool stone canyon of house-fronts. To their left ran a sort of broad canal, full of moored boats, criss-crossed with a spider's web of masts and rigging. A façade in the style of Napoléon III swam up before his eyes, and he read: 'Crédit Marinier — Fondé en 1883 — Société Anonyme — Banque Inscrite . . .'

God, he was having a dream of capitalist France. Moreover, in his dream he seemed to know what 'God' meant.

Abruptly it seemed, they were back on the beach, and she was pointing out to sea. Her hand marked out the horizon as it rose from left to centre, slightly dome-shaped, and fell curving away again towards the western end of the beach.

French poetry again: 'Ce toit tranquille, où marchent des colombes.'

'Och yes,' he was saying, 'I can see that. As you stand at the

42

edge of the water, you seem to see it sloping upwards away from you. As if the sea looms above us. It must be because of the bulge of the globe. I suppose it *is* rather like a roof.'

'And the doves of course are the white sails.'

White sails and shining teeth. 'What about that other line you quoted at me? You still haven't explained it.'

'I'll translate it for you. *Le Temps scintille, et le Songe est savoir.* "Time flickers past, and Dream is wisdom." The waves are time in the poem, you see, John, and they glitter in the sun like the passing of seconds. Like moments in eternity. There, what do you think of that?' she said with pride, as if she'd written it herself.

'And the dream?'

'That's the dream of eternity which, it turns out later in the poem, Valéry doesn't believe in. He was a rationalist, you know.'

I suppose, said Ivan to himself when he woke the next morning, it was the sunshine and the holiday. It can't have been capitalism that gave that sense of freedom. But why could he remember nothing except that single line of French poetry?

Bah, dreams were always like that! They made no more sense than poetry. Than poetry in a foreign language. A foreign language within a foreign language. And now he'd forgotten the line.

'Is your French good?' he asked Sue when the alarm-clock rang.

'Well, I learnt a smattering at school,' she said doubtfully, 'but we only had half the time that was given to Russian.'

'But do you remember any?'

'Not really. Darling, what a funny question! No, I've just always wanted to visit Sète, I don't know why.'

She looked so sad, he wished he hadn't asked her.

'But that's impossible, even though it is a communist state. Unless you're at least Grade 6.'

Event Five

*No organisation except the army
has ever controlled man with
such severe compulsion as does
the State organisation of the
working class in the most
difficult period of transition.*

———— LEV TROTSKY ————

Stalinday, 1 July 2116

Normally, Ivan never remembered his dreams. Even if he recalled an image or two on first waking, these slipped out of his ken at once, like snakes bolting for their holes in the sand, and by the time he had yawned and rubbed his eyes, they were gone for ever. But for some reason disconnected fragments of sunshine, sea and poetry kept jogging at his attention all week long. Mention of France had made Sue a little pensive too. It made no sense, the train would cost a whole week's wages, but if the sun were to come out . . .

Freeday was out, of course, for it was a normal working period. Sartreday was out too, as three out of four always were. It was a Voluntary Labour Day, on which workers raised production norms. Stalinday, however, dawned a little cloudy, and promised a sultry warmth which would be perfect for the seaside. Ivan and Sue took the first bus down to Victoria (short for Victory of the Oppressed Millions) station, and presented their Party cards at the barrier.

The barrier consisted of a barbed wire fence running the length and breadth of the station. At intervals this fence was broken by sentry-posts, each dominated by a watch-tower.

44

There was already a huge queue, and the couple had to wait for an hour before being admitted to the platform.

There they waited another hour for the train. In the meantime, the ranks of would-be travellers built up on the platform till Ivan, afraid that Sue, who was neither tall nor heavy, might be elbowed onto the track by the sullen throng behind them, pulled both of them back a little from their choice positions.

Unfortunately, as the train at last came sliding in, panting and choking on its own fumes, there was a flurry of shoving and shouting from behind. A file of People's Friends came pushing onto the platform, advancing along the edge of it, compressing the waiting travellers even more stickily and sweatily against each other. 'Special Priority!' they cried. 'Heroes of Labour and Cadres only!' They formed a human wall on the edge of the platform, thus preventing any door from being opened. Meanwhile, Sue and Ivan had fitful glimpses through the crush of workers' caps and sky-blue képis — and through the grime of the train windows, of a large number of new arrivals marching up the platform on the train's further side, and being ushered into its empty coaches.

There was no room for anyone on their own side of the platform to enter.

Half an hour later a second train groaned into the station. There was a scramble to get in, and, since the young couple did not happen to be placed exactly opposite a door, it was some minutes before they could force their way on. By this time there were no seats left.

'Well, at least we're on,' said Sue, her natural cheerfulness asserting itself.

She spoke too soon. Packed to the doors, the train remained standing at the platform as a group of railway employees gathered round the engine, like doctors who had called in a specialist to discuss the imminent death of their patient. Time was not flickering past on Victoria station this morning, but yawning as it almost failed to move at all.

'Everybody off. The engine's broken down.'

They eventually reached Brighton some three hours later.

The station was a little way from the front, and you could catch no sight of blue sea through the skyscrapers standing to attention like People's Friends between it and the railway. Inside, it consisted of a large waiting area quite innocent of anything to sit on. This waiting area (like that at Victoria) was divided in two by a double barbed wire fence and a series of sentry posts which faced both ways, outwards in the direction of the citizens of Brighton, inwards to hem in the arriving passengers. Ivan and Sue presented their tickets and identity cards.

The PF was young and pimply, with a nasty rash on his neck made worse by the rubbing of his sky-blue collar. He glanced at their documents and at them. 'Social Quotient?' he said.

The Social Quotient was a card that listed the following things: (1) Hours of voluntary work; (2) Attendance at Discussion Group; (3) Weighted Assessment of Social Worth; (4) Productivity Rating; (5) Voluntary Contributions to State Funds; (6) Attendance at Spontaneous Political Rallies; (7) Voting Record; (8) Subscription to the Paper *Truth* (twice daily).

'Sorry,' said the blue-boy without expression, handing it back.

'I beg your pardon,' said Ivan.

The PF swivelled his eyes to look at them. Sue, sweating and dirty from the train journey, burst into tears. 'Nobody's coming through today,' said the gun-jack flatly, 'except over Social Quotient 70. Town too full. Make it too crowded for the Cadres.'

'Get a move on there,' growled the woman behind Sue. 'Let accredited travellers pass. Shocking, isn't it,' she said to her husband, 'blocking up the station when they haven't the right . . .'

Ivan thought of saying that nobody had told him about this back in London. But there was one simple rule, ingrained in him since childhood: never argue with a People's Friend.

At least the man had said sorry. More, he had actually explained!

At this point, the young man did more than that. He felt in

his uniform pocket, bent close to Sue (down whose face tears were pouring, making grimy smudges on her cheeks), and (first gazing around him to check that no officer had noticed) pressed into her hand a sticky bar of chocolate.

Ivan and Sue, defeated but tongue-tied with amazement, turned around and trudged back towards the platform. Their shoulders were sagging but the shock had stopped Sue's tears dead. People's Collectives of Mexico, a whole week's ration!

They had spent a week's wages, they had not eaten all day, they had not even glimpsed the sea, and were not back in London till nearly midnight. When they reached the haven of their flat at last, they found the electricity was off. 'I should have kept my mouth shut,' said Sue mournfully, glancing at the glass house across the road.

'You go out into the country,' she added, 'and the only blue sky you see is a PF's uniform.

'Well,' she added to console herself, 'at least it was voluntary.'

'Voluntary?'

'Yes.'

'Sorry, love, I don't see what you mean.'

'Voluntary. It was something *we* did.'

'Is *that* what it means? I always thought it meant "additional", like in "Voluntary Work Day"!'

And yet, though she had wanted to see the sea so much, though the day had been such a disaster, though all she had got was eleven hours of standing on platforms with grit blowing in her eyes, four hours of standing in the corridor, being jolted and flung to and fro, somehow the PF's gesture made up for it all.

Leninday, 2 July 2116

The Brighton fiasco had taken on, at the time, the dimensions of a tragedy. But it was all blood under London Bridge (and, Sweet Marx, had there been blood under London Bridge back in 2009!). They had discovered just how lucky they were in each other, for neither had claimed it was the other's fault.

When Ivan arrived next morning at the Department of Social

Harmony (Clerical Division, 33 Warder Street), he glanced at the plaque as he entered, and erased it in his mind.

Leninday, 2 July 2116. Marxday, Engelsday, Althusserday, Freeday and Sartreday all confronted him, one after another, each with its six hours of compulsory, two of voluntary, labour. Then there was an average of three hours daily spent queuing for food — bread, milk, potatoes, meat when there *was* any. On Leninday, Engelsday and Freeday you attended your Discussion Group (but at least Sue would be with him). Never mind; there were still evenings in the pub with Geoff and Polly, there was still that moment every day when they got home and drew the curtains on the PFs patrolling the darkening streets.

The vestibule of the Department was full of newly arrived clerks of all grades, squatting on the carpet, taking off their socks and shoes. It was, Ivan mused, like entering the mosque in a Qadhafian country, only here you didn't do it out of reverence to Allah, but simply so as to preserve them from wearing out too quickly. The Socsov System, people joked, was really the Socks Off System. Though the Production Norm for footwear had been triumphantly exceeded this last year, and indeed (as public records proved) triumphantly exceeded every year since 2015, it was only sizes 8 and 9 that had been produced. The government was working on the problem and, since it had been working on it for 101 years, it would soon victoriously solve it. It was also working on the 'Problematic' (as the philosopher Althusser put it) of the sock shortage, which was due to sabotage by agents of the USA. In the meantime, only PFs were allowed to wear boots around the office, and the cond citizens would be wise to economise on shoeleather.

Carrying his shoes in one hand and his briefcase in the other, Ivan advanced towards the lift.

Though he loathed the great Department of State for which he worked, his task within it had a certain interest. He was attached to that section of the Industrial Liaison Division which collated reports from the north of England and compared them with confidential reports on those same industries sent in by undercover members of the PF. It was thus that he learned that the Production Norm for coal had been exceeded in 2014–15, but

48

that at the Arthur Scargill Pit in Yorkshire, whose output was always greater than the norm, no coal had left the pit for the last ten years. Looking further into the report. Ivan discovered that this was less unreasonable than might appear, since the seams had been exhausted. The problem was that the pit employed a large number of colliers, so that if it closed down there would have been serious unemployment. They had kept the mine busy by bringing up shale and stone which they then tipped down a number of disused mineshafts. Recently they had stepped up production by bringing up rubble that had already been disposed of, and sinking it once more below ground. There had been a grave mining disaster at the colliery two years ago, some thirty-seven miners having been trapped in the shaft — thirty of whom had died before help arrived.

As for the coal which had been dispatched — which was not coal, and had not been dispatched — the explanation was a local agreement between managers and PF chiefs, under which receipts had been filed, accounts entered, and statistics kept scrupulously up to date.

It was all very difficult, as one of the attached notes made clear. 'In the Workers' State,' the official had observed, 'there is, and can by definition be, no unemployment. In practice this is ensured by the fact that, out of our total population of 30 million, 8 per cent are employed by the Department of Social Harmony as People's Friends, clerks, etc., 5 per cent by the Red Army, and that some 0·5 per cent of the population are designated each year as People's Enemies and are under arrest in various places of re-education. It must be said, however, that the Arthur Scargill solution has a certain attractive humanity about it, though when we write "humanity" we mean, of course, "socialist humanity" and not any other sort.' Ivan reattached this document to the others, scratching his head in puzzlement, and passed on to the next case.

In this, a factory at Glasgorky had been producing warm jerseys for the Armed Forces. Output, morale and product equality were all excellent, and had been approved after an inspection by the Board of Control back in 2115. Now it turned out that there was no factory; it had not yet been built. Minister

49

of Productive Labour, Seamus Dignan, who had gone up there and presented the workforce with the Gold Medal of Heroic Effort Class Two and a certificate entitling them to a holiday in Uzbekistan, had had the woollen jersey (as it were) pulled over his eyes. Apparently the workers did actually exist and had been drawing two salaries — one from the job they had, the other from the job they hadn't. They had in fact visited Uzbekistan, and had offered a unanimous vote of thanks to the freedom-loving Soviet Union for sending them there.

What was one to make of all this? Was it even true? Was it a trap, intended to instil counter-revolutionary doubts in him, a poor Chinaboy Grade 15? If he expressed alarm and disgust, would they turn on him and say, 'Caught you, cond, believing slanders against the Revolution!' The only safe way of acting was to see how his head of department behaved when presented with the files. But he, as he had rapidly learned, showed not the faintest flicker of emotion. Was this because he was inured and blasé? Was it because he was trying to trap him, Ivan, into showing indignation? Or was it because he wanted to trap him into *not* showing indignation? Did all these contradictory thoughts pass through the mind of his boss, just as they did through his own, and was that the reason for his expressionless demeanour? After all, Tov Divisional Sub-Department Executive Manager Jones was vulnerable to report from his inferiors as well as his superiors, had both inferiors and superiors to be vulnerable *to*, and so was even less secure in his position than Ivan himself, who had merely superiors to placate.

But then, the more insecure, the more likely you were to bite somebody else. The rule worked with dogs, and it worked with bureaucrats.

Ivan raised his eyes and contemplated the huge open-plan office for a moment. It was all square corners, all glittering plastic and glass, there was (save the enormous portraits of C-M, of Len Thoresby and other dignitaries of the Revolution) not a scrap of decoration anywhere, for there must be the least space possible for microphones to hide. Since the Department of Social Harmony spied on all other Ministries, all other Ministries in self-defence spied on it. Ivan saw it for an instant

50

as a glass conservatory, a large botanical hothouse crammed with palms and pandanus and jungle-weed, full of insect-eating orchids, treacherous bogs and lurking snakes. Holy Karl! He made the sign of the hammer and sickle, and tried to drown his fears by plunging again into his work.

All at once, as if a fit of mass epilepsy had struck the office staff, everyone was making the sign of the hammer and sickle. For a hasty female clerk had tripped into the office on the grubby bare soles of her feet and was bending over the Sub-Department Manager's desk. Normally he would have enjoyed her doing that, for there was a bra shortage too and Miss Wakeford's breasts followed a very Marxist line. This time, however, she seemed to have brought an absolute silence with her. Everyone noticed the pallor on her face, the answering whiteness on Jones's cheeks as he struggled to rise, failed twice, and then hauled himself up by main force, leaning on the arm of his chair.

'T-t-tovs, I have t-t-terrible . . .'

Jones did not normally have a stammer, nor spill saliva down his chin when he spoke. He paused to collect himself, wiping spittle from his bottom lip. Emotion at last, thought Ivan, but how I wish there wasn't. Striving to speak for the second time, Jones failed once more, and motioned to the girl.

She promptly fainted, and people rushed to attend to her, supposing that if they were occupied in this way they would avoid responsibility for her message, for responsibility was an infectious and sometimes fatal disease. Ivan himself crouched over the poor girl, fanning her cheeks, listening to her heart beat, gazing askance at her sprawled-out legs with the skirt riding up so prettily. Ah now, if it weren't for Sue. Miss Wakeford was horroshensky — quite krasny — funny how Russians thought red and beautiful was the same thing! Not that she was red, she was pale as death.

Anyway, what was her message? Perhaps the Production Norms were out by 10 per cent. Or maybe the Little Green Men from Arcturus had landed (I wish they had, thought Ivan). Or maybe . . .

Now it was like Pass the Parcel. Jones whispered to Mitchell,

51

Mitchell made faces and hissed at Shadwell, who dropped it as it were, and turned right away, shaking his head and saying very loudly, 'You must be joking!' Mitchell then whispered in Turnbush's ear, who, explaining carefully that he was deaf, passed him on to Miss Seath who turned her eyes upon the portrait of Len Thoresby, and began to sob. Mitchell looked wildly about him, and passed the message back to Jones his superior with an appearance of great relief, as if he had been just in time before the music stopped.

Jones contemplated the situation for about five seconds, then, aware that all the eyes in the office were fixed upon his face, tapped something rapidly out upon his secretary's typewriter, gazed at it, shuddered, tore it out of the machine and ate it.

He looked despairingly about him.

At this moment he was providentially saved from further distress by an announcement that croaked through the intercom, in heavily disguised tones, as if the person reporting this news were holding a handkerchief in front of his mouth and pretending to be a female imitating a male voice, though male himself. Probably, therefore, he was indeed female.

'Tovs!' this voice cried jerkily. 'Terrible news!' There was a sound of struggle through the loudspeaker. Ivan rested his ear upon Miss Wakeford's blouse. It was warm, soft and pulsing down there and, despite the fact the girl was still out cold, it gave him a modicum of comfort.

A new voice made itself heard over the intercom. Its owner was holding his nose, in an effort to make himself unrecognisable.

'Tovs! Our Beloved Second-in-Command, Secretary Lenin Thoresby was assassinated at 11.15 this morning. A man has been arrested. Our Beloved Chairman Boris Clegg-Molotov appeals for calm. The guilty persons will be found. They will be rooted out.

'Long Live the Workers' State! Long live the Glorious Revolution! Employees will immediately engage in a spontaneous demonstration of affection and loyalty to our unerring leadership!'

Holy Karl! thought Ivan uncomfortably as he laced up his

shoes, I don't like that bit about 'guilty persons being rooted out'. Since joining the Department of Social Harmony he had learnt that the List of Lists really did exist after all.

Event Six

*History is nothing but the
activity of men in pursuit
of their own ends.*

———— KARL MARX ————

Leninday, 2 July 2116

Truth is power, and vice-versa. Clegg-Molotov, having the
power, had the truth. Later it would be known to history as the
July Revolution.

At half past ten on Leninday, 2 July 2115, James Colum
Doherty had presented himself at the gates of the secretarial
offices in Whitehall (now called Redhall). Two PFs with
machine-guns took his pass, examined it perfunctorily and
handed it back. There could be no doubt that it was valid, for
it bore a secret code. Doherty strode on into the building.

These offices stood on the very spot where the old Houses of
Parliament had been sited before the fire. They had survived the
Blitz, but not the Revolution. The only trace that remained was
the lofty gothic clocktower named Big Ben. This the great fire
of 2009 had somehow failed to destroy and it was still an object
of emotion for every citizen of London, the more so as the hands
of the clock stood for ever frozen upon the time of 11.59, that
moment when the heat of the flames had finally halted the
mechanism that drove them. Twisted and rusting on their levers,
they still pointed to that moment, checked and precise according
to the meridian of Greenwich, which marked the final defeat of
bourgeois capitalism. Big Ben. Back in 1984 someone had
climbed it and swung there in a hammock, pleading against the
cruelty of human beings towards dolphins. Back in 2084

someone else had climbed it, to plead the cause of humanity to human beings. The first had been ushered down by the police, who had enjoyed the picturesqueness of the stunt, and had laughed and joked with him as they took him off to spend a night in the cells. The second had been sniped out of his perch by blue-boy sharpshooters, and had made a famous splash of red upon the pavement beneath.

All this, however, did not concern Doherty as he entered the present building. It consisted of a colonnade surrounding central offices, with above them a kind of stepped pyramid in Social Realist Style resembling a Mesopotamian ziggurat, which culminated in the Party Secretary's Suite. Doherty knew that the First Secretary was not to be found there but in the basement. He walked briskly down the northern colonnade, turned into a descending staircase and vanished into the bowels of the building.

On the first floor down he was stopped again, again was waved on.

He went on down to the sub-basement. The corridor here was lighted as brightly as day, but there was a curious absence of guards. Ahead of him stretched a series of doors, which he went slowly by, checking the motto upon each of them. He came at last to one that read ADMOFF(FIRSTOFF). Doherty glanced up and down the corridor. There was absolutely no one in sight. He leaned against the wall and waited, puffing at a Shamrock.

At 11.05 there came the sound of movements from within the room. Doherty turned to face the door, plucked the cigarette from his lips and stamped it into the expensive carpet with his heel. The door opened.

The First Secretary's personal secretary, a large-bosomed blonde in her mid-twenties, could be seen holding the door open, smiling back into the room. She took no notice of Doherty who was smiling, too, like a man about to meet an old friend.

Len (short for Lenin) Thoresby emerged from the door and, as he did so, Doherty stepped up to him, still smiling that friendly smile of his. 'O'Meara,' he said softly. Thoresby, hearing this name, blenched and stepped back. Doherty, still advancing, pressed his gun to the First Secretary's chest and shot him twice. The expression on Thoresby's face did not alter. He had not got where he was today by registering the shifting phases of emotion. He sat down slowly on the floor, his eyes still fixed upon his assailant's beaming face. Doherty applied the muzzle to the man's temple and pulled the trigger for a third time.

The tall blonde secretary was screaming and screaming.

There was a short pause, during which Doherty replaced the gun inside his jacket, turned his back on the dead man and began to walk away down the corridor in businesslike fashion. He wondered whether he should have shot the Secretary's secretary, but no doubt his employers would dispose of her in their own good time. It crossed his mind to wonder whether any guards would even now appear.

The length of the corridor, doors were opening, people were coming out with alarmed expressions on their faces. Suddenly a bunch of pale blue uniforms appeared at the foot of the stairs in front of Doherty. He glanced round. The further end of the passage too was blocked by armed guards.

Dream Two

*The 'artist' must be made
redundant as a special category
of person . . . The star system . . .
stifles creativity . . . because
it also encourages the mistaken
notion that some people are born
more musical than others.*
— PROFESSOR JOHN BLACKING —

The eerie silver and black of Alkan's world — its moonlight and
its Gothic shadows — shone out into the auditorium as if the
piano were a lamp. *Comme le vent.* The 'brilliant young
virtuoso fresh from Leningrad' (that's how they were all
described) tossed his tousled mane over the piano keys to such
effect that you would imagine there was a horse galloping
through the music. At the end of the piece, when they were all
clapping and shouting for more, Sue giggled in his ear, 'Showers
of dandruff! I hope it's good for the grand!'

'Alkan,' she had said. 'He's French, isn't he? I could just
do with something French to remind me of my holiday. I bet
you didn't know he died from being crushed under a bookcase.

'Now, after the concert you can take me out to dinner. That
Chink place, you know, the one whose name I cannae mind, but
it means "Happy Food". Or so you tell me. I don't believe a
word of it!' She was particularly cheerful tonight, looking at him
out of the corner of her 'jet-brown eyes', as he called them, as
if there were some practical joke afoot.

'Jet-lag eyes,' she had replied when they got back in the plane.

They'd been stuck at the airport for a day and a half. Air-traffic controllers, this time.

And now the restaurant, strangely entitled the 'Sik Fok', out of sheer Cantonese contempt for the language of the foreign devils, their customers. Good business, though. A bamboo screen, beef in black bean sauce, the ginger in the Cha Cha Chicken enough to take the roof off your mouth.

'Stimulates the sun-tan,' he said, admiring her shoulder, Sète-brown in the candle-light. 'Which wine do you fancy?'

'You have some, I don't think I will tonight.'

He looked at her in surprise. 'I thought we Scots were always thirsty?'

'No, that's only Scottish reporters like you.' She held his hand under the table and said, 'You don't know what we're celebrating, do you?'

'Oh dear,' he said, concern shadowing his face. 'Have I forgotten something? I know women set store by these things. Your birthday, no. Our anniversary, no, that's not for another month. I give up.'

She whispered in his ear. In response, he gazed at her with real awe, as if she were the first woman who'd ever . . .!

Then, disregarding the diners, he kissed her and said, 'But that's wonderful, that's the most marvellous news, better than anything I write in the papers.' He thought for a moment. 'Listen, it must have been in France, at that little hotel overlooking the beach.'

'The baby'll be born with the sea in its blood. He'll be a Jack tar, or maybe a Jeannie tar. Which do you think you want?'

'It doesn't matter, darling. Aren't you clever?'

Event Seven

*In modern society all relationships
are subordinate to the
single abstract relationship
of money and speculation.*

——— KARL MARX ———

Sartreday, 4 August 2116

'Listen, Sue. A symphony, that was for orchestras, wasn't it?
You can't have a symphony for piano, can you? And have you
ever heard of anyone called Alkan?'

'I dinnae ken,' she said, doing her echt-Scots bit. 'There's none
of that music any more, anyway.'

'I know, but I remember hearing about it at school. If you
weren't a member of the bourgeoisie, they wouldn't let you in
to listen. Apparently they had huge big orchestras a hundred
strong, and they had to train for years and practise every day
for hours, and one piece of music lasted *for forty minutes!*'

'Must have been really boring.'

'I don't know, how can you tell? They shot all the musicians
back in 2010.'

'What did they do that for?'

'Why do you think? "The artist must be made redundant as
a special category of person." '

'Are you quoting or making it up? Sounds like Discussion
Group stuff to me. I suppose it was class-divisive.'

'Élitist.'

'Anti-proletarian.'

'Parasites are to be shot on sight. I wish I could hear some of
it, though, just to see what it was like.'

'Do I look all right?' She did a pirouette, glancing back at him over her shoulder.

'You look beautiful, darling,' he said, and then briefly tried to prove it to her.

'But what is all this about Alk . . . Alkohol? You've not been having more dreams, have you? I thought you didn't remember them. I hope *I* was in it,' she added, hamming a brief pantomime of frantic jealousy.

'Of course you were, love,' he said soothingly. 'Would I leave you out of my dreams?'

Ready at last, they set off for Redhall, hearts in their mouths, for this was their first step 'up Party', as it was termed — a reception for new members at the Palace of Proletarian Culture — rubbing shoulders with the rich and powerful — buffet, dancing, talking — they must watch their tongues. It was enough to give you the squitters, just the thought of it. Far safer to stay at home, except that a refusal would be, without a shadow of doubt, fatal.

Once you got on the moving staircase and starting climbing in grade, the staircase began to move faster and faster, till there was no way of getting off without breaking your neck. You had to cling on like grim death, playing the game of being orthodox until it became second nature, accepting all the compensations for orthodoxy that came your way. At least they were considerable. The British Republic was, it must be remembered, Truly Democratic, and therefore everyone earned exactly the same wage. Boris Clegg-Molotov himself had (apart from his expense account) only 100,000 phunts a month, the same as a miner or a street-sweeper. The difference was that they had to shop in Grade 10 shops, where potatoes cost 100 phunts a pound, whereas he could shop in a Grade 1 Shop, where a washing machine cost 200 phunts. Yes, for (unbelievable as it would have sounded to the twentieth-century worker) Sue now had a washing machine, bought in a Grade 5 Shop — where it had cost her 5,000 phunts.

Being rocked to and fro on the top floor of the red London bus, Ivan asked her, 'And Chinese restaurants, have you ever heard of such a thing?'

'Wake up, love. Sweet Marx, this dream has really got to you, hasn't it? No, of course I haven't. I suppose there may be one for the high Party cadres somewhere else in London. Can't say I've heard of it.' Which you'd think she would have done, since she worked in one of those same restaurants available to the inner Party.

'Free, gratis and for nothing, those places.' She lowered her voice. 'Meat on the menu. Every day!'

'But this restaurant bothers me. I can even remember its name, it was called the "Sik Fok".'

At this she squealed with laughter, as well she might. 'Says something about the dreamer, anyway!'

'I think we're nearly there,' he remarked, looking out of the window. The bus was just rounding Red Square, in the centre of which stood a gigantic wheel like a Ferris wheel at a fair, constantly revolving. An obvious symbol of Revolution. A living proof of the superiority of proletarian to bourgeois science, for this wheel was powered by a principle which the old capitalist physics had declared against the laws of nature — namely, Perpetual Motion. At certain crucial times in the history of the Workers' Party, it had been stopped and started again in a contrary direction, for there had always been some disagreement whether it was proper to call clockwise or anti-clockwise motion 'right to left'. Whenever a new Chairman wished to be a new broom, he would sweep the motion of the wheel the other way. But Ivan could not see that it made any difference, for 'what goes up must come down, as the wheel shows'.

'Och, we *are* philosophic tonight, aren't we?' said Sue, glancing over her shoulder in case someone was sitting close enough to eavesdrop. But it was all right, there was almost no one on the top deck but themselves.

Oddly, at this moment into Ivan's mind jumped the words 'to falga', or was it 'travel gah'? Nonsense words. He glanced to the northern end of the square, but could see nothing there but a huge proscenium arch of stone, built as if for a Roman theatre, draped in red, brightly illuminated, and bearing the outsize portraits of the heroes of the Revolution of 2009 — Will

Murphy, Brianston-Pedley, Farrell and O'Rawe, along with the martyred Arnold Briggs. Black and white under the arc lights, more than three-dimensional, the five vast sculptured heads did not look at each other. It was as if they dared not. The bulging stone eyes of Briggs and Pedley took care to exchange no glance, and gazed southwards in idealistic fashion into the future, which seemed to be sited somewhere about Redhall and at a point rather more elevated than the horizon. Their necks vanished into the marble stage beneath them. They were like giants whose bodies had been buried in the earth below the streets of London, so that now they were motionless for ever, for ever imprisoned in the year 2009. Funny, but where these decapitated heads now sat, there should have been a building, grey stone, with a Greek portico.

And had he dreamed it, or had there really been, once, long ago, a tall white pillar in the middle of the square, improbably high, with a man on top of it, distant, foreshortened, a curious hat on his head, all flaps and folds? Then he remembered the Discussion Group. They'd pulled down the pillar as an insult to the French Revolution. The old National Gallery had been burnt with all its canvases inside it. Another victory for the forces of culture, as against the forces of culture.

Nonetheless, he felt faintly disturbed. It was as if, tonight, his dreams were trespassing on solid reality. To restore his sense of the real, he settled his hand onto Sue's bare knee, and she wriggled her bottom and snuggled against his shoulder, turning her crooked smile up at him.

'Yes,' he said, as if the meaning of the State's central symbol, turning for ever here in the heart of England, had been suddenly revealed to him, 'yes, it's not just a revolution, it's a *complete* revolution. The State turns upside down. And then, of course, everything is back exactly where it was before.'

There was a joke which had been going the rounds lately. 'What is capitalism? The oppression of man by man. What is Communism? The reverse.' You told it only to people like Geoff and Polly, people who had a sense of humour.

'Sh,' said Sue, 'don't think such things. Not on the top of a bus.'

The reception was the nearest thing in modern British society to an Ideal Home Exhibition. It offered the aspiring younger members of the Party a sight of those modish dresses, those piles of meat and fruit, those special brands of French wine, champagne and Scotch malt whisky which, if they went on aspiring long and hard enough, would one day be their reward. The buffet tables gleamed with Irish Republican linen and groaned with delicacies. None of these things was on sale in the ordinary shops, only in those of the First Grade. As for those who already had such passes, they gleamed and groaned too, wiping their perspiring foreheads, revolving among their underlings, uttering words that were polite, politic and politically harmless. Here too were such striking beauties, glossy of eye, emphatic of figure, sensuous of mouth, as Rusalka Smith, Tamara Handy, Tatiana Keenan and Ludmilla Hecklestone. The chicks of the apparatchiks. For, though the advertising of all these goodies was tacit, what was being advertised was positively indiscreet.

Pâté de foie gras and truffles from Red France, armagnacs, wines, tarts and titsers, peaches, power and passion, the prosperity of the dynasties of Thoresby, Farrell, Clegg-Molotov and O'Boyle — and yet these things (the unspoken message taught) were not exclusive. You could earn them, Tov. Every Briton carried in his knapsack the baton of the Great Conductor.

The reception was not merely a commercial shop window, however, it was at the same time a passing-out parade. The principal method of examination was for a departmental chief to assemble a group of young men around him and fire a rapid succession of rounds of drink at them while keeping the conversation fixed on a political subject — a sensitive one, for preference. There were many qualities needed for success in life, and a hard head was not the least of them.

While her husband was being put through the hoops, Sue found herself taken aside by a plump dowager with a neck almost goitrously thick, who introduced herself as Mrs Varvara Clegg-Molotov. Sue's tongue immediately clove to her palate with fright, and she was for several moments unable to utter a squeak.

'How pretty you are, my dear,' purred the great lady. 'What intense brown eyes. Well, well, at your age I suppose I wasn't too bad myself, but time passes by and so do husbands. I'm a Farrell by descent, you understand, with little specks of blood through the Pedley line and a touch of the Jack-Tar-brush through the Briggses. Boris wasn't my first, you know, my dear, though of course he *has* been my most successful.'

Sue, intrigued to know just what she meant by this piece of ambiguity, but unable to think how to prompt the first lady of the State, found her tongue and complimented her on her continued beauty.

'*What* was your name?' inquired Varvara and, when she had it repeated to her, exclaimed, 'How charming! "Susan", imagine! So pretty, these old traditional English names!'

Nettled, Sue explained that she was Scottish, and thought to herself that Mrs C-M could not possibly have any ear for accents. Varvara went on with undimmed enthusiasm, 'Ah now, when I was married to Maxim, my second, we had the most lovely little datcha up in the Highlands, at a place called Ardnamurchan. I don't know if you know it?'

Sue agreed how special it was, with its extinct volcano and its ruined crater, and the view offshore to the broken silhouettes of Eigg and Rhum.

'Yes, my dear, I know exactly what you mean,' said Varvara. 'It's such a quaint place, Scotland, and the people have such an amazing accent; why, I remember I could hardly understand a word they said. Of course, I can understand *you*, my dear.'

Sue, though blazing with anger, kept this fire well stoked down, and was relieved to see another lady of Varvara's age advancing across the floor, frowning in a worried way and trying to attract her attention.

'Varvara, my dear.'

'Alexandra.' The greeting seemed somewhat frosty, but the woman was too perturbed to notice.

'Varvara, have you seen Sasha? He was supposed to be here at eight, and look, it's past ten.'

'I expect he's been kept at his bureau, Sandra, you know, in the great offices of state . . .'

'But he rang me and assured me specially. You see it's Natasha's birthday, and we were going to leave early to celebrate.'

'I wouldn't worry, my dear, I expect he's just forgotten.'

'Forgotten? Oh no, Varvara, he wouldn't forget a thing like that, he's so fond of his daughter.' Both affection and bitterness were blended in these words, as if Sandra was suggesting that, had it been her own birthday, he might well not have been there.

Sue, genuinely embarrassed, but also beginning to feel a touch of fear in case she was about to overhear things that weren't meant for her, looked around for a route of escape. Unfortunately, she was hemmed firmly into the corner between a potted palm and these two large loud Party wives.

'I imagine you've tried ringing his office?'

'The night watchman said there was nobody there. You don't suppose some of those East Enderworlders . . .'

'A mugging, dear? Gooligans? There's no crime under socialism,' said Varvara, gazing indignantly at her friend.

'I'm at my wits' end,' sighed Sandra.

'Of course, there are other explanations. I'm afraid my Boris isn't always as attentive a husband as . . .'

'Oh, Varvara, that's a horrible suggestion. Not on Natasha's birthday!'

Varvara gazed at the other woman with a curious expression, as if she understood her completely, felt triumph at having brought her to the same pitch of suffering as herself, and then hated her for daring to feel as she did. After a moment Mrs Winch-Kalashnikov began to cry. 'I'm disappointed in you, Varvara. One of my oldest friends.' Dazzled by tears of betrayal, she hesitated for a while, then strayed blindly off into the crowd.

Mrs Clegg-Molotov turned back to her captive, still pliant, still pinned against the wilting palm. 'Sandra and Sasha, Sasha and Natasha. The Winch-Kalashnikovs are too absurd!' Her resentments resolved themselves for the moment into a demonstration of inside knowledge, masquerading as a sort of abstract kindness towards the younger woman. Leaning close to Sue, she said, 'Just look in *Truth* tomorrow morning, my dear,

65

and don't breathe a word to anyone till then. Now where were we? Ah yes, talking about my datcha.'

Sue took a swig of champagne to stop her hand from shaking. She was dragged back willy-nilly into the torment of conversation.

Event Eight

The correct way to picture the world is as matter moving, and matter thinking.

———————— LENIN ————————

Sartreday, 4 August 2116

'Most impressive, Tov Doctor,' pronounced Clegg-Molotov, pumping the man's hand up and down. 'I was particularly taken with the children's section of your establishment. This notion of — what did you call it? Hypnagogia? You are doing invaluable work.'

Outside, irregular patterns of sun and shadow shifted and passed across the gardens of the old asylum. The vast expanses of Norfolk sky were full of hurrying clouds. Sunlight fell moodily inside Doctor Charlesworth's office, so that sometimes the big coloured diagrams that covered the walls were painted in violent reds and blues, sometimes a softer, more discreet light fell upon them. All were charts of the brains of apes or of humans, seen variously from left and right, from above or from below, their internal structures picked out in a variety of colours.

A large bookcase entirely concealed one wall of the office, containing titles such as *Software Engineering*, *Biological and Bio-chemical Bases of Personality* and *Cerebral Commissurotomy in Man*. The occasional volume bore a more imaginative title, and for a moment C-M's eyes rested on a book that had, apparently, fallen from the shelves and was now lying supine on the floor beside them. Its cover bore the black and white reproduction of a nineteenth-century drawing, Goya-like in quality — a man, in nightgown and tasselled nightcap, his arms outstretched, his eyes closed, advancing towards the wall of his bedroom. This wall had, however, become a yawning darkness through which mysterious shapes could be glimpsed but not identified. The book was attributed to an American Doctor of Psychology and was entitled *The Dream Wall*.

Doctor Charlesworth, clicking his tongue with annoyance at the sight of this stray volume, bent to pick it up and replace it among its fellows. To Boris he said,

'Your conduct of the Revolution, Tov Chairman, is a permanent inspiration to us all.'

'Science has made great strides since the Revolution,' said C-M, passing the compliment back, so to speak.

'In the departments that matter,' agreed the neurologist. 'Political stability demands that, technologically, we have simply been marking time for the past hundred years. Bourgeois science concerned itself above all with the nature of the material world. That we have more or less abandoned.' He glanced with satisfaction towards his library of textbooks.

'Of course. The material world is the material world. Why rack one's brains about it? Indeed, what is the point, now that the world is Marxist?' Zhdanov had had the right idea. It had been necessary to put a stop to quantum physics lest matter, investigated too profoundly, might turn out not to be matter.

'Where the mind was concerned, however, bourgeois science was unbelievably backward.'

'But I thought the mind didn't exist, Tov Doctor,' exclaimed Ludmilla.

'Well, of course, tov secretary, not as a special metaphysical category. If you follow me,' he added, gazing at her acutely. Beautiful but dumb, he thought, which is much better for all of us, herself included.

'I don't know, but it sounds otchen scientific,' she said, thinking to herself that certainly Charlesworth's confidence was real, and existed in the most solid and material way, broad-shouldered, tall, athletic, reflecting all the evident splendours of his maleness.

'There is no mind, only brain,' the neurologist explained,

'Lenin himself said so. The mind has been scientifically proved to be the result of physical interactions of an electro-chemical nature. Consciousness, for instance, is controlled by a portion of the reticular formation in the brain-stem . . . I hope I am not taking up your time unduly, Tov Chairman. The fine details of human brain-structure are too pettifogging to be allowed to concern the helmsman of our glorious republic.'

'Neetchevo,' said Boris, essaying for once a smile of his own, 'such matters are of great political moment, and I try to take a close interest in them.'

People's shit! swore Charlesworth to himself. If C-M takes an interest in our work, he'll be interfering next, laying down the orthodox line, and then where shall we all be? We'd never find out anything ever again!

'I am flattered by your interest,' he said aloud. 'Might I take the liberty, then, of saying that, despite the generosity of our funding, we do occasionally have our little problems of supply.'

'Ah,' said Boris, looking pleased. 'Your notepad, Ludmilla. The names of those responsible, Tov Doctor?'

'No, no, nothing like that, Tov Chairman,' said Charlesworth. 'I'm not referring to chemical supplies, electronic equipment or instruments of any kind, but rather to the little question of the supply of subjects for experiment. In particular, we need more children, especially those of an early age, so that . . .'

'Make a note, Ludmilla. My dear Charlesworth, you need have no worries on that score. I can assure you that all such problems are on the verge of being solved. I shall personally ensure that, within the next few days . . . What ages are the most suitable? What quantities are needed, and how frequently should they be supplied?'

A flurry of rain beat a brief rhythm against the window-panes. The August trees in the asylum grounds bent and un-clenched themselves like springs, and a sprig of green leaves tapped like fingers on the glass.

When this little matter of supply and demand had been settled, Boris went on, 'But, Tov Doctor, I'll tell you what most interested me in our discussion. While we were inspecting your experimental subjects, you mentioned the control of consciousness by the, er, by the, er . . .'

'The reticular formation, Tov Chairman.'

'Exactly. Are you speaking then of the possibility — it sounds almost like science fiction — but of the possibility of controlling consciousness by, as it were, plugging ourselves in to that vital centre in the brain-stem?'

'If only one could! But I'm afraid that does not seem to be quite practicable at present. The reticular formation, you see, contains a kind of switching mechanism, a device which selects the available modes of consciousness, the waking state, the dreaming state, deep dreamless sleep and so on. In short, I am not speaking of political consciousness in the Marxist–Leninist sense, but of . . .'

'Otchen vashny, Tov Doctor. You mean to say that science might, one of these days, be able to control our dreams?'

'Not exactly,' said Charlesworth. 'The hypnagogic experiments, I mentioned earlier, have shown that you can indeed control a person's dreaming to some extent by aural suggestion at a subliminal level, while he is asleep. In the case of children, it seems we may set up patterns of dreaming by such means. Even in their case, however, dreams gradually revert to their normal, counter-revolutionary pattern when the child's sleep is no longer "chaperoned". I am afraid that our findings in this area are only in their infancy. No, what is really encouraging is a quite different study of ours, whose results are, to tell the truth, quite startling, and whose long-term effects may be . . . "revolutionary" is not too strong a word.'

'You fascinate me, Tov Doctor. And what exactly are these results?'

'Ah,' said Charlesworth, smiling again. 'What we can determine, Tov Chairman, is not the dream but rather the fact of dreaming. We have recently discovered that it is possible, by means of a most delicate and advanced piece of surgery, to (as it were) remove the switch that turns on the dreaming mode of consciousness. The patient is then in a most curious state, which (I dare to suggest) constitutes a new and revolutionary human condition. He will continue to sleep, of course, *but he will never dream again.*'

70

Ludmilla stared at the neurologist in astonishment. Could it be possible that she had heard him aright? Her eye fell on the chart that occupied the wall behind Charlesworth's desk, and which seemed to float at the moment above the doctor's head like a garish red and blue halo. It depicted the human brain as seen from below, and into her head came the words, *turning the brain upside down*. She blinked hard and readjusted her usual expression of blank receptiveness.

'Does that shorten the time he is asleep?' asked Boris. 'How useful it would be if we could increase the waking, and hence the working, period! What strides the Revolution would make!'

'We are working on it, Tov Chairman. Naturally it would be, for practical reasons, impossible to operate on any very large number of people. Bourgeois deviationists perhaps. But other techniques are conceivable, apart from the surgeon's scalpel, and I am extremely encouraged by our present progress. I am also, needless to say, deeply flattered by your own interest, Tov Chairman.'

'It is an issue that is close to my heart,' replied Boris, musingly. 'It has long been clear to me that dreaming is *inherently counter-revolutionary*. *People dream alone*, that is the point to register. The dreamer closes his eyes and floats away into some private self-indulgent world of his own, where he creates — stratchny! — his own reality. When he turns over in his bed, wrapping the sheets around his back, he turns, in the realest sense, his back upon society, upon community, upon the loving and caring state. He becomes a Berkleyan solipsist. It is awful to relate, but as long as people dream, they will remain socialists during the day, but bourgeois individualists at night.

'Your experiments, Tov Doctor,' he said, rising and shaking Charlesworth's hand with real warmth, 'are, I believe, otchen vashny to the Revolution. I shall watch them with intense interest. I require you to send me regular reports of your progress from now on. No, no, don't thank me, we are all engaged in the same titanic struggle. If any obstacles are placed in your path, tell me and I shall liquidate them. This morning, dear Charlesworth, History has been present with us in this room.'

Outside, the rain had stopped and, across the steppe-like flatness of East Anglia, evening was streaking the clouds with red. This inspiring tint fell upon the white curtains of Charlesworth's bureau, staining them the colour of surgery, the shade of revolution. Ludmilla snapped her notebook shut and rose, offering her warm white hand to be kissed. The neurologist thought to himself, What relief! But what responsibility!

Whisked in the Rolls onto the motorway, and whirling southwards towards London through the falling darkness, Ludmilla reached for Boris's hand and cooed in his ear,

'Poor luby, have you been having nasty dreams?'

'To tell you the truth, Ludmilla,' said Boris, frowning a little, 'they *have* been disturbing me lately. A dream of bombs, a decapitated head, arms and legs flying. Highly unpleasant. No doubt they have a perfectly dialectical-materialist explanation, and are due to my untiring vigilance against counterrevolutionary terrorism. In one nightmare recently, I seemed to be spraying a capitalist bank with machine-gun fire. No doubt it shows the correctness of one's Marxist sentiments, but I must admit there was rather a lot of blood.'

'How distressing!'

'Stratchny! Atavism, I suppose. It makes me feel almost superstitious, as if these dreams were trying to tell me something. That's the betraying thing about dreams, they're so primitive, irrational, a relic of the pre-revolutionary phase of history. The logical intellect must simply discount them.' Nonetheless, he clicked on his intercom and spoke to his cavalcade of escorts. 'Switch to Route 17.'

'What's atavism?' she frowned.

'Never mind. Let's get our minds back onto something real.'

'Ooh, lubricious luby!' she cried, squirming with pleasure.

Meanwhile, Mrs Sandra Winch-Kalashnikov had left the party in a tearful state. Getting out of her taxi at the doors of her palatial home (Park Lane, now Party Lane) she found the lights all ablaze and the doors standing open. Puzzled, she paid off the driver and entered the house, calling first for Natasha and then for her servants, of whom she had eight. There was no reply.

She went from room to room, feeling at first anger, then horror, then total bewilderment. Pictures, mirrors and crockery had been smashed, the cupboards ransacked, books lay in tatters in her husband's study. Cigar-butts had been stubbed out on the Khomeinian Revolutionary Persian carpet and human excreta deposited in the middle of the dining-room table. Upstairs, the clothes of her family had been dragged out of the wardrobes, piled upon the floor and burned, being afterwards doused with water. Natasha was nowhere to be found, but on the floor of her bedroom there lay a patch of blood. Pressing her hands to her head, feeling as if she were going mad, Mrs Winch-Kalashnikov phoned the police and told them that her daughter had been kidnapped and her house burgled.

They arrived at the door two minutes later and arrested her.

'But my husband's on the Presidium,' she kept repeating. 'He's the Minister of Health and Sanity. Ring Clegg-Molotov's office, they'll tell you who I am.'

'But why, but why? And where's Natasha?' she wailed as they pushed her into a cell at the Web.

She was not to learn for several months.

Others learned soon enough, however. When *Truth* fell thump upon the hall mat the following morning, Ludmilla ran to pick it up, then remained frozen to the spot with sheer oozhass as she looked at the astounding news. Indeed, it was several minutes before she could take it in.

'Evil men! Filthy Yank-lovers! Murderers! Counter-revolutionary Shits!' were the measured expressions of proletarian indignation that stared at her from its front page. 'Thoresby's Assassins Nailed!' it cried in bright red letters. 'Top Spy Plot Foiled!'

Beneath this scarlet scream were listed the following facts. At 8 pm on 4 August 2116, two members of the Supreme Presidium, O'Boyle and Winch-Kolashnikov, had been arrested as they left their bureaux, and taken to the Web. The charges against them were criminal thoughts in respect of the Socsov System, spying for American capitalism, and plotting the murder of our beloved First Secretary Len Thoresby.

Ludmilla felt weak at the knees. She staggered into the bedroom where Boris was still snoring peacefully and threw the bulky journal onto his stomach. 'Luby, luby!' she cried, shaking him. 'Wake up and look at *Truth!*'

Even asleep, Boris knew that by 'truth' was meant *Truth*. He sat up cheerfully and glanced the paper over with evident satisfaction. 'Get me my coffee,' he said.

'But Boris, two ministers of state! How could they . . .? Where have they . . .? What did they . . .? Why should they . . .? I can't believe it!'

'Can't?' asked Boris, raising his eyebrows. 'Can't?'

But Ludmilla didn't blink an eyelid.

'I like that bit,' she said, pointing at the final sentence.

'At this unparalleled crisis in the nation's history, we salute the kindly wisdom of Our Beloved Leader Clegg-Molotov, Father, Son and Spirit of the Revolution.'

PART TWO

Dream and Reality

Dream Three

Sue panted to an anxious rhythm, clutching the sheet-top, while the nurse smiled down at her, wiping her forehead with a tissue, and John held her round the shoulders with more reassurance than he felt. 'Nearly there now. Don't push, just let it come.'

'Oh! Oh! It's starting again!' gasped Sue. Cries of mingled effort and pain were forced from her and John grimly clung to her, whispering in her ear, wondering if he were any help at all. 'Clever girl, clever girl, that's the way, here comes the baby's head, take it easy now.'

There was a moment of respite. John moved to the foot of the bed and gazed with awe at the head of the living baby that had just emerged. Its eyes were as calmly closed as a jade figurine, its complexion a transparent green. As he watched, its tongue slipped out between its lips and licked them. Life.

When the contractions started again, even though Sue was trying not to push, the infant was ejected, almost catapulted onto the bed. The baby went red and let out a wail of indignation, tears ran down Sue's cheeks and into the corners of her smile. There were murmurs of triumph and exhaustion, the midwife telling Sue what a clever girl she was and, in a moment, passing the little boy up to be held.

John felt like an explorer who till now had descended into only the first caverns of his own emotions. Watching the birth of his first child, he had penetrated into an area much further down, an area of light and fire where you could sense the earth moving. He felt shattered, torn apart, remade.

Later he walked over to wonder at the new baby lying in his

cot by Sue's bed. His eyes were darker than ultramarine, very big under the lights of the theatre, and he was gazing up at the shadows and shapes that passed across the ceiling in what looked like puzzled concentration.

'I thought they're not supposed to be able to see yet.'

'Och, they do so, Mr Lumsden,' said the nurse, smiling. 'You can see he's seeing, can't you? Looks wide awake, amazed at this strange place. It's so bright and noisy for him.'

A few days later, returning home to London Road with a brand new person in the carry-cot on the back seat of the car. Entering, the flat too seemed new. Though he had left it only an hour before to fetch Sue and the baby from the hospital, their home seemed as unfamiliar as when they had first bought it. Their new son. The universe had expanded, changing the world a little, and everything in it.

Event Nine

Great are heaven and earth, but greater still is the goodness of Chairman Mao; dear are our parents, but dearer still is Chairman Mao to us.

—— (A CHINESE PEASANT) ——

Freeday, 15 Marx 2117

Sue woke up in the middle of the night, panting and gasping, eyes big with alarm. When Ivan struggled up beside her, he saw, however, that it wasn't fright after all, but a sort of wonder, which turned to disappointment as she took in the scene around her, the darkened bedroom, the street lights falling aslant the room, the donkey-like hee-hawing of an ambulance far off.

'Sweet Marx,' she sighed, the corners of her mouth turning down. 'I thought for a moment . . .'

John caught at the floating shreds of his own dream, and they tore in his hands. Nonetheless, he could remember something. A hospital, a baby, yes, the lights, and the child's eyes the colour of a gloaming. He'd been dreaming that Sue had had a baby.

'He was so beautiful, Ivan,' she was saying, 'and I felt so tired, as if I'd been pummelled all over, but the baby was wonderful.'

Ivan was silent for a moment, unable to take in the enormity of what she'd just said. 'But, but, that was the dream I was having too. I dreamed you'd, we'd just had a baby and . . . and . . . I don't remember any more,' he confessed with irritation. 'It was very vivid,' he added, frowning.

'What was his name, can you remember that?'

Ivan shook his head.

'Neither can I.'

'I can remember a dark hot cave under the earth too,' he said. 'I suppose it must have been a volcano, with glimmers of fire through a hole in the cavern floor, and the earth trembling.'

'That can't have been the same bit of dream. But, Ivan, is it true? Did you really have the same dream as me?'

'Well, it sounds like it, doesn't it? I expect there's a simple explanation.'

'You mean we both want one, yes, I suppose that must be it. Funny though, both at the same time on the same night, isn't it? Can you remember anything else?'

'I don't know, there was a nurse wiping your forehead with a tissue paper, and right at the end there was a big dark room with nobody there at all but me.'

'Hm. Oh, darling, do you think we might have a baby?'

'Holy Karl,' he said, 'with all these arrests going on? What sort of world is that to bring a baby into? What would happen to him if . . . if I . . . if you . . .'

'You're right, of course,' she said ruefully. 'I'd forgotten about that, there weren't any arrests in my dream.' Then she cried out angrily, so that he jumped, 'But it hurts, it hurts, what right have they got? They can't tell right from left!'

'I'd be afraid,' he said. 'I know we're afraid already, but that would be worse. What would we do if . . .?'

They settled down again, but sleep had deserted Ivan for the night.

The thin high irritating wail of a newborn infant tugged Sue out of sleep. 'There, Mrs Lumsden,' the nurse was saying, 'I think we might give him just a wee suck, to get him and you in practice, you know.' Awed by his tininess, his fragility, and by the emotions inside herself, Sue put out her arms to receive her newborn son. When he tugged at her breast the sensation gave a hard, wakeful pleasure. 'Mm,' she murmured, and her son gazed up at her with concentration in his eyes, sucking and drawing life.

She was flung out of sleep by a crash from below. The door to the street had been flung back, and a regiment of booted feet were running up the hard wooden boards of the stairs. Then a tattoo rang out on the door across the hall, fists battering on its panels, shouts from several different voices: 'Marsden! Marsden!' A volley of kicks and shouts.

Sue and Ivan clung to each other in sheer animal terror till it was all over.

They had long ago given up going out to the pub. Around late December last year, just before the great festival of the birth of Baby Stalin, they had had a meeting agreed with Geoff and Polly in 'The Hammer and Sickle' down the street. They had stayed there for a couple of hours, but their friends had not turned up. You couldn't know why. Probably they had been arrested, which was frightening, because when you were arrested you were sometimes tortured, and when you were tortured you couldn't help giving the names of everyone you knew, and then they would be arrested too. On the other hand, perhaps Geoff and Polly had the kind of bravery you read about in books about heroes of the Revolution — absolute loyalty to their comrades. Though not very many had that degree of courage. On the other hand again, perhaps they had simply decided not to go out any more and meet people. For the more people you knew, the greater your risk of being arrested. Indeed, Ivan thought, you could calculate the risk mathematically. Let's say the risk is x if you know one person. Then, if you know two, the risk becomes $2x$ and so on. He wondered if the risk was greater or smaller for mere acquaintances. Would they be more likely to give you up, or less? Should the risk be assessed at $2x$ or x over 2?

These thoughts, however, did not succeed in shutting out the horrible sounds from next door.

Finally, when the nail-studded boots had receded down the stairs, when the front door had been slammed shut again, and when all that could be heard were the loud sobs of Mrs Marsden from her open doorway, Sue got up, still shaking with fright.

'What are you doing?' asked Ivan, appalled. 'Where are you going? You'll get yourself arrested too.'

'I must see Mrs Marsden,' said Sue firmly, though she was

shaking like a leaf. 'They've been very kind to us.'

'You know the rules. It's like the plague. You can catch it by kissing, by shaking hands. You can catch it by talking to a stranger.'

'I don't think there *are* any rules any more,' she said. 'I know we want to stay alive, but *how?* Just tell me *how* you can do it. If you talk to *A*, you're an enemy of the state. If you don't talk to *B*, you're an enemy of the State. Which is *A*? Which is *B*? Can *you* tell?'

He was silent.

'Even Winch and O'Boyle couldn't tell. How should we?'

'But they were traitors,' he said weakly.

She glared at him as if he were an absolute fool. 'Rubbish,' she said. 'They just happened to be there. Anyway, what's poor old Fred Marsden done? I suppose he has a secret cache of weapons under the third paving stone from the left in the street outside, and gets on the phone to the American Government every evening. I expect they've been looking through the Ms this afternoon, and every tenth one gets arrested. How can you help the name you have?'

'It's not really mine,' murmured Ivan.

'Well, everyone's name is just an accident, isn't it? And when the PF runs his finger down the list and decides who to arrest and who not to, maybe his nose is itching, and he hits on the eleventh one instead of the tenth.'

In a fine passion of anger, she slammed across the corridor and tapped at Mrs Marsden's door. 'Pat? It's me, Sue Lumsden.'

The story was so simple it wasn't a story. Pat Marsden didn't know why Fred had been arrested, and neither did he.

'If only they'd tell *him*,' Mrs Marsden kept saying. 'If only *he* knew, he'd stop all these terrible things happening.'

'Tell who?' asked Sue.

'Why, Clegg-Molotov, of course,' said the old lady, raising her eyes to theirs in puzzlement.

'Why didn't he try to run, Pat? The fire escape . . .'

'Where would we run to, dear, at our age? Besides, didn't you know? They took the fire escape away last week.

'I'm just glad about one thing,' she repeated. 'I did make him put on some warm clothes before they took him. I'm sure it'll be cold in the Web.'

Mrs Marsden was quite right. By her presence of mind she had saved her husband's life.

For about six months.

Event Ten

Freeday, 15 Marx 2117

'Can't sleep, luby? Is it these stratchny dreams again?'

She had jumped awake out of a gorgeous dream of herself
as the Sultaness Safié, ruler (through her insignificant husband Murad III) of the Ottoman Empire, to find her Boris pacing
the floor like a mother with a newborn child. Only he had
nothing in his arms but a bundle of state documents. He put
them down with a sigh and turned to her. She patted the bed and
motioned to him to sit beside her, put her arms about him,
breathed into his ear, ruffled the mane of grey hair of which he
was so proud.

'You shouldn't doodle wolves on your note-pad all the time,
luby,' she murmured. 'I'm sure it gives you nasty dreams.'

'It's not wolves I dream of, Ludmilla, it's terrorists. And do
you know, in the nightmares I keep having, it's me that's the
terrorist.'

She burst into squeals of laughter. 'Oh, Boris, that's *ridiculous!*'

His mood didn't lighten, however, so she tried a different
tack. 'I tell you what'll stop your nightmares. When you go into
the office tomorrow, get them to reduce the quota.'

'Ludmilla, don't meddle in things you don't understand. The
books have to be balanced.'

Ludmilla was an expert at conveying puzzlement without frowning (for frowning produces wrinkles, and wrinkles are bad for one's career). She enlarged her eyes and raised them towards Boris in helpless appeal. He smiled condescendingly down at her.

'Psychological economics. The quota has to be raised, or we'll never progress to the next stage of the Revolution. You want to live to see true Communism, don't you?'

'Oh, true Communism,' she said, as if wondering if it were a new hat, and which way up she should wear it. 'Of course I do.'

'Ludmilla, you don't know what I'm talking about, do you? True Communism is when everyone devotes himself and herself entirely to Community.'

'Well, I devote myself entirely to you, luby.'

'That's not what I mean.'

'Oh, if you don't like it,' she said, pouting.

'Ludmilla, you are sometimes quite infuriating. I simply forbid you to utter a word for the next five minutes while you listen to me. I'm not doing you a favour, it'll help me to get things praveelny in my own mind.'

'Praveelny. I do love all those words beginning with *prav*. I like being *de*-pravved.'

'I'm a man in a hurry, you see.'

She smirked at him silently.

'It's two hundred years since the Revolution, a hundred and eight since we had our own, and where have we got to? There are still people who disagree with us and have to be hauled off to re-education camp — 150,000 a year of the bastards. They still don't love us.'

'Oh come, luby, you're exaggerating.'

'No, no, my love, there is still dissent. Why, this is the purpose of the "thaw". Mao did it back in China in the mid twentieth century. He called it "letting a hundred flowers bloom", of all colours, you see, not just the red ones. From time to time we announce a "liberalisation programme"; the rats are invited to scuttle from their holes and squeak. We let it go on for, oh, six months or so. By then, of course, we know who disagrees with us, the thaw is declared over, and we arrest them all.'

'But, luby, isn't that a wee bit dishonest?'

Boris gazed at her. Where she was concerned it took a lot to amaze him (except in bed, where he liked it), but for once he was speechless. After a moment he was aware that his mouth was wide open. Then the humour of the situation struck him, and he began to roar with laughter. 'Dishonest!' he gasped. 'Dishonest!' He pounded the bed with his fist, then paused to search for his handkerchief and wipe his eyes. 'Sweet Karl, Ludmilla, you'll be the death of me! Dishonest! Just wait till I tell Vassily and Innokenty!' He collapsed into another fit of laughter, while Ludmilla watched him with a slight frown on her face. Very few things made her Boris laugh. When you come to think of it, they tended all to be the same *sort* of thing.

It made her uneasy when he laughed, so the moment some calm had been restored she hastened to put another question to him. 'But, luby, there hasn't been a thaw at the *moment*.'

'Well, you see, Ludmilla, thaws aren't necessary. That is one of the great discoveries I made at the Department of Social Harmony. It's not just the rats in their holes. It's worse than that, it's unbelievably serious, it's *everyone*. You get a cond in the interrogation cell. You quietly and gently explore the contents of his mind. Now of course on the surface you will find he agrees with you, he's been told by all his teachers since the age of 4 that a human being is a product of historical inevitability, that we are the passive results of social forces acting upon us, and that therefore it is the collective that is the only true reality.

'But what do you find when you dig a little deeper? You find the man is unwilling to give up another evening of his time to discuss the forward progress of the proletariat, and would rather be playing football with his son. (Cricket, Lenin be thanked, was banned back in 2021.) It's the same all the way along the line. Our psychological division can check a man's pupils under a lamp, and they invariably find that he is more excited by talking to a pretty woman than by reading the words of Marx himself.'

(But, Boris, you have the most beautiful big pupils, said Ludmilla to herself.)

'But it's worse than that. I discovered, in the course of my fifteen years at the Ministry of Social Harmony, that no matter how correct a man's views may appear to be, you will always find, providing you dig deep enough, some little deviancy, some little fault in thinking. I discovered an awful truth, Ludmilla!'

Boris paused dramatically, and Ludmilla put her admiration face on, and gazed at him with it.

'Everyone is guilty, *because it is impossible to be orthodox*. How can a man *entirely* understand the Party line, 100 per cent and in all its subtleties? Interrogation invariably reveals these tiny differences and, of course, any misunderstanding is damning.'

'But, Luby, *you* understand the Party line!'

'You see now, my sweetheart, why the quotas do not matter. No matter how high you raise them (they're 5 per cent at present) you will find in anyone you arrest the presence of personal opinions. Everyone is guilty, so everyone is equally worth arresting.'

'Luby, you do explain everything so well. But what is 5 per cent? I suppose they're mostly men?'

'Mostly.'

'What proportion of the male population is that?'

'Oh,' said Boris judiciously, 'most of them are between 25 and 40 The expectation of life is approximately 50 under our scientifically run system, so that is about one in six of all males between those ages.'

'But, Boris, I can hardly wait for you to tell me. What is the Next Stage you mentioned? What's going to happen *then*?'

'Wait and see,' said Boris mysteriously. 'All I will say is that I have, not one plan for the Future, but two.'

'*Two* things to wait for,' said Ludmilla. 'Ooh!'

She wondered if Murad III and the Sultaness Safié had been real historical figures, or were merely phantoms, the imaginary creatures of her dream. Long ago she had decided that it was her duty to survive. Her duty to History. Darwinian theory proved it so, for History was simply the survival of the fittest. But who were the fittest? Ah, that was more difficult, but again one consulted Darwin, and one found that the fittest were those who survived. Well, this was a pleasing conclusion, and in accord with her instincts.

They dressed, picked up their brief-cases, called the Rolls and proceeded to a dawn session of consultation with Vassily the principal People's Friend. (Or Principal People's friend, thought Ludmilla, depending how you read it.) For, while the State sleeps, the traitor dreams of counter-revolution. There Boris doodled wolves upon his note-pad, raised the quota to 6 per cent, and had a call put through to Charlesworth to say that he wished to be informed of his latest findings. He also left a request with Professor Sweasey of the Bureau of Words and Communification. He was to be contacted later that morning.

Vassily bowed his head and his secretary scribbled. Towards the end of the interview, he addressed these words to Boris:

'Has Tov Vorkuta of the Soviet Embassy been informed?'

No question could have been more pertinent, and Boris leaned forward to emphasise his point. 'The position of Russia is otchen clear. I have been assured of total support. As you know, I flew to Moscow a month ago to offer our fraternal congratulations to Tov Kolymski on his ninetieth birthday. Our socialist comrades are entirely satisfied with our policies, and are relieved that we are showing no softness in the face of provocation.

'Besides, you will recall that Tov Vorkuta said as much when we celebrated the 199th anniversary of Glorious October.'

Indeed. The great Ear of the State had wagged upon its flag-pole, Vorkuta, the Russian Ambassador, had stood on the rostrum beside Boris, Vassily and Innokenty, wreathed in smiles, and had observed the passage of tanks, guns, armed men and other harbingers of peace, all smartly goose-stepping through the streets below. 'I always say, nobody does the goose-step more smartly than the British,' he had observed to Boris. 'You celebrate our own Glorious Revolution with such panache, with such esprit, with such imagination. What a tribute to the great ideas that inspire us all!'

'Indeed,' said Boris. 'Tov Kolymski told me, in his own words — 90 years old, and still such a wit! — (of course, his interpreter is very good) — "A London autumn is better than a Prague spring." '

'Wonderful sense of humour,' agreed Vassily.

'If you doubt the exactness of my information,' added Boris, 'you should at once ring Moscow.'

'Doubt your information, Tov Chairman!' They all had a good laugh about this. Ludmilla watched Vassily Forson drying his eyes. Tears were so ambiguous, she thought. It was not that Vassily had any compunction. It was simply that he had his family to think of.

As for her remark about dishonesty, by 5 o'clock that afternoon there was not a Grade 1 Party member who had not heard it and whose eyes were still dry.

Sue woke at seven shouting, as if out of a nightmare. Or perhaps into one.

When Ivan woke beside her, he found her crying. 'I still can't remember the baby's name.'

Dream Four

*It must be firmly understood:
if a truly workers' government
came to power in Britain even
in an ultra-democratic way,
civil war would be inevitable.*

———— LEV TROTSKY ————

Tuesday, 7 May 2007

John wasn't there, Sue didn't quite know why, and she was pushing baby Michael through Princes Street Gardens and wondering why the Edinburgh gales were so forgetful this year. Perhaps they had got trapped inside the bagpipes of that pibroch band she could hear chanting away down in the bandstand, and so hadn't been able to blow the blossom straight off the trees in their usual manner. She could hear them howling and skirling in the most fearsome way as they struggled to escape, and, wheeling little Michael briskly through the spring flowers towards the West End, she found she was swinging along in time to the pipers' march.

As for Michael, he lay on his back, tiny, all eight pounds of him, peering up, his eyes still the dark blue of the newborn baby, gazing at the intricate patterns of twigs and flowers each tree held proudly above his head, each one offering a different puzzle. If so tiny a baby can frown, she was sure he was frowning. (Of course, she said to herself, even grown-ups can't make it out, but he'll only learn that much later.)

A squirrel ran across the lawn ten feet away, then another. Both paused, with the amazing abruptness of small rodents, frozen in an instant, as if their clockwork motors had been

90

turned off. Carefully she lifted Michael out to show him the tiny animals, which made another dart and check as she did so. One of them ran up the coat of an old man — he was standing stock-still, a familiar human tree — and down his sleeve to feed at the nuts offered in his palm. Michael stared at the scene with the permanent black wonder of the newly born.

Suddenly something was wrong with the day. From the bandstand two hundred yards away, the pipers' tune droned and sagged unevenly to a stop, leaving a solo caterwaul exposed, shrieking and dying. There seemed to be some sort of disturbance going on at the further end of the Gardens, and Sue, turning her eyes that way, saw to her alarm . . .

A band of men all marching to different rhythms, advancing up the path and brandishing a variety of improvised sticks and staves. In front of them they were pushing a cart that seemed to be loaded with broken pieces of brick.

My God, the baby! Sue crammed him unceremoniously back into the wheeled carry-cot and, tearing off her shoes, set off at a run towards the little footbridge that crossed the railway and led under the shadow of the Castle Rock. You couldn't push him too fast, you might tip him out, and fear was making her lungs breathless and her legs unsteady.

The strikers! Well, okay, their jobs were under threat, the employers hadn't consulted them, but then neither had their own union. Okay, they had grievances, but poor wee Michael, only seven weeks old . . .!

'Jeezus, am I glad to see you!' she said to John when he got back that evening. She hung round his neck, giving little skips with her feet, but when he drew back and looked into her eyes he could see there was a fleeting, worried shadow.

'Darling, what ever is the matter? Sit down, tell me all about it.'

'Okay, but hold me, John love.'

When she had finished, he got up in a rage and stalked around the room sighing and waving his arms. 'And I thought *I'd* had a bad day! It's riot and civil commotion! What do they think they're at?'

Fuelmen defending their jobs, right, and the Tories didn't give a damn about jobs. Survival of the luckiest, that was the new Darwinian Toryism. So they'd struck. Fair enough, but Will Murphy hadn't held a vote, he'd just ordered them out. As for those who wouldn't come, he'd sent in three thousand rough tough bravoes to seal off the pits and power stations. Cars had been burnt, bricks thrown through the windows of families who still were working. And now they were running round the streets of the cities, terrorising women and children.

It made you — no, it was your fear — for Michael, for Sue — that made you boil with anger.

Scargill had radicalised the miners back in 1984, with his year-long strike. Murphy — 'Our Will', as the Yorkshire miners called him — was even more radical, it seemed. His struggle, he said, was against the Capitalist State itself, and he spoke of the Russian East as 'the lands of Socialism'.

'The People's Will', the capitalist press had dubbed him. Ironically. The epithet had backfired. Murphy had adopted it with pride.

What was Murphy after? Well, you couldn't be sure, but John had done a lot of reporting, interviews with miners, and the polis, and with some of those members of the hard left who spent their time revolving on the edges of the conflict. He had a pretty good idea what *some* of the actors in this tragi-comedy wanted. Particularly after the awful day he'd just spent — his watch removed, a hood tugged down over his eyes, two hours on the road to an unknown destination. Then, when the blindfold was unfastened, finding himself in a bleak and dirty shed with a single light focused on the pad of notes upon his knee. In front of him a masked man sitting at a table — the chairman? The meeting, however, consisted only of himself and a girl, also masked, pointing a gun at his shoulder-blades. Brianston-Pedley's Red Army. Then the journey back to Edinburgh in the car, with the blindfold on again. Mind you, these details must be hidden from Sue, for they'd give her the shivers. The same shivers they'd given him.

'Better not make any sudden movements,' the young man had told him. 'The lie-di's nervous.'

John recognised this as the London slang for 'woman'. 'She's lucky,' he said. 'I'm terrified.'

This mild joke was treated severely. 'You're a lackey of the bourgeoisie.'

John talked uneasily about fairness, the right to reply. He was here to get their point of view. Of course, even *his* paper might not publish . . .

'You're a toff,' said the youth. John had been startled to hear this old-fashioned term. Only people who didn't know still used that one. People who read books. But it wasn't that which was perturbing him. That sense of *déjà vu* again — the vital thing you couldn't quite remember. 'Toff.' He noted it down. Maybe something would come back to him later.

His informant spoke in the servile whine that denotes a native of the English south-east. 'Free speech? Don't make me laugh. Free speech for fascists. Liberal democracy equals police state.'

'Just why,' said John (for all journalists begin their questions with 'just why') — 'just why are there so many revolutionary groups around?'

'God, what a bore this is,' said Comrade X, yawning to underline his point. 'Six million unemployed, isn't that enough for you? The great god Market, working men thrown on the dung heap at 35.'

'But if the economy were being handled right . . .'

'It's obvious you've never read a word of Marx or Trotsky in your life,' said the masked man with contempt. 'If you can't step outside it, how can you see it? The system has to be browken.' He pronounced it like that, for it had a special sense.

'But it's basically quite a tolerant and humane system, after all. You've just got to get a decent bunch in to run it — which we haven't got at the moment.'

' "Basically." "Decent bunch." That's the whole filthy sham of bourgeois western democracy,' said Comrade X. 'Clichés disgust me. Elections? You have to reckernise facts. The parties and the issues are all controlled by the ruling class. A "humane" legal system? Marcuse had your number, it's all just repression disguised as tolerance. It's an illusion, a Wall of Dreams. It's killing by kindness.'

You can't kill by kindness, thought John, because that's not what kindness *is*. You can't repress by tolerance, because that's not what tolerance *is*.

But you can kill by revolution. 'Back in 1984 the revolutionary left were taken by surprise,' said Comrade X. 'They still hadn't learnt the lesson of Ulster, the historic struggle of the IRA. That was the floor in their thinking.'

He means 'flaw' thought John automatically, beginning to feel more and more worried.

Retailing the interview to Sue (though carefully leaving out the guns and the blindfolds), John had got only as far as this when the door-bell rang. Peeping through the judas, he saw it was Ben and Ailsa. Their surname was Bell, and as always the obvious joke would be made.

Well, a sense of humour, even a bit dull and rowdy, was what they needed tonight. He had lost his somewhere in — Dundee? — Glasgow? — that day. He uncorked the bottle of red 'Brigadiere' Ben had brought so as to make another obvious joke, and they began Ben's favourite rhythmic process, Clink! Drink! Bums up! My round, I think! — a process which John always thought might have been set to music.

To a funeral march, Sue would say warningly.

'The glockenspiel,' said Ben, pinging his fingernail against his empty glass.

'Have another,' said John automatically.

'The truth is,' said Ben, 'I want to make you drunk tonight because I have a proposition to make to you.' He let out a klaxon-hoot of laughter. 'Not a postposition, you understand.'

Ben's sense of humour was wearying, but it was better than brooding on the state of the nation, and John was the prisoner of his friends, trapped in his armchair by his own fireside.

'These dreams you've been having . . .'

Ben Bell was the manager of a wine shop, but his heart sat behind the counter only in daytime. At night he was a prey to crazy ideas. He was a crank who delved in the library for books that were read only by other cranks and by the majority of the great British public. He claimed not to actually *believe* in telepathy, reincarnation, life after death, telekinesis, live frogs falling from the heavens, ley lines, the colonisation of Earth by spacemen from Canopus, the prehistoric rocket-port at Nazca, and the ability of 'Rosemary' (back in 1931) to speak Ancient

Egyptian. And it must be admitted he wore all this odd pseudo-learning with an engaging modesty. When he discoursed on Bridey Murphy, it was fascinating, and full of ironic deprecation, like a raconteur saying, 'Have you heard *this* one? It's *amazing*! Crease you up!'

John blamed himself. He had mentioned the nightmares he and Sue had been having, and that was a fatal thing to do in Ben's large and enthusiastic presence. He should have known better. He did know better, but he'd been drunk at the time, not to mention tired, worried, wondering if he could ever bear to take down another eye-witness report from some man whose wife had had her legs blown off by Brianston-Pedley's terrorists.

'J. W. Dunne, *Experiment with Time*, a great book, you must read it, it tells you exactly what to do, you keep a pad of paper by your bedside, and when you wake up you note it straight down because dreams, you know, sigh away — whew — like smoke, the moment you open your eyes. The only way to remember them is to write them down, religiously, the moment you wake up. And if you wake up in the night, you keep a wee flashlight by your bedside. Now Dunne's theory is . . .'

'But it'll disturb Sue.'

'No, it won't, and anyway she'll get used to it. Listen, she can do the same! You said you and she seemed to be having very similar nightmares. Now Dunne's theory is . . .'

'I bet our friend Brianston-Pedley doesn't do that.'

'I bet our friend Brianston-Pedley doesn't fuck. Now Dunne's theory is . . .'

'But what's the point, Ben? Who cares about these crazy dreams anyway, and . . .'

'Okay, John, I know, beautiful wife, wish she was mine, hope mine can't hear me, mhpffhlshwff!' said Ben, making kissing noises which made Sue giggle even in the midst of talking babies to Ailsa. 'But how can I explain why if you keep cutting me off in the middle of a sentence? Your trouble is, John, you talk too much, never let anyone get a word in edgeways. Now just stop blethering for a moment, and listen to me.' Ben held up a large plump hand. 'Dunne's theory is that there are at least four dimensions, three of space and one of time. So far so good, because that's Einsteinian enough. Now he discovered that he often had dreams which seemed to foretell events in the immediate future. He took to noting all his dreams down, and found that the effect was quite consistent, though most of the happenings he foresaw were quite trivial, and if he hadn't been on the look-out for them, he would never have noticed. Eventually he worked out the theory that our consciousness is situated in a fifth dimension, in which it is free to observe a certain distance, not only backward in time (as in memory), but also *ahead*. Now do you see what I'm driving at?'

John began to laugh. 'Look, Ben, you're not going to persuade me by going on and on like that. What kind of persuasion is that? You're a human steam-roller, no, a human steam-roller-coaster! Try and use that little speck of Jewish blood you claim you got from your old granny, and be *acid* and *subtle*, then you might have some effect.'

'Deep down I'm subtle,' said Ben. 'Have you no scientific spirit in you, man? No love of the purity of knowledge for its own sake? "And I knew the woman and behold she was big with child and bore fruit." Not *that* kind of knowledge, John old friend, not the kind of knowledge you're interested in, but pure — disinterested — speculative — truth — for — its — own — sake — do you get my meaning?'

'Well, I'm very doubtful,' said John. 'I can't remember dreaming about the baby before we had him . . . or even about Sue before I met her.'

'How do you know? The point I've been trying to make is that you don't know *what* you're dreaming about till you start setting it down. Because otherwise you just don't remember.'

'Och, John,' cried Sue, dramatic, from across the room, 'did you no dream about me and am I no your *destiny*, then?'

'Well, I agree it's very interesting,' said John, 'but if you'd been where I've been today, I don't think you'd want to have anything to do with the future.'

'Why, where was that?' asked Ailsa, a tall young woman with lots of bangles and a sort of stagey elegance.

John related his day, or as much of it as he cared to, as he had to Sue earlier in the evening.

'And what *is* your theory about Murphy's revolution? Not that we have revolutions in this country, "it jahst simply isn't *done*, may deah," ' said Ailsa, adopting the breathy gushiness of the southern boarding-school.

Will Murphy was at the time 47 years old. An ex-member of one of Britain's seventy-eight Communist parties, he was the man who had put 'New Left' into the New Left Labour Party. His main claim to fame at the moment, however, was that he was leader of the National Fuelmen's Union, which had been on strike for the last two months, and looked as if it might go on being on strike for the next twenty-two.

'Well, I can't tell what goes on in his mind,' said John, 'but this is how it might look. Conflict, that's the key. Listening to Comrade X today, the whole scenario flashed into my head. And the worst thing is, these New Right Tories have set up a situation where it really all could start to happen. Six million unemployed. Benefit reduced so as to force them to take jobs — which don't exist. More out of work every week. What do they expect? They've set the water boiling and they've jammed the safety-cock.'

'Maybe Trimmer is really a crypto-Marxist,' wondered Ailsa. 'It's taken 150 years, but Trimmer and his business men are trying to make old father Marx come true at last.'

'Okay, John,' said Ben, 'we know all this. If you've just had a revelation on the road to Damascus, you need to convert us too.'

'All right, just think of this. Murphy's called his men out for the final victory, right?'

'Rubbish, he's done it at the worst possible time, just at the end of the winter, with fuel stocks high and a long hot summer in the offing. So he can't win, can he? It'll be Scargill in 1984, all over again.'

'Ah,' said John, 'but with that example before his eyes, why isn't he acting differently? I'll tell you why, it's not winning he's after.'

'How do you make that out?'

'Well, if you were a general, how would you choose your battlefield? The foot of a slope, wedged between river and mountain, standing your men in a bog so they couldn't fight and couldn't escape? A general who does that is either a fool or a traitor, or else he doesn't want to win at all. Moreover, when Trimmer offers him a compromise, he won't accept it. Then Trimmer offers him everything he's asked for, give or take a few empty phrases, and Murphy shifts his ground and demands still more. What can you think? He must want to draw it out, he must want to . . .'

'But what's the point? He's imposing real hardship on his own people.'

'That's just it. If you suffer for a cause, you *know* it must be just.'

'But he hasn't called a ballot, a third of them are still working.'

'Yes, treachery in the ranks. Backs to the wall. The more your cause is threatened, the more intense your loyalty. The more afraid you feel, the angrier. Fight to the death, lads. It was all there today, hidden behind Comrade X's evasions. How do you get a revolutionary situation, that's the question. The secret is to have trouble, the nastiest trouble you can. Division in the ranks makes your people insecure. So they huddle closer, depend on each other more, their loyalty is deepened. Make your people suffer. The more they suffer, the more they'll hate the opposition. Stir, and wait for the mixture to start smoking. Get the police to charge in and do something stupid. There's nothing more explosive than righteous indignation.'

'But how can he win with a divided union?'

John replied briefly to this, but Ben protested, 'I'm sorry, but it's a funny thing, I get a wee bit deaf when my glass isn't full.'

'Lenin,' said John again, pouring another round. 'Split, split and split again. It's a funny thing about socialism. The purest form is always further left. A procession of crabs — Lenin moves left, and everyone scuttles along behind him. The ones who are left behind feel guilty because they're compromising with the class enemy. Bewilderment, anger, internecine quarrels, excommunication. So, when Lenin comes to power, there's no problem at all. No one trusts anyone any more, nobody has any friends, and — off with their heads!'

John was silent for a moment. 'Now you see why I'm a bit

leery of your experiment, Ben. I don't especially want to see into the future.'

'Great!' cried Ben, clapping him noisily on the back. 'I can see we've got a real enthusiast here!'

That night John took a small note-pad, a pencil and a flash-light and put them on his bedside table. And so did Sue.

Dream Five

Saturday, 11 May 2007

Professor Aimery Brianston-Pedley spat upon his hands. He heaved his pick against the sub-basement floor. In the concentrated light of the lamp that the latest acolyte was holding, sparks flew, to be succeeded by a fine spray of cement dust as the tusk of the pick began to bite. After a few minutes, B-P passed the tool to Dougie, who took his place in the corner of the cellar, the shadow of the pick swinging up huge against the ceiling as he raised it, vanishing altogether as it stabbed into the floor. B-P checked his watch. Six o'clock. Thirty-seven hours before the watchman opened up on Monday morning. He hugged the latest acolyte, who raised her mouth to be kissed. The lamp swung about, and Dougie swore.

'Put the lamp on the floor if you must do that!'

B-P reminded himself that for some — himself for instance — adrenalin was pure elation, whereas for others such as Dougie it had a rather sharper edge. Once on any job, distraction made him irritable, so that he was unsuited for any praxis involving direct contact with the public. Hold-ups, for example. On the other hand, he was an expert with explosives.

B-P took over again, and after a few minutes there came a dull shock from a point some feet below them, followed by a muffled clattering. A new split appeared in the concrete some feet from where they had been digging, and a whole segment of floor subsided by several inches. Striking the floor with the handle of the pick, B-P felt it give a hollow shudder. 'The sewer roof's gone, I think.' It was going to be a lot quicker than they had expected, and he felt almost a pang of disappointment. 'Here, let's prise these fragments out and see if we can glimpse some darkness.'

As they heaved out the first big shard of concrete, the thick foulness of the sewer hit them. 'Christ, doesn't capitalist shit stink?' joked the latest acolyte, who had a Ph.D., which B-P had written for her, on 'The Political Centre as a Disguised Manifestation of Fascism'. They carefully removed the loose fragments of concrete, earth and brick from the hole, and checked that its walls seemed secure. It was like a broken-toothed mouth, gaping, foul-breathed. Carefully they lowered themselves into the sewer's stinking maw.

B-P flashed his lamp up the tunnel, checking their direction. Somewhere in the gloom, a rat splashed, escaping.

He led them up the tunnel about a hundred yards. After twice computing the precise distance they had travelled he pointed to an area on the right-hand wall of the sewer. 'There.' They smashed a few bricks, then began to lever them out. There were splintering and wrenching sounds, the scraping of metal against brick and cement. Bricks were prised out of the wall, and fell tumbling into the slime beneath their boots. The dust whispered and ran in rivulets out of the cranny they had left.

'It won't take long to break through,' said B-P.

'Into the new world,' said the latest acolyte.

At ten to eleven on Sunday evening, a large van drew up over a manhole cover in Allenby Street. The driver got out and began to change one of the wheels, while his unseen assistant in the rear part of the van opened a trapdoor in the floor, levered up the manhole cover, and drew up a number of heavy metal boxes.

'Another blow against the international financiers' mafia,' said Dougie as they drove away. B-P smiled. He felt a pure professional pleasure, like that of the winner of a marathon, or a mathematician who has just solved Goldbach's Conjecture.

When the news hit the evening papers that Monday, it was not so much the size of the robbery which preoccupied them — though that was in millions — but rather the little present which the thieves had left behind them — 'a symbolically apt exchange,' B-P had said. When the bomb had gone off at 9.20, there had been two bank clerks, the manager and a pair of security men down in the vaults, trying to ascertain what was wrong. 'SAD LOSS OF LIFE', the papers mourned.

'Hypocrites!' sneered the latest acolyte.

Event Eleven

*The red sun lights the
world; the spring thunder
shakes the earth.*

———— CHINESE MAOISTS ————

Sartreday, 11 May 2117

Ivan and Sue were woken in the early hours by a very odd
sequence of sounds. First there would come a deafening series of
bangs at the other side of the bedroom wall, then a scraping as
of metal against stone, the splintering of bricks and the whisper
of falling dust. After a pause, the crashing would start up again.
Someone was plainly trying to break through the wall.

Sue clasped hold of Ivan in a panic, wailing to him to wake
up. He held her automatically, then himself sat up in bed as the
splintering and crashing began once more. He switched on the
bedside lamp, but the electricity was again not working, and
they remained in darkness save for the dimmest of reflected
moonlight filtering through the thin curtains.

'What's the time?'

'Ten past one,' said Sue, her teeth chattering so much she
could barely get out the words.

'Are they trying to come through the wall this time?'

But why should even the People's Friends try to do that? It
was the wall between bedroom and living room that was being
beaten upon, and though Sue automatically locked it every
night, this inner door was the flimsiest of objects, and could
have been knocked off its hinges by a single well-aimed kick.

'It's them, it's them, it's to frighten us to death,' gasped Sue.
She felt as if the heart in her breast had swollen up so big that

it filled the whole of her ribcage. She couldn't stir a muscle, she could neither breathe nor move. It would choke her. Suddenly she fainted clean away.

It was quite irrational, Ivan knew, to suppose that the People's Friends would not come through the door, and would prefer to batter the wall down. But, after all, rationality had nothing to do with any of their actions. What they ought to do was simply to get out of the window and shin down the rope he had installed after the authorities had removed all the fire-escapes from the backs of the apartment block. But now, how could they do that, with Sue lying pale and white on the bed in a dead faint? To tell the truth, he felt just as frightened. He wasn't sure that his legs would carry him, and he felt quite incapable of removing his eyes from the surface of the wall through which the thumping and hammering were coming. The wall bulged inwards slightly for a moment, and a sharp-edged fragment of plaster fell from the ceiling. It was as if some heavy animal were locked in the next room, leaping and throwing its weight against the wall.

A dog? thought Ivan. A lurcher? By the sounds, it was a whole pack of wolves from the steppes of Russia!

It was very odd, some remaining rational part of his mind was telling him. You could hear bricks falling out of the wall, and yet that wall was so thin and the whole building so jerry-built that by this time, to judge by the din they were making, they could have broken through twenty times over! Why then . . .? It made no sense.

As he thought this, the light suddenly came on again, beside him Sue groaned and stirred and the shaking and bulging of the wall together with the wrenching of the pickaxe on the further side were succeeded by complete silence.

Ivan waited, feeling Sue stir under his hand. 'It's all right, love, it's all right,' he was whispering as the blankness in her eyes gave way to slow bewilderment, and finally to the memory of who she was, where she was. 'Just lie still, love, just relax, it's all right, they've gone away.' He got out of bed, picked up a chair by one of its legs and went to the bedroom door. After a moment's hesitation, when there was still no sound at all from the other room, he threw it open. His heart was in his mouth.

Nothing but moonlight lying aslant the room, shining on the chair and sofa, a broad band of whiteness pressed flat against the inside wall, on whose cheap and faded wallpaper not a mark could be seen. Everything, chair, sofa, shelves and table, was in its rightful place, and somehow the room lay in such stillness that it persuaded you there had never been any sound at all. Ivan looked back into the bedroom, where Sue lay eyeing him with big dark eyes, still scared, pale and damp-browed from her fainting fit. He looked back again into the living-room, daring the manifestation to start up again the moment he took his eyes off it. Nothing stirred.

He made a cup of tea, turning round every now and then to eye the room. It was all perfectly normal. While he was waiting for the kettle to boil he had a sudden thought and went back into the bedroom, crouching down and searching for the tiny fragment of plaster they had seen, falling from the ceiling. Yes, that was there right enough.

No footfall, not even the faintest of steps creaking on the stairs, and no, not a sound from the rest of the tenement, which lay fast asleep as if all its inhabitants had been spirited away into some other universe.

'Maybe it was up above, not in our flat at all.'

'Must be the explanation.'

'Or in the next house.'

'Could be, I suppose. Some kind of sympathetic echo, a sounding-box effect. How are you feeling now?'

'As weak as a kitten,' she said, smiling palely.

'You'd better get some sleep. I'll just lie here awake, and watch. I couldn't get to sleep if I tried!'

Which indeed proved to be true. Sue, exhausted by her fainting fit, soon drifted off into a disturbed and restless slumber, while Ivan lay there wide awake, gazing sometimes at her but generally at the inner wall of the flat, where all remained silent and just as it should be for the remainder of the night. His mind revolved like a fly-wheel, driven by puzzlement and fear, catching on nothing. A sounding-box effect? But then you'd expect noises to have come through before — footsteps, something being dropped. But there had never been anything.

In any case, it couldn't have been in their tenement, for they had heard nothing afterwards, no footsteps up and down the stairs, no doors opening.

Is there a state, he wondered, *between* dreaming and waking? A state where you thought you were awake, but weren't?

He lay listening to the sounds Sue was making in her sleep, murmuring, sighing, and then the occasional clearly pronounced word — and he wondered, not for the first time, at the mystery of sleep, the way it locked people off from the world into a different universe created by and for themselves, and the extraordinary nature of its privacy, the way no one else could get inside it at all.

In the old superstitious days before dialectical materialism, people had believed — and in fact the uneducated still insisted — that dreams could foretell the future, or at least occasionally retrieve half-comprehensible tatters of it. The strange thing was that his own dreams had sometimes seemed to do just that — when he had dreamed of Sue before he'd met her, and then, much later, when he had dreamed of someone called Alkan, and looked him up in the encyclopaedia at work, and found that he actually had composed a Symphony for Piano.

But two cases didn't constitute any sort of proof. Besides, was either of these even a case? He could perfectly well have seen Sue in the street in Leninpool before he'd dreamed of her, and then met her again and remembered only his dream, or maybe just thought it had been a dream. As for Alkan, maybe that was something he'd known once and forgotten. 'The simplest explanation', as the scientists said, though he wondered what they meant by 'simplest'.

No, he knew just what they meant. They meant what fitted their theories. Fair enough, for what could you do with things that didn't fit, like the terrifying blows they had heard that night, the crashing of the pickaxe against the bedroom wall? They were like a piece that had wandered in from some other jigsaw puzzle and for which, when you'd solved your puzzle and fitted it all together, there was no place, so that you had to leave it lying about outside it, not belonging, a little contorted fragment of colour on which no shape at all could be dis-

tinguished. The puzzle was what people called 'reality', but odd
fragments like that didn't belong. They were there, but what
could you do with them? Throw them in the wastepaper basket.
But perhaps, like pieces in a jigsaw puzzle, even these were parts
of some larger pattern.

'Sleep well, darling?'

'I'm still tired,' she said, gazing about her with puzzlement as
she sometimes did these days when she woke — as if the one
thing she recognised in the room was Ivan himself.

But when they had kissed and when the warmth of it started
spreading through her like butter melting in a saucepan, she
found that making love was precisely what she wanted. Ivan got
out his Proletarian Pleasure Pack (known, of course, as the
People's Friend) and what to put in it, and moved over onto
what to put it in. And they made the bed creak and bounce in
the most successful way.

Some time later, he said to her, 'You were talking in your
sleep.'

'Eavesdropper!' she said. 'What did I say?'

'You said a lot of funny things, you said "the People's Will" . . .'

'Oh, that's easy to explain . . .'

'And "flashlight" and "decibel".'

'What? Well, it all goes to show that dreams don't make
sense.'

'And "Michael".'

Her eyes opened wide, the pupils dilating so that they no
longer looked brown but absolutely black. 'Oh, John, I . . .'

'Ivan,' said Ivan anxiously.

'But, Ivan, that's the name I've been looking for! That's the
name of the baby in my dreams!'

It was Stalinday, so they could make love again, and Sue
could rest, and they could talk it all over. Not that they could
think of anything to explain it.

On the next day, Leninday, Ivan went in to the office, and Sue
to her Grade 1 Restaurant. In Ivan's office there were two
chinaboys missing, and nobody dared ask where they were.

Dream Six

'Hot from la Belle France?' said Ben, whose surname should have been Decibel. He knocked back his glass and smacked his lips. 'Mm, those Frogs know a thing or two.'

'And by the way, *was* it hot?' asked Ailsa.

'There was a nice little breeze off the Mediterranean,' said Sue, smiling. 'And so long as I kept wee Michael cool . . . You should see him in his tiny sun-hat!'

'Oh sweet!' said Ailsa, her lips automatically forming in a kissing shape as she shuffled through the photos of the baby — in his cock-eyed linen hat — reaching for his rattle — gurgling at the swaying fringes of the sun-shade. 'Where's the original?'

'He's sleeping just now,' said Sue in a stagey whisper, a finger held theatrically to her lips. 'But I expect that won't last long, worse luck,' she added in her normal tones.

'He wants to see his Uncle Ben,' said Ben. 'It always makes his day.'

'I tried this dish of sea-food when we were there,' said Sue. 'I can't imagine what possessed me! I know perfectly well I can't bear the thought of eating live things, even if they do look more like little grey puddles.'

'They weren't all grey,' said John. 'Some of them were yellow, or green, or blue.'

'Shut up, John,' said Sue with a grimace. 'Anyway, I ordered this thing.'

'I said you must be mad,' said John.

'And it came, with the waiter looking so pleased with himself, shooting his white cuffs and saying "Pour Madame". It was a famous restaurant in Béziers — so they said. And I looked at it, and thought to myself "Oh". So then I thought to myself, "Courage, Sue", and I picked up the lemon they'd given me and squeezed it all over the wee beasties, and when they felt the fresh lemon-juice they all shivered and shuddered about on the plate like jellies on a wobbly table. It was as if they were a lot of soft teeth and I'd jabbed their nerves. Ugh!' She was silent.

'Did you eat it?' asked Ailsa with interest.

'I just couldn't touch it after that,' said Sue, drawing the air in sharply through her teeth. 'Terribly shaming.'

'Probably just as well,' said Ben. 'They tell me the Mediterranean's the next best thing to a septic tank.'

'Och, these were specially grown in a special lake, Ben.'

'Well, we're back,' said John, sighing. 'Nothing's changed, the strike's still on.'

'What would Britain be without strikes? The Tories are getting edgy, though. Do you know, there was a terrible case in the papers the other day — this man threw a grenade in a crowded arcade, and when they arrested him he explained he *had* to throw it, because he'd accidentally dislodged the pin.'

'And did you read about the paraquat in the chocolate bars? Marvellous, isn't it? Bankrupting the capitalists by poisoning the workers' kids.'

'As for the strike, I don't know why the government doesn't *do* something. All those pitched battles between miners and police. Somebody'll get killed soon.'

'I expect they're hoping that if they look the other way, when they turn round it'll have gone away,' said John. 'It worked in 1984. It's the good old British method of taking decisions.'

'Aye, invented by King Canute,' said Ben. 'I think they're just plain scared out of their wits. Well, I shall wait for your next sensational report, John old lad, in which you'll explain everything.'

'I don't think I want to repeat the interview with Brianston-Pedley's bunch,' said John. 'It was a pretty nasty experience.'

There was more modesty in this than frankness. Driving back

from the airport two days earlier, he had been struck by a huge piece of street art, a hoarding leaning against a church — painted in the garish red of butcher's meat, the fly-blown blue of dead animal matter, it stood there screaming at all and sundry, 'JUSTICE AND PEACE!' But the colours were wrong, and so were the guns and bayonets, the raised fists that it depicted. No, he would go on writing his version of the truth. You had to try, even though the country was tearing itself to pieces all around you.

'You know I was hauled over the coals by the Press Council for that interview? Said I shouldn't talk to terrorists. And the worst of it was that I couldn't get my paper to publish it all. My editor made me cut half of it out. "Come off it, John," he said. "You take these gunmen too seriously. After all, we're all British." '

'What kind of progress are you making on the other front?' asked Ben. 'I don't mean journalism,' he explained. 'I mean *reality*.'

'Och, the dreams,' said John. 'I don't know, they're almost more alarming.'

'Glimpsed any bits of the future yet?'

'I'm all too afraid I may have done,' said John, not meaning quite what Ben may have thought.

Sue stopped chatting to Ailsa and turned to them. 'You remember that day last month when Michael fell out of his high chair? Well, not a hint in the previous few nights. But the night after, I — well, how can you tell? It was probably for some quite different reason.'

'Don't leave us on tenterhooks, then,' said Ailsa.

'I had an image of a man falling from a fire-escape. In my dream he was being pursued by — well, I suppose you'd call them the KGB. And then finally he threw himself off the top of this thing . . .' She was silent, and suddenly drank a long draught of wine.

Ailsa, watching her narrowly, said, 'Don't talk about it, Sue, if it makes you feel bad.'

'No, it's all right, Ailsa. But do you think there's a connection?' she said, appealing to Ben as the authority in cases of precognition.

'Well, it *could* be,' said Ben, frowning. 'Hard to say, isn't it?'

Sue, however, had apparently lost interest in the subject. She drew Ailsa away to the window, where she could be seen talking rapidly, while Ailsa nodded, occasionally shook her head, once pressed her hand in sympathy.

'You see, Ben, what I want to know is this,' said John, pouring them both another drink. He moved the lamp-standard over between them, bent forward in his chair, and focused his eyes on Ben's face. Pointing his finger, he began, 'Just how much weight do you put on this Dunne thing, and how . . .?'

'Ah, the lawyer puts his case. My God,' said Ben in mock terror, hiding his head under his large tweed-covered biceps, 'I'm under interrogation.'

John came to a full stop. 'Interrogation,' he repeated. 'Christ! Ben, I wish you hadn't said that.'

Over by the bay-window, Sue was saying, 'I know I must sound *mad*, Ailsa. I must sound as if I'm away with the fairies. But would you just do that wee thing for me? You see, these nightmares, they're horrible, but they're so convincing. They all fit together one after another, like leaves out of the same nasty book. Away at the restaurant every day, and people disappearing, and the men in blue caps with guns in the streets. And that awful dream, och, I think it was the worst of all, a thumping on the wall in the middle of the night, like they were trying to break through, but there was no one there.'

'You should give up noting them down and remembering them, love, maybe they'd go away then.'

'Och, I've tried that, Ailsa,' said Sue, giving her mop of hair a determined shake. 'I haven't been making notes for ages now, but it still stays with me every morning.'

'I don't know how you stand it, Sue, I'd crack up if it was me.'

'So would I if it wasn't for Michael and John. I can stand it, you see, 'cos when I wake up every morning I come home.'

'Have you tried going to the doctor about it?'

'Symptoms and causes, love? I've a feeling doctors don't have a pill to stop the future coming.'

'Aye, but a psychologist . . .?'

'Or a psycho-*anal*-ist, I suppose?' said Sue with sarcasm,

111

drawing herself up to her full height of five foot one. 'I think it's my dreams that are frightening, not me for having them.'

'But did they go on in France, even in Sète? But you've come back looking so pretty, so brown!'

'They don't take a holiday, my dreams,' said Sue grimly. 'In fact, in my dreams nobody seems to have a holiday, ever.'

Ailsa stood looking in some alarm at her friend.

Then she said, 'My husband's an absolute fool! Him and his daft ideas about J. W. Dunne, and time, and precognition. I'm getting superstitious, Sue, you shouldn't meddle with such things, you shouldn't tamper.

'You *look* perfectly normal,' she added, sizing up her friend's ironic smile, with the teeth, crooked, standing out white against her southern French suntan, making it even more ironic.

'Meaning I'm not,' said Sue.

'Meaning you are,' said Ailsa, grasping her hand. 'Listen, Sue, can I do anything to help? Just tell me, I'll . . .'

'Just do this one thing, Ailsa love, for the present. If I think of anything else, I'll come running to you. It's just that I'm terribly afraid Ben may be right, and if he's right, och, don't blame the poor man, Ailsa, he'll have done us all a service. You see, what if these dreams are some kind of warning, just as he says — or why should they keep coming back night after night? Maybe because the warning's strong and hard and dreadfully important.

'So just do this for me.'

Ailsa nodded. 'If I hear you on the phone, and you say, "Aow, wot a lahvly suhprayse to heah yaw voice, Ayulsuh," . . .'

'That's it — Christ, you do it much better than I do —'

Was this moment comic or deadly serious? At all events, they both broke down giggling.

'Just in case those people who don't exist . . .'

'On the other side of a wall that doesn't exist . . .'

Event Twelve

*The unions become the apparatus
of revolutionary repression
against undisciplined, anarchical,
parasitical elements in the
working class.*

———————— TROTSKY ————————

Engelsday, 9 October 2117

The Party knew. That is to say, the Presidium knew. That is to
say, Boris Clegg-Molotov knew. And one of the things the Party
knew, without a shadow of a doubt, was that the best restaurant
in London was an establishment festooned with floral
curtaining, glittering with wall-height mirrors and nineteenth-
century chandeliers, and called 'The Peasants' and Workers'
Community Cafeteria'. This beautifully appointed establishment was available to all those peasants and workers who had
Party Cards Grade 1 and 2, such as Vassily Forson or C-M
himself, and to heroic servants of the toiling masses such as
Rusalka, Tatiana, Tamara or Ludmilla. It was to be found
conveniently wedged between the central offices of five
ministries, just off Westminster Bridge in a cul-de-sac named
Cannon Row. The name by which it was known to the cooks,
washers-up and waitresses who worked there was Caviar Row.

The waitresses were all prettily dressed in period garb
(miniskirt and bikini-top, style London 1968), for it is well
known that high Party functionaries are all keen antiquarians,
and make something of a fetish of History, particularly at key
moments of the pre-revolutionary past. Sue thanked her stars
she was not one of them, but a certificated cook, toiling in the

depths of the building, for the job of waitress involved both greater opportunities and greater dangers.

Particularly at times like these. Here was little Kathy Sugden with her perfect blonde legs and her frantic tousle of yellow hair, coming up to Sue. For advice, Sue could tell, by the way she was twisting her finger in her apron, and by the hint of darkness at the back of her blue-grey eyes. She knew what sort of problem it was before her friend opened her mouth. Not much fun being pretty in 2117.

'What shall I do?' she said. 'It's that Shameless Dignan, Minister for Productive Labour.'

'He doesn't have a very reassuring title,' agreed Sue.

'I know what my mother told me,' said Kathy, her mouth twisting up humorously, 'but if I say no, will he have me arrested?'

'And if you say yes, if *he's* arrested, will *you* be the day after?'

'And if I'm arrested, then so might you be, the day after that.'

'What does the Constitution say?'

There was a sound like a rapid fragment of music for soprano duet, for both girls were giggling briefly, despite their worries. The words 'What does the Constitution say?' had become a fashionable catch-phrase when the Purge began in July 2116. Its meaning may be guessed from the fact that, though the Constitution of the Truly Democratic Republic was often said to be the most enlightened in history, it was available for consultation neither in any library nor in any known bookshop.

'I think I'll just toss for it. How can you tell what to do? There aren't any *rules* any more. You can't even work out how to survive. I'd rather be a knife-thrower's girl in a circus. At least you know the boss is trying to miss you.'

'Do you like him?'

'What's that got to do with it? Heads I go to bed with him, tails I don't.'

Living with fear, Sue mused as she caught the bus home to De Valera Street, was like living with a constant nagging illness. It sapped your vitality, it undermined your courage, it made you restless and snappy, it made you — sometimes — make foolish mistakes. But then the mistakes you made hardly mattered, for the mistakes of others could drag you down just as easily. Dialectical materialism? No, for the philosophy that emerged was atavistic — it was pure and simple fatalism.

And yet — what a state of frantic despair Ivan had got into the other day, for no reason except that their clock had broken down. You see, he explained to Sue, when I'm waiting for you at night to come back from the restaurant, I need, I *need* to know what time it is, to know that I don't have to start worrying *yet*. I know, said Sue nodding; it's the same for me. He had rushed round to a man he knew who fixed chassis on the quiet, for it was no good going to the official shops with their big scarlet notices THE PEOPLE'S TIME. It was illegal, of course, but then did the law keep within the law? At any rate Ivan was back later that same day with a properly mended clock, and not exactly relief in his heart, but perhaps a slightly less acute degree of dread.

They ate the delicious meal that Sue had brought back, made of leavings from the restaurant. Everybody did it, what else could you do? If you didn't, the other cooks would look at you askance — 'Is she going to inform on us?' — and before you knew where you were, they'd have informed on you. Yes, since she'd landed this job at Caviar Row, two months ago, there was nothing but the best for her and her Ivan.

'Not right, though, is it? When you think how we used to live — how *most* folk do. Why should those bastards in the . . .'

'Sh, not so loud. At least *we're* not those bastards in the . . .'

'Sh, not so loud. I agree we deserve it better. At least we don't go in for kicking people in the . . .'

'Sh, not so loud. Under capitalism, you have to realise, people had meat only once a *month*.'

'But how do we know, Ivan?'

'Well, surely that at least must be true, because you know very well, love, they had private enterprise. So everything must have been very disorganised, with no central planning at all, and . . .'

'Sh, not so loud, they'll think we're talking about *them*.'

After supper they went to bed and made love, then lay there in the contented darkness for a while, chatting about 'Michael's World', as they called the fragmentary land of dreams that

115

slowly, over the last six months, had been building and building between them. It was puzzling and sometimes contradictory. But it did have the common feature of a child called Michael. It had a place called Sète in it, and a blue sea called the Mediterranean, and sometimes long stretches of complicated music — not just patriotic marches for brass band and the sort of pop song that people called a sex sandwich — but great mourning, exultant and enchanting noises all mixed up with pictures and images that poured into their minds just like . . . well, just like ordinary dreaming. Was it only in her dreams that Sue still laughed, was her old funny, gay, witty self?

Escapism. Besides, they would be tired after all that talking till two in the morning.

But then it was best to be tired, best to be absolutely razby, for otherwise, waiting for 3 am and the knock on the door that might or might not come, and would do either for no predictable reason, you would never get to sleep at all.

The following day, Mrs Marsden across the corridor received a large official-looking letter. It informed her that her husband had been shot on 14 September for having been implicated in the O'Boyle—Winch—Kolashnikov Plot. It enclosed a bill for 95,000 phunts to cover the cost of her husband's execution.

Two days later, Kathy was not in the restaurant. 'Oh yes,' said Gregory the chef, 'she was asked out by — oh, was it Tov Dignan and Tov Sovietsky? She went out with both, so maybe one of them was jealous, you know how it is. I wouldn't mention it to anyone else,' he added, eyeing Sue up and down. 'Best not to notice she's gone, you should know that.'

Sue felt cold, knowing he hated pretty women. Later again, she kicked herself for not have guessed, for not having felt what he would do.

Marxday, 15 October 2117

Waiting for them to come was horrible. But it was almost worse when they knocked at someone else's door and you felt that appalling sense of relief: Thank God, it's not me! Thank God, it's someone else! Thank God, it's their children and not mine! 'Community,' they said. 'All one people together,' they said. But they forced you to be glad when your friend or neighbour had his jaw broken.

If it was like this under the Truly Democratic system, what horrors folk must have suffered under capitalism!

It was two nights later, at 3.17 exactly. Sue had been dreaming of wee Michael, who was crawling everywhere like a small express train, banging tin pans with wooden spoons (though he hadn't learnt to swing yet), was into all her cupboards, and was rapidly becoming too much for a mere grown-up to handle. She had gone to sleep with a smile on her face, half delight that he was safely asleep and — please God! — wouldn't wake up till tomorrow morning, half amusement at the trouble he'd been causing all day long. When . . .

When the world shifted on its axis and They were beating on the door as if They were real and Michael were the figment of a dream.

Most people just got up and put some clothes on, and were taken out into the freezing street, protesting in bewildered tones, as if they thought the System had a system. Nobody ganged together, it seemed, collecting a few pickaxe handles and lying in wait for the People's friendly Friends. Nor did Ivan and Sue. They got their clothes on in one minute flat, peered out of the bedroom window and shinned down the private rope that Ivan had installed some months before. (It was worse to be arrested than burnt alive, of course, but best to try and avoid both.)

The PFs were creatures of violent habit. They were quite unused to people taking evasive action, and there was no one waiting in the darkness of the yard, nor in the shadows of the alley beyond it that stank of dogs and old dishwater, and was slippery underfoot.

Up above, the lights had snapped briskly on for a moment but then, as the persistent fault in the wiring took its toll again, snapped firmly off. The PFs blundered about in the bedroom, trying to see if there was someone hiding under the bed or in the wardrobe, shining their torches up and down. In the living-room, Tov captain-detective Watson was sitting on the couch,

117

groaning, holding his foot. He had hurt it while kicking the door down, which was strange, because he'd had a lot of practice by now. He hardly noticed as the sofa gently subsided under his weight, and resolved itself into six separate pieces. 'Bastard socialist—humanist counter-revolutionary rightist—opportunist terrorist—reactionary agitators!' he moaned, using all the worst words he knew. 'I think they've broken my big toe.'

By 8 am Ivan and Sue were on the train to Engelsburgh, a place they had chosen out of instinct, because they were both Scots, because you might as well flee as far and as fast as possible. The place was popularly known as the capital of Scotland, after Karl Marx's *Kapital*.

'It's no a very nice name to call the place,' said Sue, bright red spots on her cheeks, the excitement of fear having given her her sense of humour back. 'Makes it sound like an English colony.'

Ivan smiled briefly. 'But what do we do when we get there?' he asked.

'I dinnae ken, but we have eight hours to think about it.'

Actually they had fourteen, for the trains under the Socsov System had been humanised, and went in for the same behaviour as people, such as stubborn immobilism, reactionary tergiversation and reformist deviationism. Having sabotaged a whole three hours of the 5-year plan by going slow north of Darlington, the train engaged in a revisionary movement back to Leeds, from where it took a rightist—opportunist line across the Pennines to Carlisle. Its progress north to Carstairs was a matter of fits and starts.

Meanwhile, the hours rolled by and, in the unheated carriage, whose seats were broken slats of wood, Sue and Ivan debated hotly. 'Skye? Ardnamurchan? Mull? The Grampians? One of the smaller islands, what about Eigg?'

'But we'll be even more noticeable on one of them. Why not Glasgorky, and try to lose ourselves in the crowd?'

'America!' cried Sue, fantasising wildly. 'They're still capitalist, they'll think we're good propaganda.'

'Och, *Sue!*'

'And why not, pray?' she said. 'All we have to do is catch the train to Greenock, find a boat, and . . .'

'And row across the Atlantic. Fine, fine. When did you last see the sea?'

'Certainly not at Brighton,' said Sue. 'But the boat would be easy. All we have to do is steal one.' The word 'steal' was still part of the English language, for Marx had written 'Property is theft' and people had to be reminded what that meant.

'All right,' said Ivan quietly.

Sue peered at him in a puzzled way. 'Listen, you're supposed to be joking, but that doesn't sound like a joking voice.'

'It's not.' (Which do you prefer, the Atlantic or the People's Friends? Cold water's cleaner.)

'A sense of humour's a wonderful thing,' said Sue.

It would be sensible, at some point when they found themselves in a town, to buy something in a chemist's. Something final.

Just in case. Just in case the inevitable happened.

'Together is better than apart.'

Sue nodded, then tears began to slide out of her eyes. 'Why us? Why you and me?'

'Everyone says that,' said Ivan. 'Absolutely everyone.'

'All I want is to go to bed every night, sure that we'll both wake up alive. Is that an unreasonable wish?'

Nobody answered her, not even Ivan.

It was midnight. Outside the windows they could only dimly distinguish the shapes of hills and moorsides passing with painful sluggishness. Reality had narrowed down to the lighted interior of the compartment, floating and swaying upon the darkness between two identical reflections of itself, a triple image projected upon this black hillside, quite out of place in such a lifeless wilderness. Objectively, which of the three images was the real one? Why, the one they were in, of course! Ivan was reminded of the trolley-bus ride that night when his identity had been stolen. Reality seemed eerie, improbable, and at the same time more intense than ever. Irritably rocked to and fro by the motion of the train, he felt the words *scherzo diabolico* skip awkwardly into his mind. Alkan again?

The train clattered, swayed and struggled onwards, then, as East Calder approached, began to lose speed once more. This time it was as if the engine were utterly exhausted. Groaning, toiling, it shuddered to a slow and final halt. Pulling the window down, they both put their heads out, suddenly finding themselves in a night-time world full of wet grass and country smells. They could see the little station quite clearly, a hundred yards up the line, standing in its own pool of light. Everything else was sunk in darkness. Confused and indistinct sounds of shouting came from the head of the train. Glancing up as they hung out of the window, they could see the raindrops falling into the light, as if materialising out of nowhere like liquefied darkness, splashing on their faces.

'Well?' said Ivan.

'Shall we?' said Sue.

They had been extraordinarily lucky up till now. But if they could possibly avoid having their papers checked once more . . . Opening the carriage door silently was impossible, so Ivan kicked it wide, and they jumped out onto the embankment one after another, slipped through a ragged hedge and into the dark concealment of a grassy meadow full of thistles and cowpats.

Ahead of them on the other side of the field loomed the houses of East Calder, a flat dark silhouette on the horizon, which no lamps illuminated. To their right shone the small station, the only source of light, haloed by golden rain. They stepped off cautiously across the field, glancing back from time to time at the motionless train. Nobody seemed to have followed them out.

Through another hedge, then out onto a road. They hesitated before turning left towards what they supposed must be the west. They had not realised before the full absurdity of what they were doing, nor how wet the night was. Apart from a packet of sandwiches, they hadn't eaten since the night before. This flight of theirs was simple impulse, purposeless, insane.

Except for the fact that it would have been still more foolish not to run.

Why should there be darkness, total darkness in the village behind them? Whatever had happened to the street lights? The Socsov System detested darkness, for it made it harder for the People's Friends to move around.

And what should they do now? Glasgorky lay somewhere off to the west, thirty miles away behind the falling rain. The only half-rational thing was to set off in that direction. Perhaps they might find some disused cottage on the way, somewhere to take shelter if the rain persisted in falling. There was nothing to be done but improvise. But if they could reach the city, and lose themselves in the crowds, just for a few more days, that at least put off a little longer the inevitable end. Every minute mattered, now that it was threatened. Life, narrowed down so close, could be seen quite clearly — it alone counted, and as long as they remained together, counted doubly.

The darkness was soft and wet, they could feel it soaking into them as the rain soaked into their flimsy, ill-made clothes. The countryside was so silent they could hear the rain whispering as it fell. The air was like a sponge, filling and filling with water.

Then a blast of sound split the atmosphere. Unlike lightning, it was the noise that struck first, the hysterical klaxon of a PF van — 'I see you, I *see* you, I SEE you!' — as, still out of sight on the further side of walls and hedges, lanes and crossroads of darkness, it swooped along the highway towards them. Seconds later, the wet sky above them began to reflect light as well as noise, a red and white flashing that became hypnotic as it grew and grew. Sue and Ivan stood for a moment paralysed like rabbits on the roadway, not knowing which way to run. Then Ivan pulled her down with him and they fell together into the soaking muddy shelter of the ditch. Ululating wildly, in a whirl of howling dazzlement, the PF van went slamming by. Past them. Down the road.

The derisive yelling fled and faded, the stabs of garish red and white shrank away westward.

There were two bangs in quick succession, ludicrously small, like a child's toy overturning. Then a thump and a flare of light, as the petrol in the PF van exploded. Four hundred yards down the road, flames roared upwards from the van, which could be seen clearly in the blaze, upside down in a ditch at the edge of the road. A clattering sound like rockets detonating succeeded the bangs. The car must have been packed with ammunition.

Sue and Ivan flattened themselves in the ditch again, meaning

121

to lie low till it was over. Then Ivan felt a sharp prong digging into his ribs just below the left shoulder-blade.

An ironic West Lothian voice said, 'And who might you be, Jimmy?'

Engelsday, 16 October 2117

The squawking and yammering of birds, the squeaking of milk-pails, the solemn groaning of cattle, the quavering complaints of sheep — (What a contemptuous sound! It's as if they're jeering at us, thought Ivan) — the whole blended into an alien hubbub which made further sleep impossible. Only the townee knows how rowdy the countryside is — a theatre of exotic and discordant noise. And, looking out of the window, the insistent wearying green, the strange empty flatness devoid of buildings, stretching out to an unimaginable distance — that strangest of backcloths, the horizon! Though it was early morning, the scene was quite without shadows, suffused with a milky sunlight, just like the image of the People's Collective Farm given by the films that celebrate, every year, without fail, Another Great Leap Forward. Ivan and Sue gazed in wonder at the strangeness of the sight.

When at breakfast they asked Donald Duthie how he'd known they could be trusted, he said,

'You can always tell by their sense of humour. Especially when they've a fork up their backside,' he added. 'You ken, we're all together in this. Will you give us a hand, then?'

It was a test to which Yes was the obligatory answer. A hundred years of Communism had made no difference to the place of women, which was firmly in the Collective Farm soup kitchen. Sue and Ivan said goodbye behind a closed door — not knowing they would never see each other again save in their dreams. Ivan mounted into the cab beside Donald, Sue and Maggie Duthie waved them bravely off, and the lorry rumbled away down the farm track towards the main road, out through the gates of the Peasants' Collective of Murieston, and away towards the Kirknewton Pit. It was curious. Despite the parting from Sue, despite the fear at the pit of his stomach and his knowledge that it was right to be there, Ivan felt also, contradictorily, a sort of happiness. It was having a sense of purpose, he decided, it was making up your own mind and acting.

A General Strike! A spontaneous anger at the Purge, but since those words didn't have the right meaning any more, the peasants called it 'From the heart'. Something had cracked. People had grown tired of being culled like seals, and had resolved somehow to resist the cullers. The peasants had remembered how once they had been farmers, not peasants tied to the land. This was why the train had been stopped the night before; the tracks had been torn up to prevent soldiers coming in from the south. This was why the PF van had blown up; there had been a ditch dug across the road. Donald boasted that the workers the length and breadth of Scotland had laid down their tools and told the People's Friends, 'On your way!' Three days before, a group of PF's had come looking for arrestees in the Collective Farm. They'd been robbed of their weapons, tried by a People's Court, and shot.

'Oh no,' Sue had cried.

Donald shrugged. 'What does the Party say about revolutions? Seems to me, one revolution's as good as another.'

His wife had said, 'They're animals. Show me a blue-boy, I'll show you a murderer.'

Now, dominating the village, the winding gear of Kirknewton loomed above them, the lorry turned into the yard past cheering pickets. Ivan and Donald jumped down and started to unload the provisions.

'What's your name, lad?' asked the miners' leader, shaking Ivan's hand. 'Och, man, that's a Russky name. You're just plain John in future, you mind that.'

'What's your plan of campaign?' said John, clasping a tin mug, as they all settled down to a tea break. He was prepared to be amazed and frightened.

'We've sent our demands to the Minister in Engelsburgh,' replied the man proudly. 'We've asked him to come and talk to us.'

It was firmly said, but John felt simply fear and no amazement. The enormity of this General Strike. Talk? That supposed someone would listen. That supposed someone had the habit of listening. Meanwhile, they all sat here like sparrows on a fence, waiting for others to act. Aye, things would start happening soon enough.

Lunch was not yet over when there came a cry from the metal tower they were using as a look-out post. The group dropped their unfinished sandwiches and ran in several directions shouting for the gates to be closed and barred, for the pickets to get into position, for the barriers to be hauled across. Donald and Ivan found themselves marooned in the midst of an embattled but unarmed camp. They drove the lorry up to the gates to form an additional obstacle.

The brow of the hill towards Engelsburgh prickled and grew a dark crest, and the road below it began to flow like a river with khaki-clad soldiers, booted, armed with guns, heading in the direction of the pit.

'Nae bother, lads, they'll talk,' said Robertson, his face expressionless. 'They'd bluidy better.' But whether his concern was for the soldiers or his own men, he didn't say.

'Christ, they're all fucking Russkies!' he added in disgust, as the uniforms of these advancing troops became properly visible. 'It's a bluidy invasion, lads. And who's that in the front of them?'

Indeed, and this did not make it any easier, thought Ivan. Foreign troops would feel nervous in their isolation among strangers, could not be talked to, could not be persuaded. Incomprehension, jumpiness, naïvety could be seen in their young faces as they formed up behind the iron barriers at the entry to the yard. They had come to put down a bourgeois counter-revolution led by the working-class — it was 1917 turned upside down, but Ivan knew they would ask no questions. Drawing Donald with him, he positioned himself behind a stack of steel girders and waited, feeling almost calm.

A small, self-important man stepped forward from among the soldiers.

'George Millar, the Union man,' said Robertson, and spat. 'I ken what *he'll* say before he opens his bluidy mouth.'

'Conds,' cried Millar, waving his arms as if he were imitating the perpetual motion machine, 'I appeal to you to open the gates, to lay down your weapons and surrender up the counter-revolutionaries who have misled you. I promise that no reprisals will be taken against those honest Socsov citizens who see where their duty lies to the Revolution and to our great British Democratic System.'

'Call yoursel a fuckin Scotsman, George?' came a voice from the pickets.

Robertson stepped forward to argue. 'George,' he said, 'we're weel kent to each other since we were bairns together, and you ken fine we're asking for nothing but our rights. We're all solid here, and no a man among us but thinks the same. Nae more o' these arrests for no rime or reason, and nae clapping of women and weans in jail. It's a simple honest thing we're asking, George, as you ken right well in your own heart, so just turn around like the good miner's son you are, and march they Russky soldiers back to Engelsburgh, and tell old McAllister the Minister to get off his arse and come down here and talk to us like a man, face to face.'

'Andy, ye ken fine well that what you ask is impossible,' said Millar.

'Impossible?' cried Robertson. 'What's impossible about it? Has McAllister no got a tongue in his heid, then, that he cannae speak to us?'

'You're a misguided man, Andy. Ye dinnae understand what you've got yourself into. You're a terrorist and a criminal, a lackey of the petty bourgeois counter-revolution.'

'Well, they're fine long words, George, and I wonder how there's room for them in your mouth, but it's the same old tape-recording you've been playing these twenty years and more. Have you no got something to say to us all in good plain Scots? Those 12-year-olds you had arrested last Engelsday were revolutionaries too, were they? Man, if you cannae talk straight, you cannae see straight. You go and tell the Minister, because the lads here are all solid, and we'll no shift from here till we see McAllister.'

At this Millar turned to the Russian officer beside him and pointed his finger at the miners' leader.

125

Time, it seemed to Ivan, slowed down to allow the soldiers' actions to impress themselves upon the mind. The officer's hand went to his belt, from which he drew his revolver. There were perhaps five yards between him and Robertson, and he fired three times. Robertson clutched his stomach and collapsed in front of the gate. A roar of anger went up from the miners behind him, but they had made the tactical mistake of being behind the barriers, so that it was impossible for them, even unarmed as they were, even hopeless as it was, to charge the line of soldiers. As these levelled their machine-guns, therefore, and began to fire, the roar of anger turned into screams and shouts. Some stood baffled seeing their comrades fall, others turned to run. In a minute the volley had ceased, and the yard had been swept almost clean of living men. Wisps of smoke rose from the Russian guns, the sun shone calmly down, birds twittered from a nearby tree, the hysterical barking of a dog sounded from somewhere out in the village. Scattered about the yard lay perhaps a hundred bodies, all splashed with revolutionary crimson.

The officer uttered more commands, and his troops split up into groups, running forward busily, opening the gates, clearing the corpses out of the way, searching the outbuildings for more miners.

Ivan, who had been John again for a brief hour, was one of the few prisoners taken alive.

Dream Seven

Thursday, 17 October 2007

John woke with a start, not knowing where he was, in what city, in what century, in bed or lying on a hard floor wrapped in his coat. He turned towards the space on the bed beside him where Sue ought to be, and yes, to his bewilderment there she was. But of course she's there, he told himself, just like every morning, sleeping peacefully, dreaming (he hoped) of something more pleasant than he had been. And there against the wall was Michael's cot, with his 7-month-old son fast asleep in it, thumb firmly plugged into mouth.

He turned back to his own side of the bed, drew the note-pad towards him and began to scribble rapidly. As a reporter, shorthand was invaluable, and he could get quite a lot down before the nightmare faded.

There were gaps in it. But this time it had been worse than usual. A General Strike. The murder of . . . there had been a name, but he could no longer recall it. The fusillade. Himself crouching with a friend behind a stack of pit-props, being hauled out and struck across the face.

He felt his jaw now, and got up cautiously to examine it in the mirror. No damage. Of course there could be no damage. But the discovery was still strangely reassuring.

It was obvious how he had come to dream about a General Strike. There was one on at the moment, and he'd been covering it. Obvious for that matter where the rest of the details had come from — miners on the picket-lines, the pits blockaded. Not that any guns had been used. After all, this was 2007, and ancient western democracies tried to avoid that kind of thing. Nor had they called out the troops yet.

It was all quite easy to explain. The political crisis, the Brianston-Pedley Brigade planting bombs — the country was, as the papers said, 'a powder keg'. He smiled, for the clichés of his profession amused him — 'mercy dash', 'a mother's anguish', 'bomb blast', 'red terror', 'putting a match to the powder keg'. His colleagues enjoyed using them, for they reduced the horrors of the situation to a set of familiar platitudes, and evoked in the reading public a set of stock responses. Perhaps these dreams were a kind of compensation, and deep inside himself he was worried — afraid what might happen if law and order broke down. Sue. Michael. In a revolution it is the innocent who are most at risk.

Dreams. Strange things, but they came from the unconscious, didn't they? This failed to console him, for he was beginning to be sure the true explanation was quite different.

Sue at his back stirred in her sleep and cried out. It sounded, John thought, like Russian. Somehow the routes of his dreaming had crossed with hers, and this was the most alarming thing of all. For what was the test of reality? That you and other people agreed about it, had the same experiences, reported the same things. Ah now, but by that test the dreams he shared with Sue were not dreams at all, but simple reality — and that was altogether too upsetting to accept.

He wished to God Ben had never suggested this experiment to him, recording his dreams every morning. Maybe then they wouldn't have begun to make such loathsome sense. Or at the very least he wouldn't have *known* the sense they made, because they'd have been swept out of his mind on waking as ordinary healthy people's dreams were, cleansed and swilled away like dirt in running water.

Over breakfast he discussed it with Sue for the hundredth time, and she (while she spooned the baby-food into Michael's little pink mouth) said, 'Okay, darling, but did you really have the same dream? I was in a farm at the end, being arrested.'

'Well, of course, I'd *left* you on that farm, hadn't I? You see, the really worrying thing is that now, if we have separate dreams, they're accounted for by the dream-record itself.'

With the edge of her spoon she scraped lumps of food from Michael's chin and cheeks, and stuffed them back in his mouth, which kept opening and shutting obediently like the beak of a nestling. 'Cuckoo,' she said to her son fondly.

'My God, I'd rather be here than there,' she said to John.

'So would I,' he said. 'Makes you afraid to fall asleep.'

'How do you get a grip of your unconscious mind?' she wondered. 'Do you think we could make ourselves dream, och, *nice* things for a change?'

The unconscious, said Freud, is a sort of sewer, where you flush away all the foul rubbish of the soul, washing it down into the darkness below the sunlit streets of consciousness, into a labyrinth of gloomy winding passageways. And at this moment, two hundred miles away, in a street called Briggate in a city called Leeds, Brianston-Pedley was squelching and splodging through such a maze. Behind him came Dougie and Noel, the former keeping his lips hard closed but cursing silently at the stench, the filth, the discomfort. The latest acolyte had refused to accompany them. Rats were just too much for her. B-P judged that her other services to the Revolution made up for such a momentary lapse.

Today's mission was perhaps B-P's most daring blow yet at the western liberal imposture. After this, let them try to write off the Proletarian Red Army! Let them try to discount the anger of the masses! Why, he had sixteen members in his cell, quite enough to form a Presidium.

And then, next week, a further blow would fall. London Road, Edinburgh, was the destined location of that. They would use one of the techniques of their fraternal allies the Conventional IRA, take over some bourgeois flat, and . . . Soon, he was sure, the capitalist tiger would be obliged to unsheathe its fascist claws; it would be forced to change its stripes. The State's repressive tolerance would give way to honest brutality. He would make it be what he knew it was.

So Brianston-Pedley meditated, trudging onwards through

129

condoms, slime and diarrhoea. At each step he took, the large bomb he carried in his rucksack patted him lovingly between the shoulders.

Ahead of them now came a bend in the tunnel, along with a curious echoing effect. It was as if the sucking and slurping sounds of three pairs of rubber boots treading through the thick sludge were picked up by the brick archways at the bend and tossed to and fro between them. You could distinctly hear not three pairs of boots but six. Moreover, the wavering haloes of lamplight seemed doubled and reflected too, as if the walls were set here and there with slime-green mirrors.

But look, that was impossible!

Jeezus, there must be someone else down here!

The Police?

B-P held up his group wordlessly with a raised glove. He strained his ears to see if the echoes stopped. For if they did not, they were not echoes.

Dougie, however, in his efforts to come to a halt on the slippery floor of the sewer, slipped, slithered, waved his arms, tripped over a loose brick and came frothing down into the mire. It heaved and sploshed. His gun fell out of its holster and the thick sludge swallowed it, bubbling. Dougie followed the unconscionable din he had made with a string of curses ('Why can't the f—— bourgeois f—— keep their f—— sewers in decent f—— order?') and Brianston-Pedley promised himself that the lad's next assignment would be a suicide mission. Kamikaze for him.

The silence was too expectant to be borne. Around the bend ahead of them there stepped a black silhouette. It was impossible to make out much detail in the figure, but it might well be dressed rather like themselves, and it was certainly holding a gun. Noel, with more presence of mind than Dougie, at once shone his torch full in the eyes of this new arrival, who for a moment could be seen quite clearly, before his two companions followed him around the corner, each with a torch in his left hand, a gun in his right.

Stalemate. B-P and Noel held two guns and two torches, their opponents three. These were not, however, police, B-P was sure of that, for their guns had leapt too eagerly to hand. A reluctance on the part of this society's police to use weapons was one of the outstanding proofs of its decadence, or of its hypocrisy, or of both.

No, and under the layer of grime, through the fumes of nameless gases, he thought he recognised his opponent. If he was not mistaken, this was a symbolic confrontation between the Proletarian Red Army and the National Socialist Council. That face, with its close-cropped hair, its narrow-clipped moustache, its jutting chin, was that of a sworn enemy of the People.

Behind him, Dougie raised himself dripping from the muck, tried to wipe his gloves but found nothing to wipe them on, faltered to his feet and struggled not to be sick.

'What are you doing here?' both leaders said in chorus.

'Advancing the cause of the Revolution,' they both replied.

Both groups would have to retire in good order, thought B-P. But how to manage it? Aloud he said, 'May I ask if you're about to plant a bomb?'

' "Mee ay awshk"!' Beasley mimicked him.

'Perhaps, seeing the strange circumstances — fancy meeting you in a sewer! — we ought to . . .'

Beasley cut him short. 'You talk too much, Pedley. It's because you're a bourgeois intellectual, like all filthy reds.'

'Well, Beasley, you may suppose you're working-class, but you're not *objectively* working-class.'

A retching sound came from behind B-P. Dougie was being as sick as a dog. The two thugs who accompanied Beasley clung to each other, guffawing.

Their laughter, such as it was, eased the tension somewhat. 'Shall we put our guns away,' suggested B-P, 'and discuss the next step?'

'Now' — when that was done — 'may I assume your target is some red revolutionary politician?'

' "Mee ay ashume",' Beasley jibed. 'Call yourself a fucking Englishman, Pedley? You can't even talk the lingo.'

'Man,' said Noel sadly, 'you haven't familiarised yourself with the relevant theoretical equipment for meaningful discussion.'

'Never mind that,' said Pedley, hushing his comrade. 'All

131

right, Beasley, if you won't answer me, may I hazard a guess?'

' "Hezzahd" away, old lad,' sniggered Beasley. 'One of your crypto-crimson pals.'

'Ah,' said B-P, 'and what if I were to tell you that *we* are after a politician of the fascist right? Namely, Hugh Walkinshaw.'

'That's a funny coincidence,' said Beasley, suddenly a bit cast down.

'We're after him too,' said one of the neo-Nazi bully-boys from behind him.

'Shut your ugly face,' said Beasley angrily. He thought for a bit. 'Okay, wotcha say we both plant our boom-booms, one at each end of the street? That should make for a right old laugh.'

'Done,' said B-P, though of course it stuck in his throat to say it. 'No, no, Beasley we won't shake hands, that would be too much for the human frame to bear . . .'

' "Aow, the yooman freem", is it?' cried Beasley, then, reverting to his normal accent said, 'You'll fucking shake hands and like it, you red bastard, we've got more guns than you.'

A replay in miniature of the Nazi–Soviet Pact of 1938, thought B-P resignedly. The ways of History were like those of God, mysterious. Like the ways of God, however, only at first sight and before dialectical materialism had got to them. Marxist theory could handle anything, even a fascist handshake.

In a way, too, Beasley was right. The sensation this afternoon when Walkinshaw arrived and made his sentimental spiel, appealing for Reconciliation, National Unity, Work for the Unemployed, a New Industrial Charter — you could read it off beforehand with your eyes closed! The sensation when the bombs went off and closed both ends of Briggate — the fires, the injuries, the panic. Yes, it would be most effective, particularly if there were a lot of deaths.

It was embarrassing, though, for him, B-P, to be shaking hands with a terrorist.

One of those moral agonies you had to bear for the sake of a greater good. Sartrean remorse. He still had too many old-fashioned scruples, he decided.

'Sue, do you know what's happened?' said John, arriving through the door with a crash.

'Your dinner's in the oven,' she said automatically.

'Right!' He rushed into the kitchen, then, without a pause, rushed back.

'Hugh Walkinshaw's been murdered. Leeds this afternoon, didn't you see it on the telly? A bomb at both ends of the street, twenty-five people killed, God knows how many injured, it's a massacre. I've got to fly right down and cover it.'

'It's because the Alliance has been winning all those by-elections,' said Sue. 'The extremists are afraid of him.'

'Christ Jesus, our greatest man — the one who might have — he even had a sense of humour.' John sat down and began to bolt his food.

'They don't like the old sense of humour,' said Sue, watching him and wishing he wasn't a journalist. 'I wish you weren't a journalist,' she said. 'Now be *careful*, darling, don't start all that interviewing terrorists again, you can come to a sticky end that way and, besides, the Press Council doesn't like it.'

'Don't worry,' he said, not listening to a word she said. 'I know how to look after myself. Look after yourself, for that matter, and wee Michael. Listen, I must just phone up the office and check my ticket's been reserved.'

Erupting into the hall again, he picked up the phone and stabbed his fingers seven times upon the wee square buttons. Whirr. Click. Brr-brr. Brr-brr. Hurry *up*, he whispered to himself. Brr-brr. Ah.

'The reglaments are quite clear, Tov McLellan. The prisoner is to be returned to her town of domicile. Departmental reglaments are to be followed *at all times*, there is absolutely no room for *exceptions*.'

'Otchen horrorshow, Tov Harris, I just wished to obtain confirmation that the proposed course is still praveelny. One can't afford a slip-up.'

'No, Tov McLellan, you can't.'

'I merely thought that at a time when the Department of Social Harmony is under such pressure . . .'

'Are you suggesting that Reglament 17a is *ambiguous*, Tov?

I am afraid that such a suggestion would be regarded as a slur upon the clarity of Socialist thinking, and in consequence . . .'

John dropped the telephone as if it had become red-hot, and then retrieved it from the carpet. Thank God, no damage had been done. The machine was purring away contentedly, like some dangerous big cat. Calm suddenly, he dialled his number again, looking around him as he did so. Yes, the Seurat reproduction on the wall, the dark green of the canvas wallpaper, the knick-knacks on the hall table — it was all exactly as usual. It was the year 2007 and he was safe and sound in his own house. Ah. Thank God. A familiar voice fluted through the ear-piece.

'Yes, John, the 8.15 flight.' A pause. 'You sound a wee bit out of breath.'

'I've just had a nasty shock,' muttered John. 'Thank you, Louise. Eh . . . thank you. I expect I'll be back in the office in a couple of days.'

He put the phone down. He gazed around him. No, the earth was not shaking, the colour of the carpet in his hallway had not changed, it was Sue and not some other person waiting at the kitchen door, and that was Michael in her arms. He checked his watch again, pressing the buttons. It was 7.15 on the evening of Thursday 17 October 2007, in the reign of King Charles III; Ronald Trimmer was Prime Minister of Great Britain, and Arnold Briggs was leader of the Opposition. Things were perfectly normal, he told himself again, things were all perfectly normal.

Event Thirteen

*The question of the form of
repression, or of its degree,
is not one of 'principle'. It
is a question of expediency.*
———— LEV TROTSKY ————

Sartreday, 19 October 2117

It was one of the great triumphs of the Socsov System that it had
replaced the crowded inadequate jails of the capitalist era with
much larger, more adequate ones, and had further added to
these the pleasant country facilities of the moorland
concentration camp, which was as much an advance on the old
walled termer as Whipsnade was on London Zoo. Nonetheless,
even Beatrice and Sidney Webb Prison had not been constructed
to hold the thousands upon thousands of bewildered and
miserable inmates who now found themselves crammed twelve
into a single cell, sharing a single stinking bucket, shivering with
fright when the door opened and one of their number, after an
absence of perhaps two days, was thrown back onto the stone
floor, bloody, groaning and half conscious.

Sue was lucky, however. Before she had had time to grow
ragged, grey and hollow-eyed, she was called — that first day
— for interrogation.

The interrogation room was not quite like an ordinary office.
There was a desk in the middle of the floor, a metal filing
cabinet, a locked cupboard, a number of chairs, and that was
all. There were no windows onto the world, but a light angled
at the prisoner's eyes, leaving the interrogator's face in shadow.
The door was four times the thickness of a normal door.

'Sit down,' said the officer behind the desk, not raising his eyes from the report he was studying. She obeyed him, trembling. The guard who had brought her in remained standing behind her chair, where she could not see but only sense him. At least it smelt better here than in her cell.

There was the long statutory silence, designed to worry the prisoner — supposing she were not worried enough already.

Finally, the man raised his eyes from the page and consented to look at her. 'Well?' he said.

'Well what?' stammered Sue after it had become evident that that was all he was going to say.

'Well, what are you guilty of?'

'I—I don't know,' replied Sue, astonished. Absurdly, a glimmer of hope shone in her mind, for if she were not guilty . . . She did not yet know that hope is the worst of traitors. It betrays us into supposing things are not as bad as they could be. It betrays us into living when there is nothing left to live for. The interrogator's words quelled it, but it would rise again.

'I suppose you claim you have done nothing?'

'Yes, Tov, I have done nothing at all.'

'You claim, therefore, that you have been imprisoned unjustly.'

'Yes, Tov.'

'I see. In that case you are accusing the Socsov System of injustice. That is slander against the People under the terms of Article 58B, and will be added to the indictment.'

'But I am a member of the Party,' protested Sue, 'and a sincere Communist.'

'In our society,' replied the inquisitor, 'everyone says they are a sincere Communist. There is therefore no way of telling who is a sincere Communist or not.'

I have always known our society was mad, Sue thought to herself, but this prison is clearly the asylum within the asylum.

'What are the charges against me?' she insisted, trying to be brave, but her voice shaking.

'Under Article 49D, theft of the People's property, under Article 58G . . .'

'Wait a minute,' said Sue, 'I haven't committed any theft.'

136

'Chief Cook Gregory Batchelor affirms, along with two other witnesses, having seen you remove unused food from the Peasants' and Workers' Community Cafeteria on sundry occasions as listed beneath . . .'

'But that's perfectly normal practice,' cried Sue, indignation beginning to give her some courage. 'All Cafeteria employees are permitted by the chef to remove unwanted left-overs, it's part of the conditions of employment.'

'On the contrary, how can it be part of the normal conditions of employment when it has no official sanction? I am grateful, however, for your accusations against your fellow-employees. Perhaps you still have some glimmerings of a sense of duty to the People.'

Sue realised with a sinking feeling just how impossible a situation she was in. If she defended herself, she accused others. If she did not, she admitted her guilt.

'Moreover,' said the inquisitor, 'five days before your arrest you were seen smiling and talking to Cond Kathy Sugden, who was later arrested as an anti-revolutionary agitator.'

'I talk to a lot of people. I have to in my job.'

'That is not the point. Had you informed the People's Friends of Cond Sugden's unreliable political tendencies *before* her arrest, you would have been acting in a patriotic spirit. As it is, not to have reported her is a sign that you are lacking in revolutionary vigilance, and is a crime under Article 58E of the code.

'Moreover, you were picked up in most suspicious circumstances, four hundred miles away from your place of domicile, associating with known criminal elements at Murieston Collective Farm.

'Moreover, you are charged under Article 58G with having engaged in counter-revolutionary terrorism.'

'But . . .'

'In that, on 11 Marx you laid a copy of *Truth* upon one of the tables in the kitchen of the restaurant you were then working in, and deliberately dropped tomato paste upon it, so making it appear that the hand of Our Beloved Leader was stained with blood.'

'But . . . but . . . even if it were true . . .'

'Are you *denying* this fact?' asked the interrogator, peering at her, as if with a touch of surprise.

'Yes, I do deny it,' said Sue, not knowing whether to laugh or shake with terror. 'Your facts are quite false.'

'Nonsense,' said the officer, and he banged upon the desk with his fist as if he wished it were a human face. Sounding as if he were quoting some official directive, he continued in a monotone, ' "Where the file contains inaccurate data obtained from an informant, the data are not inaccurate. They are a true record of what someone said." '

Sue gazed at him, almost in awe, and found herself saying, 'That doesn't make sense. Can you people not distinguish between truth and falsity?' She felt horrified with herself the moment she had said it.

The interrogator, however, began, for some reason quite incomprehensible to Sue, to roar with laughter, and it was some time before he could master himself enough to give her any reply. When he did so, he sounded almost regretful:

'You call me a liar? You deny the truth of the indictment? Let me tell you this,' and he got up and suddenly hit her across the mouth, 'we are not going to surrender to intimidation.'

She felt the salty taste of blood on her tongue and said, 'And my husband? Where is he? At least tell me — please — that he is safe.'

'Your husband?' replied the officer in amazement. 'Your *husband*? Do you not realise, woman, that once you are here you have forfeited the rights which attach to being a Socsov citizen, along with all elements of social status such as the possession of a Party card, the status of motherhood or that of being a wife. Consequently you have no husband and, supposing the man you refer to still exists, he has no wife. Indeed, to be perfectly frank with you, you have no legal existence whatever, so that it is no good your friends and relations inquiring after you: they will be informed of what is, after all, no more than the unvarnished truth — namely that there is no such person as yourself.'

Sue realised at last — it had taken her twenty-four years to do so, all her life — just what the trouble was. She was guilty of being a human being. Guilty of living in the year 2117. Guilty of feeling, seeing and hearing. Guilty of loving, guilty of thinking. Guilty of longing for a child of her own. These were the crimes of which the State, being an insensate abstraction and not able to feel or think of love, accused its citizens. Even the interrogator, had he the wit to know it, was as guilty as the women he tormented. She said nothing, for what was there to say?

The officer rose to his feet and, pressing a large rubber stamp on the file in front of him, handed it to the guard. Speaking as indifferently as if he were discussing a consignment of soap or a batch of Zyklon-B for a concentration camp bath-house, he said,

'Category ZX. Medical. If she passes muster, Wagon 13 tomorrow morning.

'Can't imagine what they want with scum like you,' he added to his prisoner. 'Some sort of psychological experiment, I imagine. Brain surgery, perhaps. Maybe they'll cut your treachery out.

'Next.'

Despite her horror at his words, Sue was clear-headed enough to wonder why he had bothered to say as much as this. Perhaps, she thought, he enjoyed his job.

Wagon 13 was packed with women, dirty, frightened, smelly, mostly with bruises and black eyes, exchanging a variety of rumours. They were to be brood-mares for a New Race of human beings. They were simply bound for Balvrain, Borrobol, Bylchau or some other death camp. Their bodies were to be dedicated to medical science, or their brains removed and replaced by stainless-steel machinery. All the most curious imaginings of twentieth-century science fiction — which people since that epoch had found it as easy to put into practice as to imagine — whispered in the form of terrified rumour round the grimy wagon as it lurched and roared its way northwards through the fields and woods of Suffolk, and finally, without a stop for either food or drink, deposited them on the doorstep of Diss Manor, where Charlesworth held his court.

The great man came out on the steps himself to look them over, dishevelled, bruised and filthy as they were, but nonetheless a bunch of basically healthy young women. She gazed at the doctor with curiosity and fear. Not that his appearance had anything inhuman in it. He was indeed markedly handsome and upstanding, six feet in height and having the kind of features that had once been ascribed to Greek gods, romantic leads and the supermen in children's comics. That made it worse, for people still persist in finding it shocking when exterior and interior are so at odds.

Charlesworth introduced himself, and spoke to them gently, reassuringly. They would be well cared for here, well fed and tended by expert medics. If any of them had been brutalised by the blue-boys, they would be carefully nursed back to perfect shape. They were very lucky considering what alternatives were available to Enemies of the People like themselves. He required them for psychological experiments, but they need not be concerned at the sound of that. No harm would come to them, and he assured them personally that they could look forward to a happy future at Diss Hall.

Thought Sue, she had never heard anyone brandish the word 'happy' before as if it were a threat.

She felt particularly uncomfortable when, for a long moment or two, Charlesworth's eyes lingered upon her. Her eyes winced away, and she knew that the man was interested in his female patients for other reasons than the purely scientific.

Diss Manor, continued Charlesworth, considering the women with great attention as he spoke, was a haven of peace — a shelter from the uncertainties and dangers of the outside world. It lay under the personal protection of C-M himself (he lowered his eyes reverently).

Well now, what was the programme for the rest of the day? Baths, showers, inspection by the medical staff, assignment to dormitories and a slap-up meal. He'd bet they hadn't seen good food for weeks! he said, laughing as if at a joke. With another meaningful glance at Sue, he turned on his heel and left his assistants to usher them in.

That evening at 11 pm, Sue, already fast asleep in the first comfortable bed she had had for five days, was awakened by a medical orderly.

'Cond Lumsden? You are required by Doctor Charlesworth.'

Dream Eight

Sue had had a perfect day. It was true wee Michael had been sick, but he had done it on the kitchen floor, so it had been easy to clear up. She had wheeled him out to do a few bits of shopping, then driven the car to the Botanic Gardens and push-chaired him round them, stopping in the glasshouses to view the lily pond and to see how those incredibly sexual orchids were at this season of the year. But it was the trees she appreciated best: even if, floating at that misty boundary between dream and waking, she sometimes doubted which of the two worlds was the real one, she was sure that these trees stood in both and were more real than either. *Presence*, one of her French poets called it — pure *being there* would be the English. There could be no doubt at all about trees, though of course they were entities that did not turn outwards to the world, but rather inward upon themselves. The reason for their stillness was not so much that they were rooted for ever in the earth, but rather it was the other way around. Their rootedness was due to their nature as beings, as contemplatively self-absorbed as Indian sages, gazing within in watchful silence, hungrily seeking the light at the centre of the world.

She was missing John. Even in normal times he was often away for days at a time, but, as the strike bit deeper, as the Prime Minister said less and Will Murphy's challenges to the government became more explicit, she worried more. Perhaps that was why, last night, she had had that dream of infidelity. No, that was ridiculous, you often had such dreams, or if you didn't you weren't still sexually awake. This time it had been a kind of Superman, oh-so-tall and oh-so-handsome, who had swooped down upon her from a white white sky, and carried her off into the clouds. The clouds were very boring, they were just like ordinary sheets. He had had a red shirt, but then they all did, didn't they (except those who had black or brown ones). The great big S on their chests was a little too much like the two backward lightning-Zs of the Nazi SS. Somehow she hadn't really liked this Superman. Anyway, it proved how much she was missing John, so it was a good thing. Another good thing to add to her day.

Now who was Superman really? she wondered. Who had she based him on? This evening, as she fed wee Michael, she was determined to find a *rational* explanation for once, instead of the crazy speculations she and John engaged in sometimes. She cast her mind around among her friends and acquaintances as she spooned the solids into her son's mouth, concentrating entirely on both tasks and judging coolly that she preferred the second. Goodness, she was doing three things at once! Well, why not? Now would it be Sandy, or Bill, or . . . No, they didn't any of them fit. Perhaps it was someone in politics whom she'd never seen except on the telly (telly-lie, hope to die), like Will Murphy, 'the People's Will' as they called him in the press. Or what about that neurologist they'd met at the Party — hey, wait a minute, Sue, party is the word, with a small 'p' — two Saturdays ago? 'Oh, Michael's Mummy's clever boy, he's eaten it all up, isn't that clever? Michael have a nice drink now?' Michael drank mother's milk, that was why his skin was so soft; Superman drank wine, the People's wine, that was why his shirt was so red.

Yes, it would be that neurologist, what was his name? Handsworth, was that it, or was she mixing him up with someone else? Not a Scotsman, he had the most *un*canny ideas. She carried Michael, temporarily fast asleep, a tiny dribble of her own real milk seeping from the corner of his lips, to his cot in the bedroom and stood irresolute. The baby shoved his thumb into his mouth, like a bung into a beer cask, and started to suck himself deeper into dreamland. Well, that was the modern science

143

of the mind, all science and no mind. Handsworth (if that was his name) thought being conscious was just going click-click-click inside like a watch. She had a hunch that her watch didn't know she was asking it the time, though it always answered her questions quite frankly when she did.

How would she pass the evening? The news as usual was terrible. Somebody had thrown a concrete slab off a motorway bridge in Wales and killed a working miner. Oh God, how awful it was when John wasn't there. How about ringing up . . .?

Surely John couldn't have been kept in Leeds all this time. Of course, the trains were on strike, that was the problem, but if she was going to have to put up with Superman in her dreams, she surely had the right to have John here making real love to her before she dreamed them. Was that the baby? No.

Call up Ailsa, that was the thing. With her exotic island name, she could always entertain you. But why hadn't John rung?

She hesitated with her hand over the phone. If she rang, would it stop John ringing? The phone went off like a tiny bomb.

'Jeezus, that was quick,' he said. 'Is that you, Sue?'

'Yes, I was just standing over it.'

'The watched phone never boils.'

'It did this time. Listen, where are you? Are you going to be back tonight?'

'Sorry, darling, I'm still in Leeds. Should be okay tomorrow, I'm just about finished, don't think it's the sort of thing you want to hear, though.' He sounded exhausted through the crackle of the wire.

'Sounds horrible.'

'It was. The bits that weren't horrible were frightening. It's B-P's mob — those bastards. But listen, love, I should be back tomorrow. Should be the evening flight. How's wee Mike?'

'I planted him today in the Botanics, and he's blooming.'

'Smashing. Give my love to Ingres's violin.'

Ingres's violin was herself in her white winter skin, the slim female fountain of the Frenchman's painting. 'I'll send her a telegram,' she said. In the mirror above the phone-desk she could see that she was smiling. 'Listen, can you hear me smiling?'

'Of course I can.'

She wandered back into the living-room and switched on the telly, then switched it off again. Out to the phone once more. 'Ailsa, is that you? Listen, John isn't back till tomorrow, I could do with a gossip session. Are you . . .?'

'Sorry, love, I have to . . . Well, and then again, maybe I don't.' She could hear Ailsa putting her hand over the phone and shouting into the back room. 'Ben! Ben! Where *is* the man?' she asked rhetorically in Sue's ear. The phone gave out a clink as, no doubt, she put it down to go in search of her husband. A good five minutes went by. Sue sighed, stood on one leg, then, not liking that much, stood on the other. Then she spread both out in a tall triangle, and looked at the toes of her scarlet shoes, flexing them up and down. Then she examined her fingernails, bit at one experimentally and decided that was a bad idea. She felt a sudden burning desire to go to the loo, but resolved to fight it off by making faces at herself in the glass. This is my face for John, this is my face for Superman — Christ, I like *that* one, I must try it on John. She clasped one thigh round the other, and stuck out her tongue at the image. It stuck out its tongue right back, and she said to it, 'Och, you rude thing. I thought you had better manners.' The reflection shook its head, and she wondered if she had shaken hers. However, the solemnly dark brown eyes were certainly hers, and she decided she must have done. Why a'n't I worried, she thought, by all these silly dreams? Well, I am worried, but why a'n't I worried *more*? Is it because it's *all* an illusion? But, looking at myself in the glass, what a pity it would be to have warm brown eyes and a smile like that, and be nothing but illusion. No vanity, it's just that some of the illusions of life are worth having. Some of them are good, some of them are pretty, some of them are pretty good. Christ, what on earth is Ailsa saying to Ben? Big Ben, Big Ben, how I love the stroke of midnight! Hurry *up*, woman, I want to go to the loo!

She examined her teeth in the mirror next, and decided they were really bad. All up and down, and some of them, particularly in the lower range, at different angles. Little impertinent white teeth, but they didn't seem to know which way they were facing. Really, the dentist should have reformed them, and

145

had them marching up and down in ranks like People's Friends. Oh God, I wish I hadn't thought of that. Where *is* that woman?

'Sue,' said the voice in her ear, so sudden that she nearly dropped the phone. 'It's okay, be with you in five minutes. How's wee Michael?'

'Och, he's . . .'

'Och, how . . .'

After five minutes of this, Sue said firmly, 'Ailsa, enough of this nonsense. If you come over here — at once, mind! — you can see him. If you promise not to wake him. Or never darken my doorstep again.'

'All right, love, five minutes, I promise.'

Now who is outside, pulling on the ancient brass Edinburgh bell-pull? Is it Ailsa? It can't be John, for he's away in Leeds. Is it Superman the redshirt, or Beastman the blackshirt, or Molly-toff the brownshirt? Sue stood on tiptoe to peer through the judas, and saw that it was Ailsa.

'Och, hen, it was good of you to come.'

'It was,' said Ailsa, playing the bringer of gifts. 'It was okay, I bribed him, I'll tell you later.'

'Bribing a husband, tell me!'

'Sue, you know perfectly well! How's wee Michael?'

'Asleep in his cot, now Ailsa, don't *wake* him. I couldn't *stand* another session like last night.'

Ailsa went, extravagantly pussy-footed, down the hall into the bedroom, and admired the baby asleep in his cot. Blissful, thumb in mouth, not knowing what world he had got into, or even if it were the real one. Not knowing what real meant. Just being there like a tree in the garden. What he felt, he felt, that was all. And what else could be real but what you feel? And the two women standing above the warm blankets, silent, like invisible ghosts in a painting.

Then they talked about husbands for a while, and had coffee. When Ailsa pressed her about dreams, Sue turned the subject, blunting it like a knife. And about half past eleven, Ailsa went out through the door again, clashing her bangles together and kissing Sue, and promising she'd tell her how the bribery went.

Sue walked back into her sitting-room and gathered up the coffee cups and thought to herself that Michael was just about due to waken. Then she noticed the bracelet that Ailsa had been showing her, sitting there still on the coffee table, motionless and silent, not saying a word, as if it had thought it over and been determined not to be noticed.

'Och *Ailsa!*' she thought. So like her. She never visited the house without leaving some object behind. Car keys, a watch, a pound of mince, even once a present for her husband. Usually Sue went round the house before she left, picking up odd things that Ailsa had dropped and pressing them upon her. Och well, she'll be back for it tomorrow. Too late to ring. I'll call her in the morning, after Michael's feed.

The door-pull rang.

She shook her head, smiled, picked up the bangle and went to the door, pulling it open without even glancing through the judas. 'Ailsa, that's the *sixth* —' she said. And stood there, her tongue stuck to the roof of her mouth, still clasped about the fricative 'th', which had long since ceased to sound. There was a gag about her mouth, and her legs had been kicked from under her. The blue-washed ceiling of the hall reeled above her head, and she registered a muddle of impressions. One, the door had been shut, two, there were men in the house with her, three, there was a gun pointing at her stomach, four, there was some-one saying —

He was a very tall and intellectual-looking man, with an accent like a parody of Oxbridge —

Why, she thought she recognised him, from the telly-lie — a mop of grey hair, a distinguished air —

'Just keep quiet and you won't be hurt.'

Her own front door had opened, and all her private night-mares had come bursting through.

The cloth had been placed about her mouth only for a moment. She scrabbled about on the floor, looking for Ailsa's bangle.

'Just a moment,' she said. 'I must find it.'

147

Dream Nine

*But the revolution does require
of the revolutionary class that
it should attain its end by all
methods at its disposal — if
necessary, by an armed rising;
if required, by terrorism.*

——————— LEV TROTSKY ———————

They were all in the sitting-room now, and being scared out of her wits was making Sue talkative.

'So here you are,' she said. 'Nice of you to call. I'd been expecting you. Now, if you've seen quite enough, I have a baby to feed, and coffee cups to wash up. Also, it's rather late, don't you think?'

'What do you mean, you've been expecting us?' said Noel. He looked around the sitting-room nervously, as if the potted plant could conceal some sort of ambush.

'Well, someone like you was bound to drop in some time,' said Sue brightly. 'Now don't you think you'd better go away before my friend finds out she's lost her bracelet?'

'Listen, young woman,' said Brianston-Pedley. With that professorial air of his, he looked as if he were pronouncing in seminar on some abstract subject of purely academic interest. 'If you don't make sense, we'll execute you, you understand? We're here for a serious reason, a political reason, and all this talk about bracelets and babies had better be cleared up fast.'

'Do you have to keep waving those guns around?' asked Sue. 'Why don't you just put them away and let me make you

148

some coffee and then we'll all talk it over in a reasonable way.'

'Man, when you say "reason", it makes me want to puke,' said Noel. 'Reason is just an ideological practice supported and reproduced by the institutions of the capitalist system.'

'Go with her,' said B-P to the other young man. The latter rose and could immediately be seen to be a girl, dressed in quasi-military denims, hair long and lank like a boy, but sway-hipped, pout-lipped and having some male appeal.

It was hard to get into the kitchen. She had thought she would never reach it, for her breath was too short and her legs would hardly carry her. Old Nick had always been said to be a suave, gentlemanly sort of person. Maybe this was his twenty-first-century avatar. She said to the boy-girl,

'Are you the latest acolyte?'

'What?' said the latest acolyte, who didn't seem to know this word. She frowned. 'I'm I-reen. I used to be I-ree-ne, but now I'm I-reen.'

'How do you do, I-reen.' Sue shook the girl's left hand, for the other was encumbered by a gun. I-reen, embarrassed, switched her gun halfway through the shake, and then tried again with her right hand.

'Are you reds or fashos?' asked Sue, buzzing like a wasp about the kitchen. Anger had given her her legs back.

'We're Marxists, of course,' said the girl, offended.

'How do you expect us to know if you don't tell us?' said Sue.

'I should have thought it was obvious,' said the girl.

Sue looked her up and down. As a matter of fact, how *could* you tell? Maybe they had a different hair-do, maybe they complimented each other on being liberated in bed, maybe they slept till ten on a Sunday morning.

'We don't have the same philosophy,' said the girl.

'Oh,' said Sue.

She measured out the beans and set the grinder humming. 'You're not like Jehovah's Witnesses, you didn't tell me what your philosophy was before you came through my front door.'

'Maybe you'd have let us in if we'd said who we were,' said the girl sarcastically.

149

'Out!' said B-P appearing at the door. 'You're talking too much, I-reen.'

I-reen vanished, her Marxist—Leninist tail tucked between the backs of her denim legs.

'I know the signs,' said B-P in level tones. 'You're hysterical. You're a hysterical woman. Really, you're scared out of your wits.'

'Nice of you to mention it,' said Sue. 'Mind if I finish making coffee before we discuss it? I have a 7-month-old baby in the next room, and if you think this is any fun . . .'

'This is politics.'

'Okay, so it's the future of the world. Now please be quiet for just a moment and listen,' she said as he was about to interrupt her. 'You don't know the whole of it. I have a friend coming back in a minute, she left a bangle here, she's always doing that sort of thing, what are you going to do when she rings the bell?'

'Bangles? They won't have bangles when the Revolution comes,' said B-P. There was a silence, and after a moment she could see that her words had sunk in. Yes, indeed it was serious. Girlfriends had husbands or friends. Missing people would be looked for. From this point on, anything could go wrong. Bugger. Why had he chosen this flat? (He knew the answer to that: a good bow-window, a perfect vantage-point upon the street outside.) If he killed her now, who would answer the door? And if they kidnapped the woman with the bangle too, and she had a husband . . . Mind you, this girl would probably say she had a husband anyway, but you couldn't take the risk of its being a lie.

'You see,' said Sue, shrieking with laughter. 'The future of the world depends upon a bangle!'

He slapped her across the face and she gasped. God, no, it wasn't a good idea to get hysterical, not *really* hysterical. What should she do? Listen to him. Calm down.

'Is she married, this friend of yours?'

She didn't dare to hesitate. The truth must be told at once, or else he would think it was a lie. And then she would have trapped Ailsa as well in this awful, this unthinkable mess. 'She is,' said Sue.

'Listen carefully, for the sake of your baby and yourself. If she comes back, you will go to the door quietly. You will not do anything to alarm her. Just do as we say, and no harm will come to you. You will think of your baby, because . . .'

The telephone rang. B-P waved her into the hall with the barrel of his gun, then stood aiming it at her while she answered.

'Sue? This is Ailsa, listen, have I left that bracelet of mine . . .?'

'Oh, what a lovely surprise to hear your voice, Ailsa!'

'What? What was that? Listen, Sue, you idiot, have I left that bangle of mine round at your place? Och, I thought I had. I'm such a fool. Listen, do you mind if I come round some time tomorrow and collect it? Yes, some time in the evening I dare say. Sue, are you all right, you sound a wee bit strange?'

'Yes, I do, don't I, and I am,' murmured Sue.

'Okay, love, kisses to wee Michael, and see you tomorrow evening,' said Ailsa, apparently oblivious to anything but her own sense of bustle. She put the phone down.

'Sensible,' said B-P approvingly.

Sue stood holding the phone, then put it down in her turn, grimaced, and went to serve the coffee. She knew what you had to do with terrorists — she knew theorectically you had to win them over, make them see you were a human being. It could, she suspected, take quite a long time.

But had Ailsa understood? She hadn't dared to drop any other hint, not with that man with a gun at her back. Jeezus, she thought, it didn't *sound* as if Ailsa had taken it in at all. Why should she? It was all too bloody improbable.

'Now what about this husband of yours? When does he get back? Tonight? Tomorrow? Or when?'

She wondered what she should say. Truth or untruth? Which was the less dangerous? She hadn't the faintest idea, and responded with the truth. 'Well, it may be tomorrow. But you can never be sure.'

'But it may be tonight?'

This, on the other hand, seemed a perfectly safe lie, so Sue said Yes.

'What does he do?' asked B-P.

'Reporter,' said Sue reluctantly, wondering whether she

151

should, but the evidence lay about the house, plain for them to see.

The reaction was predictable. 'Christ Jeezus!' cried Noel as if in severe mental agony. '*We*'ve come to the right house, haven't we? A lackey of the existing mode of production, no less.'

'Well, they report *your* doings,' said Sue sharply.

'In this transitional phase,' said B-P, 'we must be grateful for the decadence of what is laughably called a "free press".' He rather enjoyed reading reports of the doings of the Proletarian Red Army in the papers. There was promise for the future in them; he was already putting his mark on history. 'On the other hand, they merely write what they are told to.'

Sue thought bitterly of the time her husband's paper had been censured for publishing his interview with one of B-P's own terrorists. The irony that they should be here now, this evening, was no less than grotesque. For the moment, in her horror of these people, she had forgotten the hysterical yowling of the press, its baying after sensation, the way that that associate of John's had pried into some woman's grief, and then she had committed suicide. She knew perfectly well the press was self-obsessed, trivial and meretricious. The point was, they weren't *all* in somebody's pocket. The point was, these people were so much worse.

The thin nagging sound of a hungry baby arose in the next room, and Sue, trying to get up, found once again that her legs wouldn't work. Hearing his voice, she felt empty again of anything but fear.

The latest acolyte got up to accompany her.

Please, John, don't come back tomorrow. Not till they're gone.

But I can guess what they're here for.

And please, Ailsa, do think about our telephone call. I used our private code, there's nothing more I could do. Please, Ailsa, think about it, *understand*!

John, meanwhile, was in Leeds, not dreaming of her in Edinburgh but of a stately home outside the town of Berwick. Or else in Berwick, thinking of his dreams of Leeds. At all events, his mind was far away.

152

Event Fourteen

*The Communist Party is based
on the principle of coercion
which recognises no limits or
inhibitions . . . Such a party is
capable of achieving miracles.*

———— PYATAKOV ————

Engelsday, 23 October 2117

In front of Ivan's eyes, the back of a shaven head and a pair of
shoulders, muscular but bowed, wearing a ragged jacket stained
with blood. In front of this pair of shoulders, another, and
another, and yet another. The line of plenniks, dispirited and
fearful, emerged one by one from the grey corridor into the
glaring sunlight of the prison yard. Blinking at the light, nervous
of the shouts of the warders yapping importantly at their heels
like dogs about a flock of sheep, they hastily formed themselves
up into ranks, fifty in each line. A parade of scarecrows ready
to be tied to stakes and immobilised for ever.

Five hundred men were now held there muttering and appre-
hensive under the little round black eyes of the sten-guns. They
whispered, trying not to move their lips:

'What's going on?'

'I don't know, but I wish it wasn't.'

'Is it no Ivan?'

'Yes,' he said, trying to conceal his start of surprise. The face
beside him wore a black eye but was vaguely familiar. Yes, a
farmer out of Murieston Collective.

'I've seen your Susan. She was okay when they arrested her.'

'Thank you, thank you,' muttered Ivan, and tears rose to his

153

eyes at the evidence of human sympathy. To be relieved that his wife was alive, though arrested . . . Absurd! Because Marx knew what they were doing to her. If she was alive, she could suffer pain. And if she could suffer pain, they would inflict it.

'Was that you talking?' A bear-like warder reached into the row of prisoners, hauled Ivan's acquaintance out of it by his ear, hit him savagely across the face with the butt of his gun. He struck the farmer's face as if he wanted to erase it, to obliterate its difference from other faces. The man's knees buckled, and he was dragged away by the heels, his head bumping on the paving-stones. So much for his small gesture of kindness.

The jail-blocks of Saughton Termer stood tall around the yard to north and west, the outer wall with its crown of barbed wire curved from east to south. Against this wall there were drawn up two lines of lorries, the nearer one consisting of large green box-vans bearing the legend OFFAL, the outer being a row of grey dust-carts. The prisoners gazed blankly at these two rows of trucks, and preferred not to think what their purpose might be.

The prison governor stepped forward from the ranks of guards and held up a coin. It was a silver-coloured hundred-phunt piece. He had an air of relief about him, for he was about to empty his jail a little. Time enough, for it was bursting at the seams. The small nickel disc flew glittering into the air, was swallowed by the governor's right hand — who hesitated for a second before clapping it onto the back of his left. He might, or he might not, have turned it over, it was up to him. He glanced at it casually.

'You. You.' He signed at the ranks of plenniks, indicating that the first ragged file should stay where they were, the second should move forward to the box-vans and clamber in. And so on, till the population of the square was halved, and the first row of lorries, the ones labelled OFFAL, was packed with men. Ivan was in the last line, and almost the last to enter the final box-van. The engines revved, the jail-yard filled with fumes, the gates swung open and, with much grinding of gears and grumbling of ancient engines, the echelon of lorries began to leave.

154

'Farewell to Saughton Termer.'

'Aye, but where now?'

'Who knows?'

From behind them, as the last lorry pulled out of the yard and emerged on to the public road, there came the chatter of machine-guns, magnified, ringing to and fro between the high stone walls, like a thousand nails tumbling on a sheet of iron.

Althusserday, 24 October 2117

'I am an idealist,' said C-M, swivelling in his chair and rising. Idealists can think best pacing the floor, pausing to gaze out of the window at a horizon of trees and meadows, framed there in the glass like a picture of the distant future.

Actually what Boris saw through the window was not what was there. For the moment he imagined he was not at Uss Hall in Berwickshire, but at Diss Hall in Norfolk — a forgivable mistake for an idealist. What he saw outside the window was the view from quite another window, of quite another place. Like Norfolk, the distant future was flat, infinitely flat. No hills or hollows could be seen in any direction, neither north, south, east nor above all west. Flatness crawled flatly away on all fours towards all four horizons, pressing itself submissively into its own shyness so as not to be observed. This, however, was impossible, for above it the sky arched roundly, all-seeingly, its single vast eye focused upon the shrinking earth beneath it. These were the steppes of England, where the wind cut straight in from the Baltic like a saw-edged knife and had, long centuries ago, chopped off the head of any hill with pretensions above its station. This land lay level, the image of egalitarianism. The very trees upon it were strange excrescences, and Boris told himself they should be lopped, so as no longer to detract from this vista of perfection. A land like water in the wind — that was the dream.

He came to with a start. No, the landscape before him was not like that at all. It was Berwickshire, not Norfolk. Well, it *ought* to be Norfolk. He would give orders, and have the experiment moved south.

'You put things so well, Tov Chairman,' said the nervous man, wondering if he should light a cigar. It might stop his hand from shaking. His hand would, however, shake very obviously while he was lighting it. A difficult decision. Ludmilla looked from him to Boris, then back again to the worried professor. So this was the second Great Plan. Seeing the man in charge of it, she felt her confidence ebbing. He was not like Doctor Charlesworth, who could — so obviously — bring anything he touched to a happy, shouting climax.

'And then — several years ago, while I was still Minister of Health and Sanity — I came across a most interesting little document from the capitalist past. Late twentieth century it was, a work on linguistics.'

'Linguistics, darling?' said Ludmilla, for this was her cue. Not for her Boris the wiles of feminism, that outmoded petty bourgeois deviation.

'The study of language, my dear,' said C-M fondly, for her ignorance was charming. Sounding-boards, he thought. You could practise a speech on them, or even a doubt. Not that he had any. You could bounce your voice back off a woman. Thank the Blessed Joseph that feminism was dead. We used it, of course, way back before the Revolution, just as we used animal lib, paedophiles, lesbians, coloured rights and those repugnant gommicks. We pulled in all the minorities so as to become a majority. Then, when we had the power, we didn't need to be a majority any more, so we simply got rid of the minorities. The fems of the time, a Jane, a Fields, a Sarah, an Eithne, a Trefusis (never mind how their names went together, and it didn't matter anyway, because they were all filthy bourgeois to a woman) were smartly arrested one fine midnight, lined up against the wall, and a rumba of bullets made sure that that was that. Now there weren't any fems, just women, and Vissarionovich! Was Ludmilla a woman?

'You will find this a little *difficult*,' he told her, 'but bear with me, for it is of great importance. Suddenly, scanning the pages of this book, I came upon a secret. Actually, in the course of my life, I have come upon *two* secrets, *two* possible answers to the riddle of politics.

'I have therefore set in train two experiments. In one of them — maybe in both — I feel convinced the answer must be found.'

Ludmilla thought again of Doctor Charlesworth and nodded, crossing her pretty legs as if to draw Boris's attention to them.

'Now, Tov Professor, as our greatest living expert on human speech, I am sure you will agree with me that language is exclusively a social product. It is not men who speak, but language which speaks through them.'

(But I talk to you, luby, thought Ludmilla. I have always chosen very carefully who to talk to, what to say, and all for the sake of my career.)

'Of course, Tov Chairman,' said the Professor obligingly. 'Under the outmoded capitalist masquerade, people suffered from the delusion that they were individuals. But if words like "individual", "personal", "private" and so on had not existed, they could not have believed such nonsense. Which shows that the language of capitalism was part of RISA, or the Repressive Ideological State Apparatus. As Althusser says.'

'Praveelny.'

'Thank you,' said Sweasey, blushing with relief and reverting for a moment to his normal appearance, which was the confident persona of the Dean of Marx-with-Us College, Cambridge, Chairman of the Department for Examining Acronyms and Thought-Health, originator of the Human Expression Liberation Programme, inventor of Communification Theory (COT).

'What was written,' asked Boris rhetorically, 'in this little book that moved me so deeply? Our dear Professor has already voiced its central insight: people think of themselves as individuals. They think of those around them as other individuals. But since, as Althusser tells us, the fundamental reality is society, and people are merely the "functions" that it "exercises", why do these people imagine themselves to be "real"? I will tell you in a word. *Because the English language forces them to do so.*'

'What do you mean, luby?' asked Ludmilla, putting on her face of frownless puzzlement. 'Is there something wrong with the way we talk?'

'Of course. You see, English (like all other languages) contains personal pronouns.' C-M pronounced the words 'individual' and 'personal' with an expression of disgust upon his face, as if they might choke him if he did not spit them out. 'We all say "I", "you", "me", "he", "she", "they".'

'Of course we do,' said Ludmilla comfortably. She would like to see Boris ceasing to use the word 'I'. And would not like him to cease using the word 'you'.

'Ah, but that is precisely the individualist trap into which we fall. These little words carry the whole ideology of capitalism with them, they make us think that we actually exist as "I", as "you", as "he" or "she". They make us forget we are but cogs in the Great Community. Just think of this.

'If the only word for human beings was "we", how then could the individualist commit his self-crime? Worse still, we have names, personal names bestowed upon us by our parents.' (The word 'parents' here seemed to be tarred by the same ugly brush as the word 'personal'.) 'The solution, my friends, becomes plain. I cannot understand why no one has ever thought of it before!

'We shall simply abolish the words "I" and "you", and that will be that.'

'Brilliant, Tov Chairman,' agreed Professor Sweasey.

'You see, the great Swiss linguist Saussure established, right at the beginning of the twentieth century, that language is a system of differences, quite without positive terms. The meaning of the word "hog", for instance, has nothing to do with the animals we call "hogs". Its meaning is due *solely* to its being a different word from "dog" or "bog" or "clog" or "jog" or "log". In just the same way, the meaning of "I" and "you" and "she" and "they" depends on nothing — on *nothing*, my friends, save the fact that the English language happens to contain these words!

'Luminous,' murmured Sweasey.

'According to a twentieth-century philosopher called Derrida (I must arrange to have him put into the names of the week — Derriday, what would you say to that?) human consciousness itself emerges only because we have a word "I" lying around ready for us to use. And the linguist Benveniste says — ah, listen to this!

' "It is literally true that the basis of subjectivity is the exercise of language. There is no other objective testimony to the identity of the subject except that which he himself thus gives about himself." '

'Pellucid,' said Sweasey.

Boris looked expectantly at Ludmilla, who picked up her cue: 'I'm sorry, I don't quite follow that sentence.'

'It means,' said C-M — he waved Sweasey to silence, for it was *his* job to put Ludmilla right — 'it means that the only thing that proves a man is himself is the fact that he uses the words "I" and "me" and "my".'

'Chotky,' said Sweasey.

'My!' said Ludmilla.

'And that is why I have set up this little experiment of mine,' confided Boris. 'Under the care of the celebrated Professor Sweasey, who has written so convincingly on all these subjects, and always with the strictest Marxist orthodoxy. This estate, set on the boundaries of the ancient city of Berwick, is destined to be the first flowering of the future. This is the site of the Great Experiment in Loving Togetherness, so called to distinguish it from my other project, the Final Solution. The whole estate has been surrounded with walls, ditches, barbed wire, look-out towers, mines, machine-guns, automatically exploding bombs and Alsatians trained to go for the throat. This will keep together our togetherness. Within the estate we have two barracks in which the sexes are segregated, young men in one, young women in the other. We allow them to sleep together, but never with the same person on two consecutive nights, since that would be a sign of their continuing to recognise each other as individuals. They are forbidden to use names, and forbidden to use the words "I, my, me, mine, you, yours, his, hers, him, them, theirs, she, he," and so forth.'

'But, Boris, what are they to say?' asked Ludmilla, her mouth wide open with a stupefaction that for once had no pretence about it.

'What are they to say? They are to use the word of words, the selfless syllable of Community. They are always to use the word "we".

159

'But of course,' said C-M modestly, 'I owe everything to Professor Sweasey here. It is *he* who will be in charge of my great linguistic revolution, it is he who is the teacher of Uscant, the universal language of the future.'

With Boris, thought Ludmilla, an acknowledgment was a threat. She would have been sorry for Sweasey, did she not despise those for whom she felt sorry.

'Keep me informed!' cried Boris, shaking Sweasey's frightened hand. 'You and Charlesworth are in competition, remember! I wonder, which of you will be the first to reach the Promised Land!'

'*I* will, Tov Leader,' muttered Sweasey. He wished he had never left his cosy university post. He wished he had never written any of those books, any of those learned articles full of the name of Marx taken oh-so-gaily in vain. He felt terrified to say the least. His epoch-making Communification Theory, a doctrine so subtle that it could not be expressed in words of less than five syllables! Tov Chairman Clegg-Molotov had somehow soiled the purity of his theory by trying to put it into practice. He thought wistfully of the great peroration with which his masterpiece had ended.

'Since all meanings are socially constituted and produced and therefore only become "humanly available" in dialectical fashion via the complex interactive behavioural contexts of advanced proletarian community, no discursive practice can be concretely recuperated which is not at once the material product of dialectical necessity and of systemic "human" interrelation (which, if it is not social, is not human) and therefore — concretely — may not be proffered or even less preferred under pain of the collapse of referential validity outside the Marxist perspective of a system of coordinates but only in so far as concepts are articulated through a signifying practice of fiduciary interchange ratified by the historic struggle of the proletariat. The conclusion we must draw is obvious. Thus, and only thus . . .'

Ludmilla had fought her way through two or three pages of the great man's book, for if you want to appear naïve, you had better know what you are being naïve about. Otherwise you might be exposed as being clever. Thus and only thus. In other words, Sweasey was saying, communication only occurs when people say the same things to each other all the time. Hurray for communication.

Boris felt moved as they got into their Rolls, with its little red shamrock and its instant decollapsible bed. He grasped Ludmilla's hand and whispered huskily, 'Moments like this . . . They are the summit of my life.'

'But Boris, you've just said "my",' cried Ludmilla.

She felt quite miffed. If you stopped people sleeping together, it showed you could tell they were different from each other! And what about *her*? The spectacular high-gloss brown of her thighs, tanned rum-fudge colour by Bermudan sunlight, their slim but muscular resilience, the creases tucked away touchingly pale and tender behind her knees, the elegant swell and taper of calves to ankles — her legs were very special and very much her own, Boris should know that. None of those words, and no words that could ever be invented, would describe them, but anyone could tell they were hers, so what was all this about not being able to recognise individuals if you didn't have language? Why, a congenital deaf-mute could see . . .!

Besides, why had he brought her here to the dreary borders of Scotland, to witness the experiment with Uscant? Clearly, so as to impress *her* with *his* brilliance!

A mere two hundred yards away from this conversation, through the big bow windows of Professor Sweasey's office, across the crisp-kept lawn with its carefully tended banks of red flowers, through a Tudor archway and into a dark-beamed refectory, the three hundred male plenniks of Togetherness Hall were to be found, wolfing their soup as if they hadn't seen food for a week. Which, of course, they hadn't.

With its lofty hammer-beam ceiling, its chandeliers, its trestle tables, the lovingly carved woodwork of the minstrels' gallery, these might have been pre-revolutionary times, and they the pampered student sons of the bourgeoisie, dining at some Oxbridge college — but for their close-cropped heads and their accents. This was Uss Hall near Berwick — so aptly named! —

pronounced 'Ooss Aall' by its inmates — or else in reverse, thus, 'Ass Ooall'.

'We must drink up our nice soup, mustn't we?' said the warder, standing threateningly behind Ivan, his gun under his arm.

'Okay, okay,' muttered Ivan. 'Don't worry, I'm just a slow eater.'

'One more slip-up,' warned the warder, 'and we shall be locked up for the rest of the day.'

'Why, what did we say?' asked Ivan, remembering himself (as 'one' had once put it).

'We mustn't use the imperative,' the warder explained. 'Besides, we just said "I".'

'Sweet Marx,' murmured Ivan. He wondered if Sweet Marx was a forbidden person too, but the warder wandered away, satisfied. Perhaps there were permitted exceptions. Or perhaps Sweet Marx was not a name, but a personification of Us All. He turned back to his meal, which was but one degree less revolting than the hogswill at Saughton, and tried to practise with his neighbour, a thickset man who was slurping his soup with every sign of enjoyment.

'We like the soup?' he asked. 'We find it better than where we were before?'

'Do we?' said his neighbour, incredulously.

'It was a question,' said Ivan. 'We didn't mean *we* liked it, we meant did *we*?'

'We don't follow us,' said the man, scratching his head, and looking at him suspiciously. 'Are we trying to make a monkey out of us?'

'We're such a fool,' apologised Ivan. 'We didn't put it clearly.'

'Oh *are* we, oh *did* we?' replied the Yorkshireman, losing all patience. 'Bloody monkey, *we* say!' He raised his plate and slammed it down on the top of Ivan's head so that it broke into several pieces, one of which spun off across the room like a spent arrow and skewered a warder's boot. A short fracas broke out, but the guards intervened to dissuade them from this kind of togetherness, and Ivan's neighbour was marched off to solitary confinement. Ivan, for his part, wondered if that was really a punishment.

162

He felt somewhat shaken. What had the quarrel been about? Ostensibly about the confusion that resulted from using 'we' for 'I' and 'you'. But was that really it? Perhaps the nameless Yorkshireman (but then they were all nameless here) was simply fed up with the whole charade. And was it, by the way, permissible to think of the man as 'a Yorkshireman'? Surely he was just 'one of us'. And what about those who weren't 'one of us'? Ivan shuddered, for he knew what happened to *them*.

'Gets too much for some,' said the man on his left. 'But as for ushere, wehere have found a way round it, as wethere can see.'

To his surprise, Ivan found himself smiling — for the first time since the massacre at Kirknewton Pit.

'It'll be cottoned on to before long,' said his neighbour, 'but wehere are sure we'll be able to think up something else, and something else again. In fact, we can have quite a bit of fun, if we really use our heads. Wethere must watch this.'

He got up and, standing respectfully to attention, addressed the warder in charge of their table. 'We're just going to smoke a cigarette, aren't we?'

The warder, the packet of Shamrocks open in his hand, the cigarettes emerging from it in pipes-of-Pan formation, paused with his hand halfway towards them. Foolishly but automatically, he replied, 'Yes.'

'Thankus,' said Ivan's new friend with warmth, and took one from the warder's packet.

Only then did the warder realise. A worried look upon his face, his own cigarette still untaken, he hurried away to the corner of the refectory to consult his superior officer.

'Wethere had better not try that with a gun,' commented Ivan.

All eating had come to a stop. The plenniks, the same blank expression on every face, were watching the warders with attention, like a bushful of birds eyeing a cat. After a while, the chief warder marched over to Ivan and his neighbour, who got to his feet respectfully. Sticking out his chest, the officer barked:

'What the Gulag do we mean by taking our fags?'

'We're very sorry,' said the prisoner in a tone of humble astonishment, 'but we don't understand. We see — we are allowed to take our cigarettes, aren't we? Besides, we offered them to us.' He repeated verbatim the conversation he had had with the guard. Scratching his head the chief warder retired, muttering, to consult higher authority.

'It's called taking the guard off guard,' remarked Ivan's neighbour. 'We'd better not try the same dodge twice, though.'

Smiles had broken out around the trestle tables. There came the strange sight of prisoners gently applauding, noiselessly clapping their hands together.

After lunch, the male prisoners filed out into the sunlight past the wall that had WE WE WE WE WE WE WE WE WE WE written all over it in red — when you got closer you saw that it actually read Warrant of Equality over and over again — past the opposite wall that announced OUR LOVE IS LIKE A RED RED FLAG, past the placard on the smooth-cut lawn that asserted WE HAS OVERCOME and the placard opposite that advised one to TALK TOGETHERLY. Ivan and his new acquaintance sat down under a tree to which were pinned the words WHY NOT TRY THE PASSIVE VOICE?

At their feet a grassy slope but a brief yard deep abutted on to a lawn cropped as neat and miserly as a convict's pate. Beyond the lawn and to its left stood two wings of the stately home, now stately in quite another sense, but much as it had looked five hundred years before, arrased in dark ivy through which peered mullioned windows. It was as if someone had taken a machete to the creepers and delivered the windows from their blindness. Ivan was indifferent to their beauty, for the mullions reminded him of bars. Where patches of wall were free of the ivy's clutch, the late October sunlight lay chill and grey upon them. He thought — he and Sue had visited it last summer — of Henry VIII's execution ground at the Tower of London, stretched between buildings, overlooked by windows. There people had crowded for a view — for a holiday of cruelty.

But here was no executioner's block. Swathes of sunlight lay flat upon the lawn, as on an empty illuminated stage on which nothing would be shown. Figures would pass, mouths would utter words, but anything that happened would be offstage, in the wings, or at a distance — miles away behind that twenty-foot stone wall to their right, standing sharp and tall, painted black with shadow. It was like a French tragedy. Offstage, blood streams, throats are cut. Occasionally a terrible scream is carried to the audience's ears. Ivan remembered the leaving of Saughton Jail. The rattle of the guns in the yard behind them, above it a noise like a gale of wind. He had not understood it at the time, it had sounded natural, not human.

This little stretch of neat lawn was a space of respite. Reality had, for the moment, been rolled back like a carpet, to reveal a world of theory in which words were all that mattered. Even the actors on this stage were like spectators. The play continued somewhere else.

Sue. *She* still inhabits the real world. A gust of wind ran violently down the garden, and Ivan shivered, as if he had heard a voice that he knew, borne in from the countryside behind the wall, crying out in fear.

The women prisoners were emerging from their own refectory on the other side of the lawn, and sauntering out across the grass; the two groups of plenniks, male and female, began to mingle. It was Fraternisation Hour. From the vantage point of their bench, Ivan and his friend watched in a detached way. Some of the women had toddlers with them, and one small blonde girl was nursing a newborn infant. She sat down on an unoccupied bench a few yards away, unbuttoned her blouse and began to breastfeed. With a painful mixture of emotions, Ivan gazed at her. He felt moved, protective, faintly lustful, but torn by longing for Sue, agonised by the baby they had not had, by the memory of 'Michael's World'. Looking again, he saw that the girl was not a blonde at all. She had dark brown hair and dark brown eyes. Why had he thought . . .? She radiated a golden aura, perhaps that explained it. No, it did not, for what did he mean by it?

After a few minutes, he could not resist getting up and crossing the lawn towards her. She looked up at him and smiled dreamily, as if it were still the baby she was seeing. The child's small greedy lips sucked and nibbled, its eyes fixed firmly on its mother's face, its fingers fumbling gently at the pale curve of her breast.

'What's he called?' he whispered, sitting down beside her.

'Sh,' she responded, alarmed by the forbidden word. 'We're called "baby",' she said. The infant paused a moment in its sucking, then noisily redoubled its efforts. The girl turned her face to Ivan and moved her lips clearly, deliberately, mouthing a name at him. Halfway through the word he could see her tongue lifting to touch her palate, then darting forward to settle behind her teeth. Sweet Marx, he thought, feeling a warm pain like a blow. Yes, he had known all along that that would be the baby's name.

'One thing's clear,' he said after a pause. 'We have to feed us, so we're not *ours*. Babies are special anyway.'

'Yes, *we're ours*,' the girl agreed, understanding him perfectly.

Dream Ten

'Rabbit's clever,' said Pooh
thoughtfully.
'Yes,' said Piglet, 'Rabbit's
clever.'
'And he has Brain.'
'Yes,' said Piglet, 'Rabbit
has Brain.'
There was a long silence.
'I suppose,' said Pooh, 'that
that's why he never understands
anything.'

———————— A.A.MILNE ————————

Thursday, 24 October 2007

'I am an idealist,' said Brianston-Pedley, swivelling in his chair
and rising. He paced the floor, taking care not to approach the
window too closely. His eyes rested thoughtfully upon it, as if
what he saw there was a vision of the future, seen from a safe
distance. But what was actually visible in the glass was
Edinburgh's extinct volcano, Arthur's Seat, gloomy under the
early morning rain — with Salisbury Crags enclosing it like the
ruined rampart of some huge feudal stronghold — and his own
reflection projected upon it in the glass, dim but enormous, a
genie made of moving smoke.

Sue sat on the settee chafing her wrists and watching him.
Michael was back in his cot again after his 6 am feed. How good
he was being! She had been tied to her bed by the wrists all
night, and it was obvious now, she thought, where those dreams

of rape had come from. Perhaps after all Dunne's theory was right, and images of the immediate future could be cast upon the walls of your dreams. She thought of what had happened to that girl down in Hampstead last year, when the National Socialist Militia had broken in. B-P's mob had not touched her, but . . .

Meanwhile, she gazed wistfully at the windows of her own sitting-room, and through them at the silhouette of Edinburgh's private mountain, on whose peak she had stood so often, looking north towards the Grampians, or east towards Norway. Her windows no longer belonged to her, no longer gave her contact with the beloved city that surrounded her, with its sudden panoramas of sun, its canyons of grey stone, its memories of schooldays, boyfriends, discothèques and music, its charge of living friendships. They had turned instead into a prison of glass. The houses across the street no longer looked familiar. She walked by them every morning as she went shopping. But now they had been kidnapped from her, they were as inaccessible as an avenue of palms in the Bahamas. The vista of grey slate roofs, of hunched and grassy mountain-top, was like a still upon a screen, transmitted via satellite from some other planet. She could not touch it with her mind. Raindrops slid across the glass, blurring it, locking her into the room as if she were trapped in a diving bell. How deep would they plunge? How high would the pressure build? A blatter of rain gasped against the glass, the view of the mountain was blotted out. His vision removed from him by the weather, B-P turned from the window.

'It is obvious,' he said, 'that this is not the way the world should be. Poverty, inequality, the conspicuous consumption of the rich, the misery of the unemployed . . . How can that be the natural state of things? The bourgeois social order is merely a swindle, resembling the Veil of Maya which the ancient gods of India spread across the world, so as to hide its true reality from those who dwell there. Western democracy is a vast confidence trick.'

The latest acolyte had been her guard last night, sleeping against the door wrapped up in Lumsden blankets. I-reen (who had been quite talkative once the two men had closed the door behind them) had not yet entirely broken free of bourgeois morality, and guarded over her sexual favours to B-P with a jealous eye. Another woman in the house. In time the latest acolyte could become almost an ally.

'Yeah man,' put in Noel. 'The greatest thinker of our era. The scourge of the bourgeoisie.' He gazed at B-P like a lover.

'The rule of law is a confidence trick,' said the greatest thinker of our era. 'Confidence trickery, *escroquerie* as Sartre calls it, is not a mere sickness that strikes some of its practitioners. On the contrary, it reveals the profound nature of the beast. Profit obtained under pressure, exploitation exercised through the hidden use of state force — the police used as strike-breakers, for instance. Middle-class judges pretending to be impartial. But we shall tear off the velvet glove and reveal the iron truth.'

'Yeah man,' said Noel, 'the signifying practices of official culture are reducible to the interests of the bourgeois *as a class*.'

Sue had seen last night what they were here for. She had seen it the moment they came through her front door. Arnold Briggs, leader of the New Left Labour Party, was due here this very afternoon, marching down London Road to the Meadowbank Stadium to address the strikers and the unemployed. Let her guess what B-P and his comrades would be up to. A volley of shots from the window, a miner and a policeman killed, perhaps, a battle breaking out between workers and polis. Both sides blaming each other, the rift in society growing still deeper.

'In short,' said B-P, arriving at his peroration, 'the society we live in is a cheat and a sham. It is a bad dream, and we in the Proletarian Red Army are pledged to destroy it. We shall shatter the wall of dream by main force, and break into the reality which lies on the further side — love, humanity, equality, the world of socialist Community.'

Sue thought, I see! He thinks Utopia's been hijacked. He doesn't think of goodness as something you have to *do*, he thinks it's *there*, like a big golden tiger in a cage, and the cage is the world that we have, and you just smash the world and let the tiger out.

'Yeah man,' quoth Noel, like a baptist at a negro prayer meeting.

'Noel' — didn't that mean 'good news' or 'Christmas' or 'birthday', or something?

169

'Och, I agree with a lot of what you say,' said Sue brightly. 'I don't like millionaires any more than you do, and I do agree the world is an unfair place, what with the unemployed and everything. It's time the government did something about it.'

Noel began to shriek with laughter. 'You haven't understood a word the Prof's been saying! And why? And why? Have you seen the pile of bourgeois class-ideological shit she reads — novels, poetry, books in French . . .' He waved his hand, still with the gun in it, at the shelves that clothed the right-hand wall of the Lumsdens' fireplace. 'I bet there isn't a single Marxist—theoretical discussion among them.'

'Well,' said B-P, gazing loftily at the bookshelves, 'I admit that most of it is loaded with class—bourgeois ideological signifiers, such as the term "personal relationships". The term "amour" keeps cropping up in its individualist sense, and not in its objective significance as "social togetherness". On the other hand, I do see some of the works of our own — well, nearly our own — Jean-Paul. Not his important books, of course, on Being and Nothingness and on the Critique of Dialectical Materialism, but still . . .'

'Althusser was a Frenchman, wasn't he?' said the latest acolyte suddenly.

B-P looked at her sadly as if in some respect she didn't come up to expectation. While looking at her he brightened a little, because in other respects she did. 'But it's time to turn on the breakfast news.'

'Switch it on, Mrs Meedjah,' yapped Noel, 'and keep away from that window. Can't have you making V-signs to the neighbours.'

Not that anyone would have noticed. On a day like this, no one had his face turned to the sky.

On the television screen there appeared, first a crackle of shifting dots, then a misty face, completely still except for its jaw, which was moving up and down in a strictly vertical direction. This resolved itself into the face of the New Right Tory Prime Minister, the Right Honourable Ronald Trimmer, who was saying,

'. . . these Alliance people are just sentimentalists. All this

170

unemployment is very sad, and no one regrets it more than myself, but the laws of the market-place have to be observed. As my predecessor said so wisely and so often, "There is no alternative." But why are we talking about them? Let's discuss the *real* opposition.'

It's a funny thing about the stiff upper lip, thought Sue. It really *is* stiff. Goodness, if we all kept the space between our top lips and our noses absolutely rigid like Trimmer, *we could all talk just like him!*

The picture of Trimmer's face (bland, blank and puce) vanished, and all that stolidity was instantly replaced by frantic movement — massed lines of police and miners, drawn up like the phalanxes of some ancient Hellenic battle between Argives and Thebans, holding shields, belabouring each other with staves. As the opposing armies shifted and wheeled, an opening was torn in their ranks and through it ran a single miner, his boot outstretched, kicking a policeman in the groin.

'. . . two thousand pickets at Bilston Glen, seeking to prevent the entry of three blacklegs . . .'

'They're showing things that aren't happening!' cried the latest acolyte, outraged.

'I'm sorry for *anyone* who's hurt,' said Sue.

'Ah, but who are the *real* victims?' asked B-P. 'The unemployed!'

'Of course, there's a lot in what you say. But . . .'

'Isn't that just the autotypical expression of decadent liberal ideology?' cried Noel, tickled to death. ' "There's a lot in what you say. But." '

'Sh,' said the latest acolyte as the picture changed.

'. . . will be marching through Edinburgh this afternoon at the head of a demonstration. Mr Briggs will address the crowd at Meadowbank Stadium . . .'

'Bang bang,' uttered Noel, making as if to fire his weapon at the screen, on which was projected a still of Arnold Briggs.

Oh my God, thought Sue, light suddenly dawning. You fool, it's taken you a long time to realise. Of course, the thing to do is have the leader of your *own* side assassinated. Well, not that Briggs is anything like these people, he's too far to the right for

171

them. But those Trotskyists in his party, what a field day for *them*! 'Socialist leader assassinated! The fascist right accused!' Here comes the Revolution! My God, what a fool I've been. And when Briggs comes marching down the road, proud and drookit under the banners and the pouring rain, there'll be a wee rifle and a telescopic sight and a silencer, pointing out of my bay window. This'll really put the panther among the pigeons!

This was the authentic stuff of life, thought Brianston-Pedley. *Brains*ton-Pedley, they'd called him at school, little knowing how the brain was nothing without a passion to kindle it. The thrill of action like a kick in the guts, the adrenalin flooding the blood-stream. This beats rock climbing and water ski-ing and hang gliding and sky diving into a cocked hat. It beats cocaine. Gives you the authentic buzz. Action.

Action altruistic and disinterested. For he did not delude himself he would survive much longer. The SAS would get him, or some other arm of the oppressive state. As the Christian martyrs of ancient Rome had known so well, self-sacrifice was the ultimate excitement. The lions were hungry, History sat watching him like the Imperator Augustus in his Colosseum, B-P's heart was in his mouth, and the chemistry of his brain responded. Up, up. This was cloud nine, the Imperial Roman Carnival.

Noel lounged in his armchair caressing his gun, out of the barrel of which Revolution would burst and blossom, glowering across the room at the media man's consort, the beautiful bitch-bird. Breakable like porcelain, eatable like a plum. You were either part of the problem, or you were part of the solution. *She* was part of the problem. Bleating to B-P about 'poor innocent wee Michael'. Couldn't she see that the whole *point* of terrorism — class-revolutionary activism, to employ the correct terminology — was killing innocent people so as to frighten other innocent people? You didn't kill the guilty, of course, you killed the innocent, because that was what created the real fear and chaos. You couldn't talk to her, for she made no sense. There were only two things you could do to her, and it was a pity old B-P wouldn't let him do either. Kept talking about their 'insurance policy'. As these strong and colourful visual patterns passed through his mind, white, golden, pink and brown, with a fine triumphal splash of scarlet to drench and redeem them all, his eye fell again upon the French books on their shelves. He spat neatly into the centre of Sue's rather threadbare sitting-room carpet.

Being part of the Cause, thought the latest acolyte, was just so dreamy. My public school had nothing on this. If you're really part of the Cause, the really-really-Cause, then nothing can dismay you any more, because you know that everything you do is right. Makes you feel so sexy afterwards. She'd never known what sex was really like till she'd done it just after a piece of revolutionary praxis. The sewer had been foul, but what a compensation to think how shocked her parents would be. Were, for she was on the wanted list now. Yeah, Praxis first, then Sex, it was enough to make your toes drop off. Better still, she had a Super-Cause, the cause of causes, the meaning of meanings, the great THING that explained it all and, because it explained it all, the source of all moral values. So, if you acted in ITS name, anything you did just had to be right. So, if you slapped a bourgeois face, it served the bastard right. If the bourgeois slapped yours, you could shoot him. Provided you were a *real* Socialist.

IT, the great Cause, was rather like a rocket-launcher standing on its base. That was how she visualised it. Bri and Noel and she were the launcher fuel. They'd give IT lift-off.

If he asked her to kill Susan, she'd do it at once. The only thing that bird knew about was babies. She'd had quite a chat about them with her last night. She wondered what would happen if she broached the subject to Bri. She'd never heard him say anything about babies or children at all. He was a very old man after all, 50 at least. Perhaps he would be flattered.

'Shall I get breakfast?' asked Sue. 'What do you want, an egg, cereal, a slice of toast?'

'The lot,' said B-P. 'We're on active service.'

'I'm not sure I have enough for everybody,' said Sue. 'Perhaps if I were to slip out to the shops.'

'Don't try to make jokes with us, man,' said Noel, scowling. 'I had a look in your freezer last night, it's full of stuff.'

'What shall we order for lunch?' said B-P. 'Sole Mornay? Venison à la romaine, Pork à la manière de Monsieur de Chaillot? I see you have an impressive shelf of cookery books,' he said to Sue.

'Our working-class brothers are out there starving on the streets,' remonstrated Noel, 'and you talk about Sole Mornay?'

'Hush, Sole Mornay is the simplest of dishes,' said B-P. 'Don't be so insular, Noel. Ours is an international movement. When Pierre Lavallière and the rest of the French Committee go to visit Etienne Baliberne, they are served only the best cuisine.'

Class-prandial élitism, Noel grumbled to himself. Aloud he said, 'Just coffee for me.'

As they were all four sitting round the kitchen table in the final stages of breakfast, Noel gazing blackly at his black coffee (he didn't really like black coffee), B-P ravenously stoking his mouth with bacon, eggs, sausages, tomatoes, beans and fried bread, while Sue tried to engage him in diplomatic talk about the plays of Jean-Paul Sartre — they all suddenly jumped.

Then they realised why. The door-bell had rung.

Noel slipped out into the hall and, from the end nearest the kitchen, covered the front door in professional manner, aiming his gun, steadying his arm with his other hand, the way it was done in the Libyan handbooks.

'Keep her covered,' said B-P to the latest acolyte.

He went out into the hall in his turn, and advanced towards the judas. They had jammed the door the previous night and blocked up the letter-box, so he was slightly concerned to see that the latter was now yawning open. As he got closer he saw, however, that it was stuffed full of the morning newspapers. He hoped that meant it was all right. He applied his eye to the peep-hole and squinted out.

Nobody. Nobody at all.

Well, that was odd, and faintly disturbing. Probably there was nothing to worry about. Whoever it was had just got tired of waiting.

When he reappeared at the door of the kitchen, looking thoughtfully at Sue, she piped up, 'Was it Ailsa, come for her bangle?' She had a mental picture of Ailsa, kneeling on the plain stone landing, peering through the flap of the letter-box. She knew that was impossible for she had seen them seal it up.

'There was nobody there,' said B-P, biting his thumbnail.

'I don't like it,' said Noel, fiddling nervously with his gun.

'Put that bloody thing away,' snapped B-P, who was in the direct line of fire. Marx and Jeezus, why are my activists so jumpy?

If only it was Ailsa, Sue muttered frantically to herself. I don't believe in God, but if You are there after all, God, though God knows you can't be, seeing what a horrible place the world is, then make it be Ailsa, make it be Ailsa. The bangle. The message. Surely Ailsa must have caught that!

Calm yourself, Sue. No good supposing there's help coming. Ailsa won't suspect anything, how could she? If it was her, she'll think I'm out with the baby, and oh, how I wish I was. It was more likely the gasman, or Mrs Kilsyth across the stair.

Michael woke again in the back room, and wailed angrily, as if he knew somehow that his mother was anxious and afraid. It was that irritating nasal sound that babies make, designed to jangle the nerves of women, of mothers in particular.

Go and see what's wrong with wee Mike. You've done all you can, last night on the phone. And if it isn't enough, God (if He exists) knows where he can put His Providence (if He has one). (Sorry, God, if You're listening.)

B-P and Noel checked that the door was secure, and Sue and the latest acolyte went to see why Michael was crying. His nappy needed changing. I-reen begged to be allowed to change it, but Sue wouldn't let her. What right had she to concern herself with real nice nasty things, with a definite living baby with a definite dirty bottom?

If only I'd dreamt of John last night, she thought. But he wasn't there at all, so I couldn't tell him. I couldn't tell him in my dream what was happening in the real world, so that when he woke he could ring the polis, and tell them to come and rescue us both. Jeezus, why are dreams no good when you need them to be? What sort of J. W. Dunne theory does that fit? And where are you, John, if you're not even in my dreams any more?

When they had changed Michael — she let the latest acolyte

help after a while, maybe it would humanise her — he needed to be fed. Then he needed to be played with. Never had Sue felt so intent on the present, she could feel it shifting by under her feet like sand as she amused her tiny son. God knew what the next hour, what the next two hours might bring. These 'Marxist activists', as they called themselves, were plainly incompetent and so all the more frightening. Her son. She would concentrate on him, make sure she did not convey to him any of the terror she felt whenever she thought of those two men in the next room — the fierce young extremist with his head packed full of abstractions. When he looked at her, what did he see? A cardboard cut-out with 'lackey of the media' daubed across it. And B-P, grey hair still full, receding with dignity, increasing the size of his forehead, giving him an image of wisdom that, when he looked in the mirror, deceived even himself . . .

She had watched an Oxford philosopher on the telly-lie the other night — 'Our greatest thinker' — he had called Brianston-Pedley that — 'until he turned to terrorism, of course.' How weird could you get? Didn't these people see any connection between ideas and actions? As for the latest acolyte, squatting beside her on her heels as Sue cooed and played with the baby, I-reen was like a huge empty room, with posters pinned upon its walls. She was too naïve to have any secrets.

'So it's Arnold Briggs you're after?' she said casually, as Michael and she pushed his pink play-ball to and fro between them.

The latest acolyte answered quite frankly, as if she'd forgotten that Sue wasn't supposed to know. 'Yes, his sort is the worst of all, Bri says, like the Mensheviks in Russia. Pretends to be a Socialist, but doesn't even want a Revolution. He's been tried and sentenced by a People's Court.'

'Who's the People's Court? Is that you and Brianston-Pedley and Noel?'

'Of course,' said the latest acolyte.

'What are you being so long about?' said Noel, bursting in through the door, so that the baby gulped with fright and began to wail again.

'Michael has to be played with,' said Sue, picking him up and cuddling him, 'otherwise he'll cry and cry, and then the people in the other flats will wonder if something's wrong.'

'Michael?' said Noel stupidly, as if he hadn't remembered the baby's name. 'Well, bring him into the other room, it makes me nervous you being out of my sight.'

'It makes *him* nervous, seeing those guns,' replied Sue.

Lunch came, and Sue made it beautifully. She found to her surprise that she had quite a hearty appetite. Maybe that's a good sign, she thought superstitiously. Maybe my body knows something I don't. At one o'clock B-P rose and turned on the telly, and Sue noticed that his hand was shaking.

As he turned from the set, she saw him glance out into the street, then check. Automatically he said, 'The rain's stopped. That'll make it easier.' Swivelling his eyes in the other direction, he said thoughtfully, 'A lot of pigs out there. Armoured vehicles, and they've blocked off the street. Good, that means the procession's on its way.'

He thought to himself, Briggs rhymes with pigs. Up to the time we execute him, this bourgeois family is our insurance policy. Once we're safely out of here, the woman is a threat. This must be seen as a murder by the Right, so we can't have this hostage telling the press — her own husband, ha? — who we really are. He preferred to think of 'hostages', not of 'the woman and her baby'. Thinking of people as 'people' was bourgeois-individualist. It didn't impress him that she and her husband were obviously not well off. If you're poor, and not a revolutionary, you've sold out to the enemy.

So, provided we make our escape, we'll be obliged to execute them. The child was too young to tell tales, but somehow it was neater, cleaner, more . . . symmetrical . . . to eliminate it as well. Thought was such a powerful tool, it made you see things so clearly and calmly, utterly without false sentiment.

'. . . Thistle, the latest thing in dishwashers,' enthused the telly-lie across a fuzz of grey, which dissolved to reveal the surrealistic scene of a plate (willow pattern, Wedgwood-blue) spinning in the midst of a whirlpool, the cliffs of Hoy rising grand and red behind it.

'Commercialism, man, it makes me sick,' said Noel.

Won't they have dishwashers after the Revolution? Sue wondered. Only labour-making devices, maybe. She didn't say anything, because Noel was making her more and more nervous. Even B-P was glancing at him, she noticed, in a funny way.

The news came on, complete with pictures of Arnold Briggs descending at Waverley station and being cheered into the North British Hotel for his lunch. The reporters pushed and shoved, the arms of a constable could be seen, as if he were trying to swim through the crowd. The image tipped, then righted itself, and someone was saying, holding the microphone close,

'Mr Briggs, can you tell us what progress you hope to make this afternoon in your discussions with the Scottish Secretary? Do you think this strike will be resolved soon?'

'While there's life there's hope,' said Briggs, smiling at the camera. His smile was his greatest asset, and he aimed it particularly at cameras. 'I'm sure the good sense of the Scottish working man, linked with the government's pragmatism, will pull us safely through in the end. After all, we are all British.'

The activists groaned and grimaced. 'Agreement! With the class enemy!' said the latest acolyte. 'A dangerous man,' nodded B-P. 'Briggs,' said Noel, 'has just declared war upon the British people.'

There came some pictures of a riot in a mining village in Yorkshire. Miners were overturning other miners' cars, petrol bombs blazed along the street, you saw the mob breaking into someone's house. Finally several men came running straight towards the camera. The image jerked and turned upside down. Rapid shots were seen of sky and pavement, of a pair of boots and a gutter.

'Our reporter was dead on arrival at hospital.'

Oh John, thought Sue, come back. But don't come *home*, she prayed.

Then the telephone rang.

The activists looked from one to another, and B-P shook his head at Sue. Nobody moved, but the telephone went on shrilling and shrilling away in the empty hall beyond the door — twenty, twenty-five, perhaps thirty times. Noel's frown became deeper as the sound persisted, and soon they all ceased to notice the television news at all, but were straining their ears for the anxious ringing to stop. When it did so, B-P sighed, then got up and switched off the set. Stooping, his hand still poised over the button, he froze as the sound of a loudspeaker blared from the street outside the window.

'The house is surrounded. This is a police message. The house is surrounded. You will wait for the telephone to ring, and you will answer it.'

B-P straightened up, a strange expression on his face, almost as if he were relieved. The latest acolyte shrank into her chair, quite pale and scared. Noel, muttering darkly, grabbed for his gun, but B-P motioned to him calmly. 'No,' he said. 'Discipline is the only way out of the situation in which we find ourselves. You will follow my instructions to the letter.' Taking care not to go too near the window, he gazed out of it, loftily, like a man trying to identify a distant landmark.

Sue felt no relief, but a violent dread. For a moment not a thought went through her mind.

'Go and look out of the kitchen window,' said B-P to Noel. 'Report what you see, then return here.'

Noel, his head down, black in the face with anger, complied.

B-P turned slowly from the window and stood there looking at Sue contemplatively. Frightened, she lowered her eyes. There was a long silence. Noel appeared at the open door.

'The pigs are round the back as well,' he said.

'Well, there is no cause for alarm,' said B-P quietly. 'We have our insurance policy and, remember, we are dealing with sentimentalists. It will be best if you return to the kitchen and stay on guard.' He tapped his teeth with a fingernail, and continued to stare at Sue.

The telephone rang for a second time.

'Yes,' said B-P at the phone.

'I can see the house is surrounded.'

'Say what you have to say.'

At this point there was a long silence while Brianston-Pedley listened, no doubt, to what the man at the other end of the line was telling him. Eventually he began to speak in his turn.

'I'm afraid your terms are not reasonable at all. You forget we have a trump card in our possession, namely this young woman and her baby. I warn you that if you make the slightest attempt to break into this Red Army military post, both of them will be executed. Now listen to me. I want a bus to convey us to the airport. The woman and child will, of course, accompany us as guarantees against treachery. At Edinburgh Airport you will provide us with an aeroplane to carry us to Libya, or any other friendly socialist country nominated by me, and the woman and child will go with us on the plane. No, don't interrupt me. We also require a ransom of one million pounds, to be paid in US dollars, used notes only. You will reply positively to our reasonable demands within one hour from now, or we shall execute the woman.'

Sue, listening to all this through the open door of the sitting-room, felt a pure abstract anger. B-P was not having it his own way, however, for there ensued a second long silence. At the end of it he swore, then put the phone down. It was the first sign he had shown of anything other than the calmest confidence; and the pause that ensued before he reappeared at the sitting-room door was, so Sue supposed, to enable him to recover it. At any rate, sang-froid was all that could be glimpsed below the thick grey hair as he stood again, framed in the doorway, and replied to the latest acolyte's questions in the most soothing of tones:

'Don't worry, I-reen. There is no reason for us to alarm ourselves. I have asked for a ransom and a plane to take us to Libya.'

'But how did they know we were here?' cried the latest acolyte. 'Did *she* tell them?'

I-reen had a stiff upper lip too, thought Sue. When it trembled, it became dangerous. No, there was no female fellow-feeling here after all.

'I don't see how she could, can you? I don't know,' said B-P, tapping his teeth. 'Perhaps we were followed from Yorkshire. Perhaps they found the car.'

'How do they know it's *us*?' whimpered the latest acolyte.

'Oh, that's easy,' said B-P, the inbred assurance in his voice still more resonant, more incongruous. 'They have surveillance

180

devices, and can tell what people say inside a room by picking up vibrations on the window. But there's no need to be anxious, we don't discuss classified matters on active service. It's disappointing, of course, but taking the long view, it is merely a small hitch in the glorious progress of the Revolution. We shall have to wait awhile, naturally. These people always try to temporise, but in face of proletarian determination they are always as soft as rum fudge. In the long run, they know we have the upper hand.

'It's all pretence, of course. Publicity. They don't really care about human life, they just keep up a show of it to delude you.'

'I don't call it a show,' replied Sue tartly, her courage having suddenly returned. 'Not if I'm still alive at the end of it.'

B-P looked at her and, for once, made no reply. This bourgeois woman and her brat would have to be kept alive, so much was clear. Till they got to Libya. Unless the fascists looked like cheating him. In the meantime, there was a long wait ahead of them all, for they had demanded that her husband speak to her. No deal, they had said, could go forward until Mr Lumsden, now on some plane lost somewhere in the skies between Yorkshire and the Borders, had identified his wife's voice positively, and was sure she was fit and well. He looked about him almost wistfully.

This third-floor flat in Edinburgh, a town which he had never visited before, full of old-fashioned Scottish drabness, shrouded in pre-revolutionary grey skies and Calvinistic commercial principles — this capitalist–imperialist three-roomed flat with its threadbare carpets, its curious air of not being part of England — almost a foreign country, but how could that be? — it didn't make sense! — this flat was for the moment his own personal Marxist state. He felt like a nineteenth-century missionary arrived on a desert island. It was called U-To-Pi. The natives had greeted him as a living God and invited him to dictate their destinies. The trouble was, it wasn't yet truly Marxist, he couldn't do exactly what he wanted, for the forces of reaction had assembled a fleet offshore, just as they had massed about the borders of Lenin's Russia after the October Revolution. It was they who would be responsible if anything happened to the hostages. The infant Revolution had to defend itself. As the highest and most humane form of government yet known to man, its duty was to balk at nothing.

Every hour the phone rang again. John, it seemed, was still lost somewhere among the clouds of northern Britain. The Scottish Secretary was having difficulty arranging for all that American money, and had not yet obtained the permission of the Libyan government to land a plane at Tripoli. The latest acolyte seemed almost used by now to being frightened, and Sue was glad she could find out how it felt. Noel alternated between fits of swearing and a rather menacing despondency. Sue had never known before how much she loved wee Michael, who spent the afternoon awake, playing — she hoped it was a good omen — quite cheerfully. The hours dragged painfully by, tense with the combination of adrenalin and total inaction.

At about teatime, Sue, following her policy of fraternising with the enemy, so as to make him realise she was human after all, engaged him in a discussion on Scottish Nationalism, which seemed to disconcert him. No, he knew little of it. It was an outmoded perspective dating from the epoch of post-feudalism. He had a Scottish grandmother himself, but that didn't make him want an independent Scotland. Was it like the Irish? 'No?' he repeated in some puzzlement.

The other thing of note was that, out of the blue, towards half-past ten, Sue asked him,

'Dis. That's the old Latin word for Hell, isn't it?'

'Is it? It's a place in Norfolk. The village of Diss. Henry VIII's poet Skelton lived there.' Then it was as if another thought had struck him, and he looked positively bewildered. He gazed at Sue for a long time, as if he were trying to remember if they had ever met before, long years ago, in childhood perhaps. Suddenly he got up and walked out of the room. She could hear him flushing the loo.

The phone rang every hour and at last, towards eleven, it was John on the other end.

Yes, Sue assured him with a calm that amazed her, they were both all right so far. Yes, she loved him. On putting the phone down she burst into tears.

At this point they had got little further than they had at half-past one. Negotiations were going on in all the relevant departments. Professor Brianston-Pedley would know how long bureaucracies took. Five hundred thousand dollars in American currency had been arranged. However, a landing place for the plane was still uncertain. The Libyans had demurred. Was the Professor really quite sure that it was an agent of *theirs* who . . .? Very well, they would try Iran. But the Professor knew it was hard to tell who precisely was in charge there at any given hour of the day.

'They're trying to stall us,' said B-P. 'Don't worry, tomorrow morning we'll be out of here and on the plane to . . .'

'To Dis,' said Sue softly. He stared at her in the same way he had before. She was sure now he would not shoot her or wee Michael. It wasn't the discussion over Scottish Nationalism or even the fact that he had got used to seeing her alive. It was the word 'Dis'. What a shock B-P must have had to find that someone else was real.

How in the midst of all this could she sleep? But it was like the night before. She was tugged into sleep as if by some force stronger than reality. Maybe after all her dreams were true, and *this* was the nightmare.

Event Fifteen

There had never been any question of resisting the man. First, he had explained to her exactly what would happen if she refused. Quite simply, he would call in a couple of 'male nurses', as he preferred to term them, and force her anyway. He described this to her in detail. But that was not really the point, he added, baring his teeth in that handsome smile of his that conveyed so much manly assurance. He looked, when he smiled, so much like Superman to the rescue, that she could hardly believe her ears when he went on to mention Bylchau — 'You know what'll happen to you *there*,' he supposed. The equable good humour with which he mentioned such things made her flesh creep.

Unless she were tired of life, she told herself — and because she treasured her dream — and because Michael's World had to be kept alive . . . Besides, even outside the gates of jails, asylums and concentration camps, the sensible modern young woman expected this kind of thing — the Nomenklatura were the jailors of that world too.

Evidently he liked to keep his women frightened. On the following morning, as she and a group of female prisoners were taking their statutory exercise, being marched up and down the grounds by a couple of nurses with guns, an orderly approached her. He gave no explanation, and Sue followed him, feeling (as she put it later) pale inside.

Sue and the orderly went through the main building and out through the wide front doors of the mansion, where they paused at the top of the steps and gazed down at the scene in the

184

courtyard below. The stench was appalling, and after a glance Sue turned aside and hid her face in her hair. Fifty or so figures were lined up on the gravel guarded by a posse of pink-cheeked young gun-jacks. Are they alive, thought Sue, or are they ghosts? For all were mere walking skeletons, none seemed to have a tooth in its head, and their skins were as grey as the tatters they wore. Worst of all was the fact that she could not tell, even when she turned her head again to look at them more carefully, whether they were men or women.

Charlesworth appeared on the steps beside her. 'Well?'

'What *are* they?'

Pleased by the horror in her voice, he turned his sunlit smile upon her. 'From Burston Camp just up the road,' he explained, then marched off down the steps again, shouting angrily at the gun-jacks, 'I'll have you all in the Web! What do you mean bringing me pigs' offal like this? I'll be on the phone personally to Clegg-Molotov himself.' He went on bawling and swearing at them till, sheepishly, they rounded up their charges and bundled them back into the van that had brought them.

He liked his women guilty, too, thought Sue with a flash of insight.

Doubtless she shouldn't have mentioned the episode again, for when, that night, she did so, his reaction was curious. His handsome lip started to tremble like that of a little boy about to cry, and he struck her across the face. Just so the lesson sinks in, he told her. It was not the blow that surprised her. No, it was that when she dared to look up at him again, she saw quite clearly that he had real tears in his eyes, though they didn't seem to mean what tears usually do.

Later he had talked, as if nothing could fill the room so pleasantly as the sound of his own voice. To her surprise, however, Sue found herself pricking up her ears. In some way she did not yet understand, his words had a bearing on her fate — and maybe on that of Michael.

'The old bourgeoisie,' he said, 'made such a fuss about experiments on human beings. They even had a movement for animal rights, imagine that! Dialectical materialism has put a stop to all *that* nonsense. You don't have a soul any more than

185

I do. We are conscious, I grant you, but the whole absurd idea that we are ghosts in machines was definitively refuted in the twentieth century by the great psychologists of the time. Ghosts, *Soochka moya*, are a superstition, and there is nothing inside our heads but nerve tissues, synapses, chemicals, electrical discharges and so forth. Guilt is simply a chemical reaction, fidelity is a neurological habit.'

So was fear, Sue supposed. What if she dared to intervene? Would he hit her again? On the other hand, it might be as well to show some interest.

'But I don't feel like an automaton,' she said, watching him warily. 'I can make up my own mind, make decisions, you know.'

He raised his head as if offering his noble profile for inspection, and bayed with laughter. 'Is that what you think? Who's been making your decisions these last two days?'

'But I've never been able to understand how . . . If we're made of nothing but unconscious matter, how does it become conscious?'

'That's easy,' he said with an air of generosity. 'Think of the brain as a series of electrical pathways, full of switches and alternative routes. Now if switch A is tripped, pathway A is activated. In just that way, if light shines on a nerve fibre in your eye, then a message is sent to your brain saying "React". Then the brain sends a message back to the eye, saying "Blink".'

'But that's just automatic.' Apparently it *was* safer discussing such things. It took you away from practical issues, like the prisoners from Burston, or the fate of her own fellow-serfs — human questions which might provoke him to violence.

'Of course,' he said, laughing again at her naïvety. 'Everything's automatic. The difference between that and what you call making a decision is only that the latter is more complicated and you're conscious of such a lot of it that you suppose you're "doing it yourself". And you are, but only because *it* is the "you" that's doing it. When you have a decision to make, what happens is simply that the messages go round and round all the relevant pathways until, finally, all the switches fire one way, and that is your decision.'

'It's just more complicated, you mean?'

'Yes, and speaking of complicated . . .'

When he had left for the night, she lay in the darkness, fingering her cheek where he had hit her, hating him and feeling ashamed. But not guilty, for the duress had been too great. She had to admit, however, that she had made some progress. She had got him talking to her, admittedly about his personal obsessions, and she had managed to control the exchange, gauging when she should not push him too far, discovering that he liked a certain amount of close questioning — provided it seemed to flatter him. But she would have to be watchful. He didn't believe that people existed, not in the same way that she did. Even your doubts had to feed his egotism.

More complicated still were events the next morning. As she and the other 'patients' were taking off their clothes to get into the shower, the women kept teasing her. 'Where were *you* last night?'

She opened her mouth to reply, but nobody was listening

'What's so wonderful?' asked one girl, looking her up and down. 'Two saggy tits and a patch of furze, just like the rest of us.'

'Better than mine, are they?' said another, stepping up beside the first woman, and balancing her breasts in her hands. Indeed, they *were* better than Sue's.

She opened her mouth to reply again, but still no one heard her.

'Boss's scrubber, *she* is,' said a third, stepping up in line with the first two.

'Doctor yobber Charlesworth's prize heifer,' whined a fourth naked recruit, adding herself to the ranks. The opinion had formed, the bodies were lining up beside it.

'Mandy,' pleaded Sue. But Mandy, eyes down, had sidled up to join the other four.

'What's he think's so special?' said a fat girl, as the other women drifted in from the spaces of the changing room. 'Or is she just trying to stop her brain being torn out like the rest of us? Wants to stay human, does she?'

'What's it all about, Susan? What did he tell you? We'll pick your brains.'

187

'Out.'

'In little pieces.'

'That's friendship, we'll do it gradually, slowly.'

She was now surrounded by a half-moon of young women, all naked, all bristling and sneering like tabby cats, advancing. Trapped in the centre of a triangle, she stepped back towards the corner behind her, and the triangle contracted as she did so. It was like a slow ballet, sixteen eyes fixed on her, feet stepping accurately forwards, cat claws at the ready. God, this was no good, she'd come out of this in shreds, little bloody shreds.

Like a tabby cat herself, she began to caterwaul, shrieking and dancing, She ducked as Milly on the left stepped up and went for her eyes, fingernails unsheathed, stabbing upwards. Thank God, she'd missed, but would the guards come? Fancy wanting them to! Christ, whose side was she on any more? And how could you choose? You couldn't, it was all set up, it was chosen for you. She went down on the slippery floor in a tangle of thrashing limbs, as the whistles blew and the warders came in, one getting a gun out in his excitement and shooting the rose off a shower, pinning it to the wall with a hole inside it where the bullet had embedded itself.

The warders took her away, stark naked, and fitted her up with a private room and a guard out of respect for Superdoc.

They might not have come at all. They might have waited five minutes. They might have come simply to stand and watch. Maybe they had a residual instinct for order. Maybe they'd been given one. Maybe their officer still had a secret kindness in his heart. As for her, what could she do, between being hit in the face by Charlesworth or dismembered by her friends the Maenads?

He, on the other hand, had an ambiguous expression on his face that evening when she told him of the skirmish in the cat-cage.

'How do you want me to punish them?' He liked that idea. She could swear that his eyes were wet again.

'No,' she said, 'just leave them alone, they're perfectly normal women.'

'Perfectly normal women?' he said. 'All the better.'

188

'No, Mark,' she said, obliged to use his forename, 'please, no.'

'You can come and watch,' he said.

She saw that he'd wanted something like this to happen. One of the amusements of power — make people angry for the right reason, then throw them the wrong scapegoat. Besides, now he'd made her grateful to him. Gratitude, hatred and fear, all wrapped up in the same stinking bundle. And now she'd have to spend half an hour on her knees, begging him to let her friends off.

While she did so, the bedroom pondered its feelings in a dapple of shadows. Time could be felt, not ticking like a clock, but burning slowly, whitely, like the electric light barring the floor. At last he said graciously he'd think about it. Thinking about it stressed his power over her. It wasn't that he didn't mean to punish them, *later*. Discipline had to be maintained. This thought seemed to please him, loosened his tongue, and he began to talk science again.

She fed him submissive questions, glad to be off the subject of the bath-house, letting him feel how macho-maxi-dominant he was, how son-of-a-Vissarionovich. But, despite herself, despite this morning's terror, she was getting interested. There was a flaw in his argument, and she wondered if he'd seen it, or what he would say if she pointed it out. Finally, she couldn't hold the question back any longer.

Setting up four cautious fences around her, she said, 'Do you mind if I ask . . . I don't know anything about science . . . It's hard for me to . . . Of course, you explain it all so clearly.'

She felt how ridiculous she was, sitting up in bed naked, feeling always at the back of her mind the nagging discomfort of fear, politely discussing with the man who had raped her, the question of the Human Soul. But he was her only defence against the cat-pack, her erstwhile friends. Besides, maybe one of these nights he would start to tell her the answer to the biggest question of all — what she and those other women, and the men in the other wing of the asylum — what they were all here for.

'But when the light flashes in my eye,' she was saying, 'not only does my brain react, not only do I see the light, but I am *aware* of seeing it. Now — I expect I haven't followed you quite, but it seems to me you've left out how those reactions cause the *sensation* I have when my brain reacts. You've explained my reactions but not how it is that I *experience* them.'

'Well, that's easy,' said Charlesworth. 'What you experience is simply a *feature* of the brain reaction.'

'A feature?' she said, frowning. 'What do you mean?'

'It's just one of the things the brain *does*,' he said, as if that explained it.

She looked at him, deciding it would be risky to push him further. She could not prevent herself smiling, but that was all right for she could see him taking it for a smile of assent. But couldn't he understand? You can't set off to explain how my experience arises *out of* electric currents, and then just say that it *is* the electric currents, or that it's one of the things that, mysteriously, they just happen to produce. Because that leaves the question exactly where it was before.

She was definitely making progress, however. Before he left her room he promised to take her on a tour of the asylum. This was his own pet scheme, the holy of holies, the Ark of the Covenant, and why was he showing it to her? Could it be that she had been promoted from Lucretia to Aspasia? Thoughtfully, she got out of bed, wrapping the dressing gown around her, and wandered over to the window. The moon shone furtively through it, striping the room with black and tigerish yellow. That was precisely what she was trying to do — ride the tiger. Or rather the tiger was riding her. The question was, who would ride whom, or who would be thrown to the cat-pack? Why was she thinking like this? Perhaps fear and danger were more corrupting than anything, even than riches. She fell asleep, imagining she could hear a chorus of grimalkins yowling and shrieking outside her room.

She was surprised next morning when Charlesworth kept his word, summoning her to his office and ordering her into a pair of bleached white overalls in readiness for her tour of the research wing. Despite her fear of the man, she couldn't help feeling flattered, and had to tell herself that the compliment was an ambiguous one — was it to show he trusted her, or to blackmail her into complicity? More likely to frighten her still more.

190

As they turned a bend in the corridor and advanced down the long west wing of the mansion, the sound present in the rest of the house fell away into silence behind them. Here was a single-minded cleanliness, a starkness swept clear of all living disorder. No pictures interrupted the smoothness of the walls. The occasional glimpse of a corner of the asylum grounds through a window was like a still upon a screen, transmitted via satellite from some other planet. They proceeded onwards in total stillness, the rubberised floor betraying no sound of their footfalls, the uniform matt whiteness of the walls and ceilings as empty as blank paper. It was a kind of sensory deprivation, as if (when you entered the sanctuary of Charlesworth's science) you might very well begin to witness hallucinations. And this was strange, for Charlesworth's philosophy was solidly materialistic. Sue found herself imagining she could hear cries and screams from elsewhere in the labyrinthine wings of the house, and she felt chilly inside her fresh overalls, for, listening with her ears, and hearing nothing coming through them, she thought it must be her own fear that was screaming. But that was odd, too, for she did not feel frightened at all. Simply on her guard.

Ahead of them, a sister rounded the corner of the corridor and advanced towards them, her feet as silent on the rubber floor as were their own, so that it was like an encounter in some world not yet totally realised. Three white figures floating on silent feet, converging on each other, their faces politely expressionless, the whole scene painted upon a field of white like an artist's canvas in the making.

'Good morning, Tov Lindsay,' said Charlesworth, 'and how is our patient today?'

'We're doing very well, Tov Doctor,' said the sister. She was, as far as her boss was concerned, quite without the usual aloofness and simpered at him unashamedly. 'Eating, talking, going for our walks. All activities absolutely normal. And not a hint of REMs!'

'Excellent,' smiled Charlesworth. 'Mind if we take just the merest gladz?'

Stopping at one of the line of doors, he peered through the

glass panel and, satisfied, beckoned to Sue to follow suit. Sue at once recognised the young woman sitting on the chair within as one of her own companions from the Web a week before. Sarah, had her name been? There she was now, sitting on an easy chair reading a work of Marxist–Leninist theory with a kind of methodical and even-paced deliberation which Sue found vaguely disturbing.

'*She's* recovered quickly,' she commented.

'Ah,' said Charlesworth, with a smile at once proud and secretive, 'the operation is quite painless, you know. We don't use anything so crude as a scalpel. No post-operative shock, indeed, if anything, the patient feels all the better for it.

'And our pianist?'

'Come and hear us play,' said Sister Lindsay, and turning on her heels led the way further down the corridor.

'We'd so love to hear us playing the piano,' she said, entering the room.

Cond Johnson, a buxom young woman with a permanent bright flush in her cheeks, rose immediately from the chair in which she had been sitting, reading precisely the same text as the previous patient (*Kapital*, commented by Althusser and Balibar) and followed them obediently into the corridor, saying first, 'Good morning, Tov Doctor, good morning, Tov Sister, good morning, Tov . . . Tov . . . Tov . . .'

'Tov Amanuensis,' said Charlesworth, for the word 'secretary' was beginning to have the wrong connotations. ('Tov whore,' he whispered in Sue's ear, and she felt her heart jump unpleasantly.)

'Tov Amanuensis,' said the girl impassively. She walked ahead of them to a T-junction in the corridor, turned without hesitation into the left-branching passageway, pushed open a third white door on the right and, still leading them, entered and sat down at the grand piano that was to be found there. Turning the pages of the music on the stand till she got back to page one, she began to play, rather well, Sue thought. If it was possible to play these pieces well, for they were a medley of favourite patriotic tunes, beginning with 'Marx Save the Wo-orkers' State', which was always top of the pops, and ending with 'Rule (two-three) the People (three), the People's Rule that Saves', whose grammar was significantly ambiguous and which was always number two in the charts. The girl played the whole thing through to the end quite faultlessly, then got down another booklet of music and began to play that. It was, as accident would have it, an identical copy of the same pieces, and Sue looked at Cond Johnson's healthy blushing cheeks in some curiosity. Really it was very creepy, not to say uncanny. She couldn't see any sign of a bandage or a scar, though. Of course, Charlesworth had said . . .

'Perfect!' cried Charlesworth when she had finished. The word seemed to mean more than it usually did, and the girl turned her bulbous blue eyes on him and smiled gratefully.

'Thank you, Tov Doctor.'

Perfection, thought Sue. What a colourless thing to aim for.

'Would we like to tell the Tov Doctor what we've been doing this morning?' asked Sister Lindsay.

Cond Johnson went into a long list of her activities. The way she had got up, the shower she had taken, the marmalade she had spread upon her toast, the toothpaste she had spread upon her brush, the book by Althusser she had spread upon her knees. She began to quote verbatim from it, and the minutes groaned to a halt as she did so. Total recall, thought Sue, though she couldn't understand a word of it, and was pretty sure in the firm-locked secrecy of her own mind that nobody else could either.

'An important finding,' said Charlesworth to Lindsay. 'Tov Clegg-Molotov is delighted. The removal of the somni-switch prevents the brain evaluating and discarding information.'

Sue had known the Abominable Superman disbelieved in persons, but until now she had not guessed how firmly. Luckily he would find it flattering if she showed an interest.

'What are you going to do tomorrow, dear?' she said to the patient, in much the same motherly tone that Sister Lindsay had used.

The girl did not seem to notice. She looked in no way offended. She smiled obediently and explained that she was going to get up and have her shower, her breakfast, read

Althusser for an hour, then come here and play the piano . . . and so on.

'And what would you *like* to do tomorrow?' asked Sue.

No shadow of disquiet crossed the girl's eyes. She repeated word for word exactly what she had just said.

Charlesworth and Sister Lindsay stood smiling, exchanging the glances of those who are in league with each other and know much more than those outside the league. They did not seem perturbed, for why should they? The experiment was Mark-edly successful.

'And when you leave this place — I know it's a very nice, comfortable place,' said Sue, thinking that this wasn't all that it was — 'but when you leave this place, what would you like to do, and where would you like to go?'

Cond Johnson stood quite silent, the red in her cheeks becoming a shade brighter, and contemplated Sue with attention. It was not that she had not understood the question. It was not that she feared to express her personal wishes, for there was no cloud of alarm in her eyes, no struggle to suppress her thoughts, no struggle to suppress any sign of *that* struggle either. After a while she opened her mouth and said,

'I'm sure it will be very nice. I'd like to . . . no, I'd sooner . . . on the other hand, it would be so pleasant . . . then again, I'd be quite happy . . .' She faded into silence, and an emphatic frown of indecision appeared above her eyebrows.

'Perhaps, dear,' said Charlesworth, 'we'd like to take my advice as to our future?' There had been a pause during which no one had uttered a word. 'It will be entirely in accord with Socsov principles.'

'Oh thank you, Tov Doctor,' said Cond Johnson, smiling as if she were a very small girl who had just seen a flower open.

Charlesworth scowled at Sue, whose face was transparent to her feelings. 'Seen enough, Tov Amanuensis?' he suggested.

The plump, overnubile and all-compliant Miss Johnson was dispatched back to her room. They watched her treading her way towards it. Unerringly, thought Sue.

Her fear of Charlesworth had for the moment been almost overwhelmed by anger. She kept quiet until Sister Lindsay had withdrawn, then burst out,

194

'What have you done to that poor girl?'

'Nothing. Or rather something quite rapid and painless.'

'They say that about putting down rabbits,' said Sue.

The moment after she could have bitten her tongue off for saying it. But he seemed to notice nothing. The expression on his face was somewhere between smugness and cruelty as he replied, 'And what's wrong with that? Naïvety, Soochka, is both stupid and dangerous. However, in this case no one has been hurt. On the contrary, everyone is happy, indeed much happier than before, Cond Johnson most of all. You could see the cheerful glow in her cheeks, the enthusiasm with which she played the People's Glorious Tuneful Medley, the . . .'

'But she can't make up her mind any more,' whispered Sue as if she were communicating a shameful secret. 'She can't decide. She behaves, well, all too normally. But when you face her with an alternative, she doesn't know which way to jump.'

'Squeamishness,' said Charlesworth with contempt, waving one muscular arm so that Sue winced, thinking for a moment he was going to slap her face again. 'She knows now. She has no more illusions. She knows where decisions are made, in the bosom of the Party. She's simply done with dreams for ever.'

There was a longish pause. When a man like Charlesworth protested his kindness, you knew what to think. Sue's fear of him was back, and she'd better go gently. 'Sweet Karl,' she breathed at last, 'you don't mean to say you've . . .?'

'Of course,' said Charlesworth, stiff with self-satisfaction.

'Is that what REMs mean?'

There was a pause, then Charlesworth said with sarcasm, 'You're astonishing!' — though Sue thought he meant it. 'Yes, REMs are rapid eye movements. You make them when you're asleep, and it's an infallible sign that you're dreaming.'

'Vissarionovich! So she . . . so it . . . so you've *amputated* them!' She shook her head so as to rattle her mind back to sanity, thinking that she was herself having a dream, from which she would wake up in just another minute.

'Not "amputated", Soochka moyá, we don't use a knife. Such a crude word.'

Sue thought how sensitive a brute could be about words. 'How is it done, then?'

'We send an electro-magnetic pulse into the root of the brain, a pattern of waves which disrupts the dream mode of consciousness, eliminates it, liquidates it if you prefer that. Pattern ZX, we call it. Our subjects are released from dreaming for the rest of their lives. As you see from Cond Johnson's behaviour, nothing could be better for their contentedness, sense of realism, psychological stability and conformity to basic social norms.'

Another minute, Sue thought disgustedly, and he'll be talking about happiness. She shook her head and said, 'She's a Pavlovian dog. I hope there aren't any of these rays flying about the music-room here.'

'No, no,' replied Charlesworth loftily. 'They're under firm control in the operating theatre.' Why did he look at the same time bumptious and uneasy? His lip was trembling, and she had better be quiet.

As they continued their tour of the snow-white West Wing, she was thinking hard. My God — it was an expression she had picked up in some dream or other, for it certainly wasn't current in the Truly Democratic Republic — what if I *had* resisted him? I'd have had that done to me, and then what would have been the good of resisting? And I'd never have seen Michael again — my dream-baby. Sentimental rubbish, she thought fiercely, but somehow that dream of mine is important, somehow it has a sort of reality, though how that can be . . . She recalled with a shudder last night's dream. Even in her private sleep-world, Michael was threatened now. Sentimental folly, and you a full-grown woman! How can you threaten a figment of the imagination? I'm thoroughly neurotic, it's a phantom pregnancy of the mind.

And if he'd done that to me, I wouldn't have been *able* to resist. Superman's got you either way, she sneered at herself. Heads you succumb to me, tails you *must*.

She referred to it again that evening in her private bedroom. She resented the irony of its décor, all hung about with virginal white, embroidered with little pink flowers. She even resented the bottle of wine Charlesworth had brought with him.

196

'That girl,' she said. 'She can't *decide* any more. You haven't just cut out her dreams, you've cut out something else as well.' She watched for the tell-tale trembling of the lip.

It was safe for the moment, though. He let out his bay of amused contempt. 'Byessmisslitsa!'

(Calling it nonsense in Russian doesn't make it any better, she thought.) 'My God,' she said aloud, as a new thought struck her. The look in Cond Johnson's eyes when she'd asked her what she'd like to do when she left the asylum. She was listening, aye, the words went in, she had understood. But she hadn't . . . *understood*, if you know what I mean. 'People's shit!'

'Do you ask them if they're conscious, Mark?'

You could see he was astonished by such a silly question, but after a pause he said, 'Yes.'

'What do they say?'

'They say Yes.'

'Always?'

'Always.'

A little thrown, she said with a sarcasm that she kept quietly to herself, 'I suppose that proves they are.'

He took it straight, suspecting nothing: 'Of course. What other proof of consciousness is there? Long ago in the twentieth century, Turing — the computer man, you know — said that if you can't tell the difference between them and real people, then they *are* real people.'

She pouted. She could see through that fallacy from five miles away, even if she knew nothing about computers. Besides, there was another problem. 'Ah, but you can.'

He frowned at her. 'Can what?'

'Fat little Johnson — she doesn't say the same things as normal people. She doesn't make up her mind.' A thought struck her and, aware of the danger of baiting him, she tried to adopt the tone of the fawning female votary, the phallus-worshipper. 'Have you been to bed with her? I bet she's turned into a right little hoori, the way she is now.'

He was silent again. Superbrain was actually listening to her, thinking maybe of Cond Johnson, admitting maybe she had been easier than usual. 'What's a hoori?' he said at last.

197

'In the Mohammedan Heaven — you know, when there *were* Mohammedans and not just Qadhafian Socialists — when you died, and if you were a man, you went to Bliss.'

'And?'

'Well, what do you suppose Bliss is, for a man? You were attended by gangs of hooris — sounds lovely in Scots, I'll tell you — who were soulless demons, automata you'd say these days — and you spent eternity drinking wine on a carpet of soft twining limbs. They had to be soulless, because men prefer it that way.' (She'd overstepped the 'Mark' now, she knew it! She felt part terrified, part exhilarated by her own silly daring, her own silly wit. It must be the wine, she wasn't used to it. Better hurry on.) 'What's the Muslim *women's* paradise, do you suppose? I imagine automata come in both sexes.' (No, that was worse. She sat trembling, waiting for the blow to fall.)

For the moment, however, he made no move. 'You're not in bed with an automat, Soochka.' He stopped short, as if aware of the enormity of what he was saying. Gulag! Was he of all people asserting he wasn't an automat?

'Where did you learn all that about the Muslim Heaven?' he asked, sounding both puzzled and annoyed. When they had abolished Christianity, they had tried to suppress all references to other religions too. This was one of the reasons why it was a crime to possess any book that had been published more than fifty years ago.

'I don't know, it's a memory from childhood or something.' In a society like theirs, in which so many important things were taboo, a lot of information had to pass by word of mouth. That was perhaps how she'd picked it up. Or quite possibly she'd dreamed it. But that didn't matter. The important thing was not to challenge Superman with her eyes, but to watch him like a lynx — sidelong. And above all to get her native buoyancy back under lock and key before the wine did any more damage.

'What do you suppose has happened to Amy Johnson, then?'

She said something evasive, but he dragged her back to the point. There was no wriggling out of it. She would have to tell him. 'I think . . . you've cut out dreaming all right, but somehow at the same time you've cut out consciousness. Maybe the two are interconnected. Maybe one depends on the other in some way. Or maybe the switches are side by side.'

'How did you know that?' he asked uneasily.

'Well, since this has happened, I imagine they must be.'

'Ah, ah' (he was grasping at straws, Sue thought to herself, and the straws wouldn't hold him, and then there would be trouble), 'then that proves it's nothing but machinery, doesn't it? It proves that you *can* cut it out.'

'I don't think so,' said Sue. 'When you cut the telephone wire, you can't hear the voice any more. But that doesn't prove the voice wasn't there.'

'And *in your view*,' he asked, underlining these words with sarcasm, 'what is it like not to be conscious any more?'

'Well, that's nothing, isn't it? No feeling, no thinking, no knowing. Just blackness.'

Now his lip really was trembling. Sue didn't know what to do. Things were quite out of control.

But the violence, when it came, was not physical. He simply began to say, watching her carefully all the time to see how she liked it, 'Well, if you're right, my little Soochka, that's exactly what you have to look forward to. Yourself. Tomorrow afternoon.'

She gazed at him open-mouthed. She had quite expected to be hit again. But not for one moment had she dreamed he would do this to her. Not after she'd slept with him. Why, selling your body was supposed to prevent this sort of thing. Of course, these people never played fair, that was the whole point of the power they loved so much. My God, I wish I didn't feel so terrified. In the handsome face staring into hers she could see the pleasure of the cannibal, the lust of the torturer. And, most horrible of all, this torturer's eyes were wet.

She began to weep herself, pleading with him, taking his hands in hers, kissing him, calling him 'Mark', abasing herself in the most shameless and cowardly way. I feel as if something's broken inside me, I feel as weak as . . . as cold as . . . as if I were being strangled. He stroked her hair, being at the same time implacable and sympathetic. He was visibly moved. She descended step after step of degradation, from pleas to promises

199

to endearments. The more she crawled to him, the greater his delight, till finally he began to bay with laughter. Dogs after a fox, or a hound insane under the moon.

'Ha ha! Perfect! What a little fool you are!' The laughter spasmed out, the tears streamed, his face was like a window-pane.

She recoiled from him, weak, appalled, asking faintly, 'What is it, Mark? Do you mean you'll not do that awful thing to me after all?' Almost she felt disgusted with herself for seeing a glint of hope.

He wiped his eyes, the laughter spaced itself out into hiccups, he explained, 'Sweet Karl, that frightened you, didn't it? You see, you don't know. You don't know what's going to happen tomorrow. Clegg-Molotov himself is due here at eleven. It's the final stage of the experiment.' He began to laugh again, explaining breathlessly through the noise, 'You'll find out tomorrow. We'll *all* find out!'

'*All?*' she repeated, gazing at him mistily. His face was distorted through her tears, Superbeast's features had melted slightly, and his neck and bare shoulders looked enormous. 'All? Whatever do you mean?'

Of course, he hadn't gone into this with his eyes shut. It was just that it was impossible that opinions like Sue's could be right. *Scientifically* impossible, that is. Tonight, however, watching the blue sky turn red, then bloody crimson and then black . . . He had listened to the little bitch's naïve, instinctive objections. Vissarionovich, how it excited him to see them helpless with fear! *She* had some absurd idea that the world would be blotted out — just a lot of machines clanking up and down with no one to see them. Like a dark enclosed space in the universe with lots of things going on inside it, but nobody would ever know what, for nothing would be conscious any more. Grotesque!

He turned to look at her now. Naked, pathetic, shivering, looking at him with those big brown eyes, like a dog that's been beaten. (How accurate platitudes always were!) How he loved being sorry for her, and how he loved being the reason for her sorrow! Why then did he too for a moment feel a ridiculous twinge of doubt?

200

She hated him. It wasn't possible to hate anyone more than she hated him. He ought to wear a red shirt with Superman's S splayed out wide on the front. S for Sex and Sure and Sleep and Socialism. S for Sadism and the scarlet French word *Sang*. S for Stupidity. S for the nasty Secret she'd been looking for and now at last had found. Not just me? Everyone? 'What are you talking about?'

Outside the sun had long since set, leaving a full white moon alone in the sky. Space was vaster here, and the Norfolk countryside beneath it lay flat, like a frightened young woman hiding herself from the eye. Long shadows thrown by the clumps of trees scarred the fields black and white like the tattoos on a savage's face. Wealth and pain, fear and power. The terrible flatness of people's lives, and above it the all-enveloping sky, dark, with its single luminary. From a distant farm came the sound of a dog, maddened by the moonlight, barking and barking.

'What is it, Mark? What is it you haven't told me?'

Dream Eleven

As for us, we were never concerned with Kantian-priestly and vegetarian-Quaker prattle about the 'sacredness of human life'.

————— LEV TROTSKY —————

Friday, 25 October 2007

At 5 am on Friday morning, the window of Sue's bedroom fell quietly out onto the street, where it smashed into a thousand pieces. The outline of a man blocked the hole, flat against the greyish light, holding his revolver pointed at a bundle of blankets on the floor. The bundle squealed and rolled, kicked and bent double. Eventually a bare round female arm emerged, hand waving, reaching for its gun.

'Freeze!'

Meanwhile, there came a dull thud from the front hall, as if the door had fallen off its hinges. From the kitchen came a rattle of machine-gun fire, then silence. This was succeeded by a thin slow trickling of glass, as the mirror Sue had hung last year on the end wall to make the hall look bigger, peeled gently away from it and descended in jagged rain upon the sanded wooden floor.

'You'll be Irene Thompson-Williams,' said the SAS man. 'Just lie still and think of Daddy and Mummy. Perhaps they might speak up for you at the trial. I wouldn't worry, if I were you. We're a civilised country, we don't hang murderers.'

To Sue he said, 'You okay, lady? Baby all right?'

'Oh yes,' said Sue. 'Oh yes, *thank you*. Och, I am so glad to see you.'

'That's all right, lady. All in a day's work.'

Distantly, from the direction of the sitting-room, there came the loud caw of B-P's public school voice, volume turned up rather higher than confidence-level: '. . . breowken our agreement. This is an eowtrage.'

'Hark at him,' said the SAS man, and gestured the latest acolyte out of her blankets. 'Come out slowly. No sudden movements.'

'But I'm not wearing anything . . .'

'So what? Pure as the driven snow, I am. Besides, if you think I'm interested in a nasty little terrorist like you . . . That's right. Now stand up.' He snapped a pair of handcuffs over her wrists and the two other men who had now come in through the window behind him scattered the pile of bedding, searching for more guns. One of them took out a knife and severed the bonds that held Sue's wrists to the bed.

The first man shook his head sadly at the latest acolyte. 'Undressing on active service?' he mourned. 'Highly unprofessional. How did you get into this, then? Daddy got too much money? Makes you sick, doesn't it?'

'Y-yes,' said the latest acolyte, her face twisting, contorting into tears.

'I feel really sorry for you,' said the man unsympathetically.

Handcuffed, a blanket thrown round her, weeping, she was led away, strange counter-image of the women of 2117.

B-P had been taken alive in the sitting-room. Noel, on the other hand, had been shot dead as he leapt for his gun. Sue was happy about that, and even fairly happy to be happy about it. She had no time for any such feelings, however, for they were all bustled out and down the common stair, as if the SAS thought there was danger of a bomb in the flat.

John was waiting on the opposite pavement of London Road with Ailsa beside him. From the immense distance that it seemed across ten yards of street, they both looked tiny, dark and motionless, like figures in a black-and-white photograph. Sue stepped onto the surface of the road and at once they came to life, smiling, gesturing tentatively.

'Oh John, Oh Ailsa,' said Sue, hugging them both and bursting into tears. 'Oh John, Oh Ailsa.'

Her husband took the baby, who was smiling and shouting. After a while he noticed something, reached out his hand in a puzzled way and, finding his mother's cheeks were wet, offered his mouth to be kissed.

'Oh God, I'm so glad to see you,' sniffed Sue, fighting with her handkerchief. 'You were wonderful,' she said to the SAS man who was standing there expressionless.

He was not the kind of person who smiled, except if you looked quite hard at the corners of his lips. 'We're paid to be wonderful,' he said. 'Don't thank me, thank your girlfriend.'

'Och, I do, I do,' said Sue, digging in John's trouser pocket for a hankie that was large enough.

If Sue was weeping with relief, Ailsa was smiling with guilty tension. 'Sue, will you ever forgive me, I heard what you said quite well, I heard you say "Oh-what-a-lovely-surprise-to-hear-your-voice-Ailsa," and I didn't think a second thing about it, will you ever forgive me, love, I knew that was what you had said, and I thought at the time you sounded funny, but I just didn't *think*. Till later. Till hours later, when I woke up like that − ouch! − in the middle of the night, and Ben stirred beside me and made an awful fuss, and I thought to myself, Jeezus Christ! What if it *isn't* a lot of taradiddle after all!'

For in the disorientation of sleep, when you're not bustled to and fro by habit and expectation − in the darkness when the walls of dream are down, all sorts of fears and craziness seem possible again − often you see more clearly in the dark. Connections are made that daylight blinds you to, and . . .

'Och, Sue, I was so slow understanding. But then I rushed round before breakfast, thinking to myself, You're a fine idiot, Ailsa, thinking Sue's joke is for real, but I had the sense not to ring the bell, you see, I looked through the letter-box. And then I knew, because the letter-box was all nailed up, so I pushed it and it didn't budge, so I took off my shoe, like this, and put my hand inside it and − I was so surprised, Sue, cos it actually gave way. Mind you, I hit it pretty hard. So then I rang the bell, and

204

through the box I could see this young man with a tommy-gun. Sweet Jeezus, Sue, I ran like mad down the stairs.

'God,' she said, 'if only I'd done it the night before. Sue, will you ever forgive me for being so stupid?

'Sue, can you hear me?' For Sue's tears were running down into her smile.

'Of course I can, Ailsa. You were wonderful, love. Don't you see that only somebody like you would *ever* have understood — it had to be somebody like you, a little bit daft, a wee bit sanely mad. With anyone else the penny would never have dropped at all!

'You know, I think it was my fault really, when we made the compact it was one of those deadly serious things that seem like jokes, and I didn't dare say it on the phone with that Southern English pawshness, though I suppose if I had the Wicked Professor wouldn't have noticed, cos he has that kind of accent himself. In fact, he's not very clued in to accents, he kept asking me what "the polis" meant, and talking about Plato. And when you . . .'

'When you're ready,' said the plain-clothes man who had been hovering all this while in the wings. 'We need a full statement, Mrs Lumsden. You feeling okay? Baby all right?'

'Yes *thank you*. He's marvellous. You're marvellous.'

'We all need a holiday,' said John as they got into the police car.

'Sète?' wondered Sue.

Two days later there was a complaint in *The Guardian* that the SAS operation had involved unreasonable violence. Noel, they pointed out, had been a young man of great promise before he had been led astray by Brianston-Pedley, and it must always be remembered that these terrorists, however misguided, were sincere idealists whose actions, however misplaced, were done out of altruistic motives. One deplored their methods, but the whole terrorist phenomenon was due to a deeply felt indignation at social injustice.

The treatment of Miss Thompson-Williams had been shocking. Apparently she had been deliberately humiliated, being hauled up naked out of her bed, though she had already surrendered and was very frightened.

205

Event Sixteen

It is not men's consciousness that determines their being, but their social being that determines their consciousness.

———— KARL MARX ————

Freeday, 25 Oct 2117

'You bloody *fools!*' Sue had said, almost speechless with rage. 'How could you *do* such a thing?' She clambered out of bed, completely naked, and wandered about the room, gazing at bits of the wallpaper as if she had never seen them before, ruffling her hands through her black hair, looking utterly distraught. In command of herself again, a thought struck her. Pausing in her wanderings, she said, 'Maybe it won't work, most launchings don't.'

She was speaking quite frankly now. For one thing, Charlesworth's experiment was so thoughtlessly, insanely dangerous that nothing else mattered now. For another, the doctor had indulged his cruelty so selfishly tonight that it had brought even him a sort of realism. The sadist, assuaged, was for the moment almost conversable.

'How did you know that?' he said. 'It's a state secret.'

'Ordinary folk aren't such fools as you think, you Party magnates. We can all tell truth from lies, you know, the System's trained us to it. We've all got to know that a lie's a lie at the same time as we say it isn't, otherwise none of us would survive. Why, the moment the teletruth says a satellite's been launched, we know fine well it hasn't.'

'I can't believe it,' she said. 'It's sheer science fiction, and in very bad taste.'

206

He gazed at her in some puzzlement. He had told her what would happen tomorrow, and she was no longer afraid of him. As for him, he had no doubts — no doubts whatever — about the correctness of his theories, and yet this absence of doubt, this nothing that he had never paid any attention to, and had locked away in the same darkness where he locked away everything irrational — it had been swelling all this long while in the obscurity, and had now emerged full grown. He had locked away a kitten. It had grown into a big black panther, and was breaking down the door.

He said, taking a firm grasp of his beliefs, 'It's just the dreams it stops. Not anything else. This consciousness you talk about, it's just an epiphenomenon, a product of matter.'

'You daft scientist!' she spat at him. 'You think you know such a lot! Maybe the mechanism will jam, most things do in the TDR.

'Have you told the Russkies?' she asked, with sudden hope.

'Of course. Can't go letting off satellites without informing them. But we haven't told them *what* they are.'

'I see, they think they're teletruth satellites or something?'

'Right.'

'What about the Yanks?'

'Well, what *about* the Yanks?'

'Isn't there a chance they might shoot it down when it goes over their air-space?'

'Why should they do that? You little fool,' he said, light dawning, 'you don't mean to say you take all that propaganda seriously about the Americans still being Capitalists, do you?'

She looked at him amazed. 'You don't mean to say . . . And I thought I had it all sized up. But why do they tell us that? It's in all the history books . . .'

'Nobody's allowed there, so what does it matter what they think?'

'But such a complicated lie! All those pictures of American teletruth, showing elections for president, and military manoeuvres threatening the peace-loving Soviet Union, and atrocities committed in Surinam . . .'

'People need something to hate, so we give it them.'

'But they don't hate it, they want it.'

'Exactly. Keeps them on the edge of their seats.'

A terrible thought struck her. 'But then what *is* going on in Surinam? I thought they were freedom-loving socialists being massacred by imperialists? Are they imperialists being massacred by freedom-loving socialists?'

'When you see people being tortured, can you make out their ideology?'

'But then the labels are wrong!'

'Ah, but it's the truth *behind* the labels that counts.'

'But it's like at the movies!'

'That's right. The USA's been communist for nearly a hundred years. I'll prove it to you, if you like. You remember the Great World Famine in the history books?'

'No,' she said.

'Started in 2030. Ah no, of course only the Inner Party are told. Well, how do you suppose it happened? Because the agriculture of the USA was collectivised.'

Sue, remembering she was completely naked, and that she hated him, covered her breasts with her arms and began to hunt around for her nightdress. He was trying to change the subject. She said, 'What I want to know is, what are you going to do about those satellites?'

'*Do* about them?' he asked, baffled. Surely she couldn't mean what she seemed to!

'Yes, do about them. You know how those radiation machines work, you invented them. You can say there's something wrong with the mechanism. Or you can just switch them off on the quiet.'

He must get the panther back into its box before it frightened him to death. He was bewildered too by the fact that his victim, who just a few minutes earlier had been reduced to despair, had now recovered all that buoyancy, that waywardness which was her chief attraction — since destroying it was his chief pleasure.

'Don't be absurd. Only Clegg-Molotov can stop them now. They're going off from four separate spots independently — Dounreay, Fakenham, Bannamore and one across the Channel in France. It would take a phone call from O.B.L. himself . . .'

'Clegg-Molotov,' she said. 'Ring him. You know what a cleg is, I suppose,' she added irrelevantly.

He replied with a contemptuous silence. She looked at him and nodded her head sadly. 'A capital crime,' she said. 'Bamboozling the People.'

'You're a hysterical little fool. There's nothing to worry about. Materialism is communism, and communism is science, and science is materialism.'

She had a sudden vision of Superman hanging upside down from a telephone line, like some ridiculous red and blue bat. 'That all goes round in a circle like the perpetual motion machine in Red Square.'

He had explained to her the other day — explaining things to women was one way of dominating them — how there wasn't any such thing as perpetual motion, how everyone knew (though no one ever said) that capitalist science had been greatly superior, how there hadn't been any scientific progress since the start of the twenty-first century, since the Revolution, and how from then on things had gone backwards rather than forwards. In fact the PMM, proud symbol of Eternal Revolution, was driven by a small clockwork motor concealed in the pavement below it. It had to be clockwork because the electricity supply was unreliable.

'You're not talking logically,' he said, dressing in some haste. 'Those patients down in the white rooms, they're all quite normal. All the neural tests are in agreement. Just as normal as me, as Clegg-Molotov . . .'

He didn't understand it. An hour before, she had been at his mercy, writhing in the ultimate agonies of terror, and now she had the upper hand.

'You'll see tomorrow,' he threatened as he left. He would do something about those women — Mandy and the cat-pack. Make a public example of them. That would put the relationship back on the right footing. Yes, he would arrange it for next week. Besides, it would give him something to look forward to.

And now it was morning, the morning of the Final Proof of Pure Materialism. As if it had not a trouble in the world, a cheerful sun blazed down from out of a dauntlessly blue sky. As far as the eye could see, the fields lay sedulously flat, hoping not to be noticed. The trees, like cat-o'-nine-tails, quivered in the wind with pleasure. The doors grinned open, the windows twinkled like shelvesful of short-sighted spectacles. The boundary walls grew bushes of barbed wire. Under them the booby traps lay buried, clenched like springs upon the code word 'death'. The birds sang with their usual enthusiasm, like clockwork the guards stamped and twirled, pacing out the confines of the park, like clockwork the blank-faced patients in the White Wing rose and went about their business.

Superman brushed his teeth and stepped singing into the shower. Why had he allowed himself to be browbeaten by a female plennik? It must have been all that sex and wine. Titsers had to be *shown*. It was fatal to listen to them, fatal to give them the slightest encouragement. No, he had no doubts, he repeated to himself, staring into the mirror as he shaved his determined jaw. Blast! He dabbed at his chin with a piece of cotton wool. When his great experiment had triumphed, Sue (like the rest of the world's peoples) would continue to survive quite consciously, even after the passage of his muttering satellites across the sky. And then she would recognise that, after all, she was nothing but a — no, he mustn't put it that way, it was an *incorrect expression* — she was that supremely rich and complex object, a machine. A soft, wayward machine. He must arrange for them both to visit the Bahamas. In total sun tan she would be the total sexual trophy, to be worn and envied like a medal, the panther, not black but brown, caged at last, and biting the hand of her keeper only so as to excite him.

As for Sue, she was frightened. Just when she had woken from one nightmare, she had found herself in another and, while she was inside each, each felt equally real. It was hard to say which was worse — the fact that her dreams were about to be taken away from her for ever, so that she would never see Michael again — or the probability that she would become, that they would all become, like the wide-eyed zombies in the White Wing. Mind you, perhaps it was a kindness Charlesworth was doing to the world, imposing on its pain and madness an eternal anaesthetic.

Och, but probably the rockets won't go up, she told herself, trying to be cheerful. As she'd said to Charlesworth last night, in the TDR nothing worked. It was one long succession of monumental bardacks. And maybe Superman is right, and pure materialism is true. Maybe Superman is right, and fancy hoping he is!

The trouble was, Supermen were never right. That was one of the laws of science, or if it wasn't, it ought to be.

Charlesworth called for her at ten, looking his usual assured and knowing self, and she accompanied him to the front hall where an élite group of the medical staff stood waiting, along with a spruce detachment of armed guards. High on the flagstaff above the hospital, the golden Ear of the People, hearing aid and all, wagged vigilantly on its crimson flag. Shortly before eleven a howling of sirens could be heard in the distance, like a mechanised wolf-pack coming up the road from the village of Diss. Our Beloved Leader was on his way, and the assembled company began to shake with fright. So affectionate were their feelings for Clegg-Molotov that several nurses were overcome with a dose of the trotskies, and had to flee to the lavatory, where they remained locked in until long after the great man had seen round the building.

As the First Secretary and his paramour emerged from their bullet-proof Rolls-Royce, the waiting party burst into spontaneous applause, a young group of nurses offered a gift of spontaneous red roses, and the Director, Tov Doctor Mark Charlesworth himself, stepped forward to give a spontaneous speech of welcome.

Clegg-Molotov favoured them with his famous smile, baring his teeth and looking round the serried ranks of the faithful like a wolf that wonders which little lamb it will bite first. As if thinking better of it, but with a faintly disappointed air, he allowed himself to be ushered into the building for a short tour of the White Wing, before joining the Director and his most private of secretaries for coffee.

Charlesworth's sitting-room was an impassive cream-grey, the pictures on its walls had been chosen for their muted tones. The upholstery squatted, dimpling, like so many fat comfortable knees — a row of soft sculptures, seated Pharaohs, headless every one. Nothing in the room was emphatic or offensive. Such discreetness made Sue uneasy, and she found herself glancing at the lampshades, and wondering what they were made of. The four of them settled themselves in luxurious chairs in front of a wide-screen teletruth, watching the reports from the rocket sites and waiting for the countdown.

The countdown to zero. Zero indeed! She did not know how it had been in capitalist times, but in the TDR these things were never on time. Nonetheless, C-M looked more and more pleased as the minutes ticked by and lengthened into hours, and they had to have lunch brought up to the Director's sitting-room, and then tea. From time to time he would pick up the telephone at his elbow, and ask for the political reliability of one of the technicians in charge of the launchings to be investigated — '*after* you've shot him, of course.'

'The saboteurs are all around us, Tov Director,' he murmured to Charlesworth.

'Just as you say, Tov Chairman.' Even Charlesworth was beginning to look slightly alarmed.

Sue, however, found her spirits rising as the hours passed. Perhaps it wouldn't happen after all. Perhaps there would be a reprieve, and Murphy's Law would direct the launching as it seemed to direct everything else. She began to smile prettily around the room, and C-M had time to admire her in his own dialectical—materialist way. Not tall enough, of course, not like his own statuesque Ludmilla, but her charms were for that reason perhaps more concentrated. Her teeth were crooked, but there was something attractive about that. Her brown eyes and the tensions of impatience in her body both hinted at hidden wealths of bedwilling sexcitement. He reckoned her whole body was an erogenous zone. He must arrange with Charlesworth to spend a night with her. Strange. She looked somehow vaguely familiar, but how could that be? He wished after all he hadn't brought Ludmilla.

By way of light conversation he remarked, 'Hitler is a much-maligned man, in my view.'

'Just as you say, Tov Chairman.'

'One must be clear that his political views were quite incorrect. But one has to admire his *method*, the *efficiency* of the SS. Efficiency is one of the greatest of virtues, I often think.'

'Just as you say, Tov Chairman.'

'And speaking of efficiency . . .' Boris picked up the little red telephone again, and instructed the removal of another scientist. Then he changed his mind. 'Order countermanded. Arrest him and send him to my office in London. Next Althusserday. Let him cool off in the freezer till then.' He tapped his teeth thoughtfully.

Putting the phone down he grinned round at their surprised faces. 'He'll be scared out of his wits, the bastard. Little does he guess I'm going to appoint him head of a research establishment.' He roared with laughter, for what a joke it was! — just the kind he understood.

Sue listened, puzzled, wondering whether the removal of all these officers from the launching would not make its problems even worse — hoping that it would. Ludmilla, on the other hand, smiled faintly and crossed and recrossed her legs, shifting in her seat so that the sunlight fell at a flattering angle across the two warm bulges inside her blouse. 'Could we have some more tea, luby?' she yawned. She understood these urges towards power, and one of these days she would — if she survived — show Boris himself how well she could pull the puppet-strings. She knew what such arbitrary acts of mercy were about. It was the ultimate satisfying proof of a Leader's power that he could be inconsistent with himself. That final and most subtle touch made him absolute.

Besides, there was the marvellous flattery of *gratitude* — from one who morally should hate you!

And then, at close on six o'clock, just when Sue had been sure that they wouldn't get those rockets off the launching pad today, one of the count downs, and then another, began to approach zero.

'Blessed Joseph,' she murmured, and sunk her head in her hands. Then, hoping against hope, she said, 'Are you sure the radiation will blanket *everyone*? What about people down the mines?'

'Everyone,' said Charlesworth, worried for a moment lest she should make a scene. With C-M here, it was unthinkable. Surely even she was scared stiff of Our Beloved Leader. Yet — he wondered — such a determined young woman! 'Everyone,' he repeated. 'The men down the pits have to come up some time or other. Animals, birds, fish, the entire living population of the globe. Supposing they dream,' he said, laughing. 'The satellites will orbit the Earth and blanket it with Pattern ZX.'

'And the final privacy of dreams will be removed from men for ever,' said C-M smacking his lips. 'No more escapism. An end to atavism. No more counter-revolutionary yearnings while the socialist vigilance of the conscious mind sleeps. No one will ever be off duty again.'

They pursue individuals with a steady burning hatred, thought Sue. But dreams are deeper than the personal, so even more disturbingly beyond the State's control. They were terrified that, far out of reach within the mind, something inalienable might live which would for ever contradict their 'truths'. So terrified that they must know that, within their own hearts too, something could be found. So terrified that they must know their truths were false.

'But you too,' she said.

Charlesworth looked at C-M, expecting anger, but the latter, after a moment's surprise, decided to laugh.

'Of course,' he said. He thought with pleasure of his dream of the night before — the frightened mother, the intention to shoot some Humanist—Socialist or other — the worst kind of crypto-bourgeois, he always thought. A pity it had all become so muddled at the end, had turned, indeed, rather sour. That was the trouble with dreams. You couldn't make them obey you. Did she perhaps resemble the young mother in his dreams? He really couldn't remember. A venturesome young woman, rebellious even. In bed now, it was very likely . . . Yes, he would arrange it with Charlesworth. One day soon he would return to Diss without Ludmilla, and . . .

A gush of light blotted out the screen. At last the first rocket had taken flight, rising with preternatural slowness from the ground, like a hot air balloon on a windless day. All that explosive force, yet how slowly it lifted, how intense were the seconds ticking by. And then the screen shifted to the launching pad at L'Arbre-aux-Mouches in France, and there too the screen began to glow, the long thin stem of the rocket to rise like a heavy kite.

'Down with dreams!' giggled Ludmilla, clapping. To herself she thought, I could certainly do without some of mine.

'When will it start broadcasting?' asked Sue. Then, since no sound had emerged from between her lips, she cleared her throat and tried again.

'Around midnight,' replied Charlesworth, checking his watch. He smiled imperturbably round at them all. 'And look, there's the third one going off at last!' He had recovered all his confidence. Sue's words last night about human consciousness had been a simple case of nineteenth-century bourgeois reactionism. He would pay her back for that! Yes, he looked forward to it. He tapped his watch. *That* was what the world was like. He hoped it hurt his watch when he tapped it.

Amazing, thought Sue, how four people could view the same event with such contrary feelings. She felt nothing but fear, they nothing but glossy assurance. There were no shadows in their world, nothing but the glaring light of certainty. They had predicted the future and understood the past. They were temperamentally impatient, meddlers with truth and reality, thirsty for instant perfection.

And hungry for dinner.

'Shall we order?' asked Charlesworth.

She found she could hardly eat at all, which was a pity, for nerve-racking acres of evening stretched before them. It was impossible to excuse yourself and go to bed, for while C-M was awake, none of his company must drowse. It was equally impossible to console yourself by getting drunk, for you had to keep your wits about you when OBL was present. Fortunately both he and Charlesworth were exceptionally fond of the sound of their own voices — even for men, thought Sue — so she could sip her wine, and wait, and brood in relative silence.

'Freedom,' Boris was saying. 'You remember, Tov Director, the sublime Karl's luminous words: "The abolition of religion is

215

a demand for men's real happiness. The call to abandon all illusions about their condition is a call to abandon a condition which requires illusions." What a brilliant analysis! That's exactly what we of the TDR have done. Without religion, how can religious freedom be a problem? Without parties, how can political choice be an issue? Without music or novels or poetry, how can you prefer one thing to another? Yes, yes, a brilliant analysis. True freedom dawns when you abolish all the things you need freedom *for*.'

'Praveelny, Tov Chairman,' said Charlesworth, hastening to cap that with another quotation from the Sacred Book. And so, like two card players, they dealt and bid, tricked and trumped each other's divine texts till the clock drew on towards midnight, and Pattern ZX was due to start broadcasting, submerging the world in its electro-magnetic darkness.

'Here's to the Revolution,' cried Boris, raising his glass. 'The two hundredth anniversary of glorious October!' For here came the 26th of that month, one second after midnight, zero hour. Chorusing 'Glorious October!' they kissed and clinked, sipped and swigged. 'Here's to the New Era!'

Sue glanced round at the paintings on the walls — an expensive motor-launch roaring at speed across a peaceful bay; a pheasant shoot with guns smoking and a dead bird clamped in the jaws of a gun-dog; an eighteenth-century Scottish datcha, crowned in medieval pinnacles, its back to a Stalinist sunset; a girl sprawled on a West Indian beach clad in less than a bikini, and painted in such attentive detail that you could see the drops of sweat between her breasts. Lastly a beribboned march past, the funeral of some Socsov dignitary, the guards around the gun-carriage performing the goose step in sinister slow motion, like mechanical puppets stretching and subsiding on wires, their faces expressionless, staring straight ahead, painted eyes in painted faces, their military caps glued to their wooden hair. The meaning and aspirations of Socsov society were summed up on Charlesworth's walls. But there was a blank space too, where a picture had been removed. There had been an act of censorship. Sue felt the solitude of this room, tonight, hanging two storeys up in the darkened central wing of Diss Hall, floating suspended in the silence of the asylum, in the silence of the Norfolk night, as if the truth behind this little cube of light in which they sat, the only thing that supported its reality, was the darkness, without which it would vanish like a dream.

She rose and went over to the window. Though she had drunk almost nothing, she thought it must be her eyes when she parted the curtains and gazed out into the night.

The sky was dark but icy clear, and here in the empty countryside the stars were endlessly bright and numerous. The only lights in the room behind Sue were the purple flicker of the teletruth screen and the shaded lamp over the table where bottles of vodka and malt whisky stood among the remnants of their feast. C-M was saying,

'Who cares about the private lives of machines?'

She had momentarily lost track of the conversation, but the others were evidently finding it funny, for they laughed uproariously. Mind you, supposing you could tell it was a joke, you did laugh when Clegg-Molotov made one.

I wish they'd put that light off, thought Sue, cos you can't really see properly. She didn't dare to ask them, so she stepped right out onto the balcony, closing the curtains behind her. The laughter from the room at her back was suddenly stifled. She stood there, her shoulders to the window, straining her eyes at the sky.

Strange, there were no clouds. Why then . . .? There seemed to be bands of obscurity in the Milky Way, to the north the whole constellation of the Plough was missing, and . . . Across the borders of her vision, the scarlet spark of an artificial satellite passed like the point of a laser, scoring its track across the darkness. She thought of those oxyacetylene cutters that are used for shearing sheets of metal. Oh God, I was right, she thought in a horrified rush, and turned back to face the room. There through the chink in the thick velvet curtains she could see Ludmilla, sexpertly decorative, her long elegant legs crossed; the rodent grin on the Party Leader's face; the egregious Superman smiling and nodding as he acted the scientist, ratifier of orthodoxy, courtier of the State — the handsome male façade, not to be examined too closely lest you put your fingers through

217

the paper. Here is truth, never mind what's going on behind it. The scene, taken in at a glance, frozen like a photographic still, floated there within the enveloping darkness for a few instants, then began to fade.

She was saying to herself, Oh yes, I hope this is a dream. I hope the veil of Maya spreads ambiguously in all directions. The spider's web. Arachne, the spinner of stories.

Oh yes, I hope it's none of it true.

Oh yes, I hope.

Ivan, Michael

Oh yes, I

Oh

In the black sky behind her, the satellites spun vibrating on their way, and gently, slowly, imperceptibly, as the shadow of final eclipse expanded across it, the world began to disappear.

Tu es éteinte . . . au bleu de la croisée. The words hung like floating sparks in the blackness, before dispersing, dying.

Dream Twelve

*Communism . . . is the final
solution to the riddle of history.*
———— KARL MARX ————

Christmas Day, 2007

'And the dreams?'

The fire in the hearth was whispering away, rapt and wrapt up in itself and puffing out scarlet and gold in token of such burning concentration. Flame-shadows wavered softly on the walls in the early Scottish twilight. Sue and Ailsa squatted on rugs, their shoes off, a little sleepy with wine and Christmas pudding. Michael (now nine months old) was exercising in his baby bouncer and babbling away in his mother tongue — which seemed not to be English, or even French. Ben, having made his regular yearly joke about the anatomy student who was erectile only once a twelvemonth ('Tonight! Tonight!') was savouring his regular yearly cigar.

'The dreams? Well, you remember we weren't having any during that fortnight we stayed with *you*. We still aren't.'

'And I can't say I'm sorry,' added John.

Ben looked disappointed. 'You mean to say you don't dream any more?'

'Of course we dream,' said Sue, 'but just the normal kind, or so it seems, with lots of confusion and flicking to and fro. No more of that awful obsessive world.'

'So you've never been back?'

'You make it sound like a holiday resort,' said Sue, 'Whereas it was really Utopia.' She shivered.

'It's as if it doesn't exist any more,' said John.

Outside, the blue of the sky had deepened and stepped down into the streets. It was already as purple as an Orkney midnight. They had not lit the lights, but this was purely because the mood was recollection, and not because of any fear of power cuts. For when, at the end of October, the news had broken of the attempt on the Labour leader's life, the strike had collapsed, Murphy and the whole Marxist leadership of the Fuelmen's Union had been swept away.

This might well explain why the dreams had stopped, and Ailsa said as much. 'You're not worried any more.'

'They take politics too much to heart, these two,' said Ben, shaking his head.

'So would you if you'd been through what we have,' said Sue. 'We take it seriously because of all the things that are more important.'

Michael, as if knowing he was what she meant, girned loudly, and Sue unstrapped him from the bouncer and plumped him down like a top-heavy jug among the Christmas toys. Ignoring them, he grabbed for an empty tea-packet and began gnawing at its edges, watching the grown ups through enormous round blue eyes.

'Hard to say how much was Dunne, though,' said Ben. 'The problem is, you've both read Zamyatin, Koestler, Orwell, Solzhenitsyn. Any glimpses of the future you might have had are inextricably confused with that.'

John shook his head, smiling. 'I don't see *that* as a problem. Nor would you, Ben, if you'd lived those dreams as we did. They weren't all higgledy-piggledy — just a mass of memories and terrors in no kind of order. Besides, we *both* had the dreams . . .'

'Till we got separated at the end,' said Sue. 'John's right, I can even remember wondering if *this* world, Michael's world, the one we're all in now, was real. Maybe the difference between dream and reality is this: reality is just a dream that's shared.'

'Sounds superstitious to me.'

'I'm not superstitious, touch wood,' said Sue, reaching for the edge of the coffee-table.

'Ah, but is it wood or is it plastic? Very worrying. These days you can't even trust your superstitions.'

220

'Maybe you ought to trust them,' said Ailsa. 'Maybe those dreams were fixed to a *place*.'

'I'm not sure what you mean,' said John. 'Do you mean we just did it to our minds by living in London Road?'

'I know what she means, John,' said Sue, who had special access to her friend's mind. 'She means, Can you have ghosts of the future as well as of the past? Well, maybe.'

Ailsa's idea was that they no longer had them because they had left their flat on London Road, with its layers of nightmares, its Marxist ghosts, its memories of Sue's ordeal. Their bedroom, she thought, had been like a spiritualist cinema, where pictures of the distant future were, once you were asleep, projected on the walls of your dreaming mind. They had left it, for it had been fouled and desecrated — not to mention the broken windows, the bullet holes in the kitchen cupboards, the small explosion in the hall. Its nature as a home had been profaned, and they had moved out, first to Ben and Ailsa's, then to other friends', and finally into the rented house on the edge of the country where they were staying at present, while the flat was set to rights and put on the market.

'Will you get much for it?' asked Ben. 'It's the quiet season of the year for house-buying.'

'It's been besieged,' replied John. 'It's a tourist attraction, a piece of instant history.'

'We've even kept the special lock the terrorists put on the door. Seems it's a selling point.'

'Bourgeois acquisitiveness,' mourned Ben.

'Extra protection against burglars,' said Ailsa.

'You don't think they all just come for a scream and a quick shudder? Like the room in Holyrood where Rizzio was stabbed.'

Sue nodded. 'That's exactly how it feels to me, Ben. But the lawyer assures us we'll get an excellent price.'

'We need it too after that holiday.'

'Don't begrudge the money, John, you know you like Sète just as much as I do. All those lovely southern French voices full of sunshine and rolling r's . . .'

'And wine,' said Ben. 'Isn't it wet in autumn, though?'

'Sun and cloudbursts on alternate days,' said John.

221

'Don't change the subject,' said Ailsa, clashing her bangles imperiously. 'I want to know what you think of my theory.'

'The ghosts? Well, I'm sorry, Ailsa, but I always went on having those same nightmares even when I was away reporting. That week in Leeds, for instance. All that WE-ness.'

'You see,' said Sue gravely, 'I think it was worse than ghosts.'

'What's worse than ghosts? Banshees, maybe.'

'I'll tell you what's worse than ghosts,' said Sue. 'Real flesh and blood men. Och, I know I sometimes got all sorts of bizarre images just as in ordinary dreaming. I can remember — a night or two before it all stopped — right bang in the middle of being in bed with . . . with that man . . . I can remember seeing Superman hanging from a telegraph line. It must have been Superman, he was all red and blue like a silly upside-down bat.'

Ben roared with laughter. 'How's your sex life, Sue? Sounds Freudian to me.'

'According to Freud, everything's Freudian. So how does that help? No, it's like John says. We both had them. It felt just as real as this.'

She peered around her at the cosy sitting-room with its corners of warm shadow, and out through the window where the first star could be seen, like a bright pinhole in dark canvas. The sun's blue veil of daylight had been withdrawn, and soon the evening star would be joined by millions of others as the skies of Earth darkened and made one sea with the light-years, the vast dislocations of space-time. Sue got up and, going to the window, gazed into the night across the outside balcony. She sighed, and the sound of the curtains as she drew them prolonged the sigh.

'No, those dreams were real,' she said. 'But of course they're not real any more.'

Ailsa and Ben frowned at her. 'Now I can't see what *you* mean.'

'Well,' said John, 'you remember Sue's final dream — the weird one when the rulers of the state turned off everybody's dreams.'

'That's pure Zamyatin.'

'It isn't, actually. In Zamyatin they cut out the human

imagination, in Sue's nightmare they were switching off everyone's consciousness. Do you see what that means?'

'Well, they succeeded, didn't they? They found out their own lives were a dream.'

The four of them were still for a while, but the shadows danced in the moving firelight, as if it were more real than the people musing beside it.

'Yes, but I meant something different. How could you have a world without consciousness?'

'Very easily, I should think. How about the universe before life began? I can quite easily imagine a world with nobody about to look at it. It's that tree in the quad thing, isn't it? Do you remember how it goes?

> There was a young man who said, God
> Must find it exceedingly odd
>   To think that this tree
>   Should continue to be
> When there's no one about in the quad.

Why is it odd? We all know that the tree in the quad is still there.' Ben smiled cheerfully at this common-sense view of the matter. It was not J. W. Dunne's, but for the moment he was playing devil's advocate.

'Yes, but we can only prove it's still there by going back to look at it. You see, it exists in a universe which does contain consciousness. The point is, if there is a universe without consciousness, then how could it be known to exist? If no one could ever witness it, no one could ever know it was there.'

'And then, *would* it be there?' asked Sue.

'Och surely, this is pure Berkleyism,' said Ben, laughing. 'Of course it would be there!'

'I'm not so sure,' said John. 'Just think about this. You can perfectly well imagine a different world from this one. You can imagine it running according to the same scientific laws, but with different stars, different planets, a different earth with a different civilisation on it. Okay?'

'Okay.'

'Let's call it Eukrea. Now how do you tell it isn't real? All the

223

laws of science operate on Eukrea just as they do on Earth. Water boils at 100° centigrade just as it does on Earth, the brakes of cars work by the same coefficents of friction, when a volcano explodes it does so according to the same physical principles. So what proves Eukrea isn't real?'

'Och, that's quite easy. You can't *observe* it erupting. Or, say, you might look at the sky to see if the constellation up there is the Plough or the Eukrean Hammer and Sickle. You can't see the Hammer and Sickle, so Eukrea isn't there.'

'You're making my point, Ben.'

'Am I?'

'Yes, what you've just said is that the test of reality is whether someone is conscious of it. Worlds that aren't *witnessed*, however closely they conform to the laws of science, are just sheer imagination. They fail the test.'

'But I could imagine a world where the laws of science didn't hold, where it was surrealistic, and the craziest things happened, like in *Lanark* or in *Alice Through the Looking-Glass*.'

'Of course. But if we all actually experienced that world all our waking hours, and not the self-consistent scientific one, then it would have to be the real one, wouldn't it?'

Ben's cigar had gone out, and he was frowning. After a moment, he relit it.

'You see, whether the world is real or not has got nothing to do with whether it behaves scientifically or not. It has in *our* world, but that's only because when we look at the world we happen to find that it *is* scientific. The test of reality — the *only* ultimate test of reality — is that someone's around to be conscious of it.'

'My mind is boggling,' said Ben, 'and when my mind boggles, it tells my stomach it wants more whisky.'

John leaned over for the bottle of Macallan, and Ben added, 'I'm a great believer in Balance. If you eat to excess you should drink to excess, and that'll produce a Balance.'

When John had poured him a new glass, he stared through it at the flames which looked, through the filter of peat-golden alcohol, brilliant but diminished. 'I can tell you've got a theory coming up, and I think it'll be more convincing on two glasses than one. Where are you going with all this? You're about to tell us that you really did experience the Truly Democratic Republic one hundred and ten years from now, is that it?'

'You tell me,' said John. 'When the rulers of the state turned off consciousness, what happened then?'

'Well, according to you,' said Ben, 'because consciousness is the test of reality — whew! — the world simply ceased to exist!'

Yes, thought Sue. On the second morning after the siege of our flat was raised — when I had dreamed of nothing all night long — I woke and realised . . . or suspected . . . or hoped, that that other world beyond the dream wall had gone for ever. And I thought of Alkan's piece the *Allegro Barbaro*, that frantic hastening of time, that chase where it is impossible to say who is the pursuer and who the pursued . . . and which does not come to an end, but to a sudden chasm, absolute and final. All at once there is not even darkness and silence. You are brought face to face with nothingness.

'Ironic justice,' said John, looking at his wife. 'Those materialists in your dream . . . they found a way of making the world *really* materialist, the way Marx said it ought to be — nothing but insensate matter — and by so doing . . .' He smacked his hands together.

Michael, laughing, clapped his too, then heaved himself over to his new rattle. This was shaped rather like a rocket. You dropped plastic balls over the top of it, then the baby pressed a lever, and the brightly coloured balls were shot up into the air. Sue wasn't sure she liked it. It looked too much like the rockets in her dream.

'A bit careless of them, wasn't it?' said Ailsa. 'I mean, supposing you're right. Daft of them to take the risk.'

'I told Mark,' said Sue, 'I told him just that. But he said he couldn't be wrong.'

'That's what stupidity *is*,' said Ailsa.

'I've been reading it up a wee bit,' said John. ' "Consciousness", as far as I can see, isn't a Marxist notion at all. Except "political consciousness", of course. They think human beings aren't conscious until society creates it in them. And individual consciousness has got to be an evil, as far as they're concerned, because it means we're all separate. We all have our own little individual consciousness, all flickering away like those billions of separate stars out there' — he waved his arm in the direction of the window — 'and that's a terrible obstacle to a collective state. So close your eyes to it, erase it, say it isn't so. Consciousness is an evil, Boris thought, because it means separation. They thought they were just destroying dreams. But deep inside, they knew what they were doing, they *wanted* to do it, and — bang! — out goes the sun.'

'Are you really trying to suggest,' said Ben, 'that you've been peeping in, the two of you, at the world's future? That this is how the world is going to be in, och, another hundred years, with universal communism and then — nothing but robots clicking away in endless darkness? That's frightening.'

'Funny too,' said Ailsa. 'Think of all those unconscious machines, clanking around saying "the functional mechanism of bourgeois democracy, my dear", and "in the old days we had repressive freedom", and "Dear robot, you have nothing to lose but your chains". '

'Ah,' said Sue, 'but we told you that part of the dreams too, didn't we? It was in John's early notes, soon after he started doing the Dunne experiment. The Revolution started in 2007 after Briggs was assassinated. Everybody thought it was the Right that had done it, and so they elected the New Left Labour Party on a wave of indignation. And you know, the really creepy thing is that, if that's so, then in that other world, Michael and me — we must have been murdered too.'

It hadn't happened. And the Revolution would not happen now. At the November election, the public, sick and tired of social dissension and monetarist detachment, had elected the Alliance. Northern Ireland would not be evacuated and left to civil war. The nuclear bombs would not be thrown into the sea, the American defence of Europe would not be withdrawn. Something would be done at last to heal the social rifts, to employ the unemployed.

'Public harmony,' said Ben sarcastically.

'Of course not,' said John, wincing, for that touched on too many memories. 'Just trying to get people to shake hands, instead of kicking each other in the face.'

'Private harmony, then.'

'Well, you can't have the public kind without the private.'

'Or the pubic kind!' said Ben, roaring with laughter. If you saw a terrible joke, the thing to do was crack it.

'We've decided,' he said, clearing his throat once or twice, then clearing it again in case they hadn't noticed. He took a sip of whisky to repair the damage caused by clearing it. 'We've decided that the sight of conjugal bliss and the smell of wet babies is too much for us. Maybe it's why Ailsa leaves all those things behind. It's a subconscious longing for a baby.'

'What do you mean, subconscious?' said his wife.

'Ailsa is . . .'

'Shut up, Ben,' said Ailsa proudly, as Sue kissed her.

John said, 'This calls for another drink.'

'That's why I mentioned it,' said Ben. 'Funny thing,' he added, gazing at the two wives, both squatting on the rug in little Copenhagen mermaid position. 'Have you ever noticed, women get slimmer as one gets drunker.' Barks of laughter burst from him again.

Sue was thinking, This whole thing raises awkward problems. What I did in reality when I thought it was a dream, and how I half excused myself, half thinking that it wasn't one. What you dream, what you deem. It was under duress, of course, and I was saving Michael's world. As a matter of fact, if I could only have got the upper hand over Charlesworth, I could have ended up enjoying it, a bit like Ludmilla Whatshername. Power and sex — I was just beginning to see it could be an exciting game.

But I don't believe in Voltaire's morality, and neither did he, with his sweet blue-eyed little blonde Breton lass suffering 'a fate worse than death', and then dying of shame. There are things a lot worse than shame, and people like Brianston-Pedley prove it. Besides, if they hadn't gone and snuffed out the world, I would have gained some influence. Charlesworth called me 'Soochka'. I thought it was an endearment (bastard that he was). Later I looked it up in a Russian dictionary. It means 'bitch'. The strange thing was, he was mad about me, and I might well have got him to rescue Ivan from that Us-Camp.

Okay, well, here it is. When I went to bed with Karl

227

Marksworth, I sacrificed private morality for the public good. Put that in your pipe and smoke it, cumrad.

Marksworth didn't hear that, though. He's a dead robot.

Ailsa stretched her long arm and slipped off her bangles. 'This is the one,' she said, holding it up to the fire so that it glowed red highlights. Michael held out his hands for it, babbling in his private language, and Ailsa gave it to him, bending down and cooing back nonsense syllables in reply.

'Ailsa, my love,' said Ben, 'I think they're trying to tell you something. When you looked through Sue's letter-box before you rang the bell, you changed the course of history.'

'Of course she did,' said Sue, taking her arm, 'not to mention saving Michael and me.'

Ben raised his eyes to the ceiling in a comedy of despair. 'You should never have told her. She won't be fit to live with after this.'

'Aye but, Ben,' said Sue, 'it was you with your crazy notions about seeing into the future . . .'

Ben, actually embarrassed for once, savoured his malt.

Sue and Ailsa hugged each other, and Sue thought: Saving Michael might even be as important as saving Arnold Briggs. To me it's much *more* important, and if they'd killed Briggs they weren't going to leave Michael and me around to tell the polis who they were. But it's more than that. After all, I used to call this Michael's World. She couldn't express what she felt for Michael, still less what she guessed about this, but just as the mark of goodness is to be revolted by people being hurt, to be specially gentle to the small, the helpless . . . so to have saved someone small and helpless was perhaps to touch some chord of sympathy in things.

'Do you think the Jews were right?' she said suddenly. 'They used to say that if you save one person you save the world.'

Rising, she went to the window and, parting its curtains, stood against its cold black pane, her nose pressed to the glass, gazing out into the night. Then, as somewhere else and at some other time, perhaps in dream, perhaps in strange reality, she opened the French window and stepped through into the freezing cold of the balcony. Above her the stars floated in their

228

ocean of night. And all of them were there, though flickering as if light itself, though it is the scale and measure of the universe, is subject to uncertainty. You think you understand? says the darkness. Look at me.

From the room behind her, Michael let out a hungry wail, and she turned and went in to feed him.

Appendix

The Uscant Experiment

The book which first roused Chairman Clegg-Molotov's hopes of effecting a Marxist Revolution by means of altering the English language, was not (as the reader may think) Orwell's *1984*, for by the late twenty-first century all known copies of this shocking slander upon *homo socsoviensis* had been hunted down and destroyed. It was, on the contrary, a learned work of fashionable literary theory published in London by Methuen in 1980, entitled *Critical Practice*, and written by Catherine Belsey, who was at the time a Lecturer in English at University College, Cardiff.

Chapter 3 of this remarkable work explains that, according to Saussure, the founder of modern linguistics, language 'consists of nothing but differences' and 'is not a function of the speaking subject'. The individual, as it were, does not 'speak', but is rather 'spoken by' his language. With numerous references to contemporary thinkers such as Derrida, Benveniste and Althusser, Belsey expounds the theory that language is a system of differences with no positive terms. It follows, therefore, that there is nothing positive to which we refer when we use personal pronouns such as 'I', 'thou', 'she', etc., and that the only reason why we think ourselves to be individuals is because our language tells us so. Derrida is called upon to suggest that consciousness itself depends on differentiation, and that without language we might very well not have any consciousness of self. Subjectivity is 'constructed' by language.

We all *feel* ourselves to be conscious individuals, but Belsey explains that we see ourselves as unique, autonomous and irreplaceable only from within the distorting glasses of the capitalist ideology through which we have gazed since childhood. We have been brainwashed into thinking that we are ourselves. Capitalist ideology, according to Althusser (a great French philosopher who murdered his wife), depends on this strange delusion; and once we rid ourselves of it, we shall see that there are no individuals and — one assumes — the collectivist millennium will dawn.

It must follow that animals cannot be in any sense conscious of themselves, i.e. that no cat can tell it is different from any other cat, and that no man could have told he was different from any other man — until the personal pronoun was invented. The naïve bourgeois individualist may wonder how in that case personal pronouns ever came to be, but the doctrine ties in very neatly with statements from Marx himself, such as the epigraph to *Event 16*, where he explains that it is *society* which produces consciousness in us.

Ms Belsey had not suggested in so many words that one might seek to dispense with personal pronouns. Chairman Clegg-Molotov had, however, an entirely logical mind, and saw that a policy of liquidation and extermination was obviously called for. After all, if language is suffering from gangrene, you should do as you did with Chairman Potter-Krasnovsky's leg, and have it off at once. He therefore hastened to set up the celebrated experiment at Uss Hall. Contrary to what one might naïvely suppose, there is nothing in the least bit improbable or crack-brained about this experiment, for it is firmly based on the thinking of four of the most admired philosophers of the twentieth century.